Without a Prayer

Jonathan Thomas Stratman

Other Books by Jonathan Thomas Stratman:

§

The Father Hardy Alaska mystery series
Indecent Exposure Book 1
In Gold We Trust Book 2
Holy Oil Book 3
The Old Rugged Double Cross Book 4
Without a Prayer Book 5

The Cheechako Alaska adventure series
Cheechako Book 1
Float Monkeys Book 2
Musher! Book 3

§

I knew why they included the marriage-counseling clause. It was because of the admittedly rare instance of the young unmarried priest who meets someone in the village and falls in love, or maybe lust. In a panic when they end up pregnant, the couple would decide to marry. A proactive session like this one would be the missionary district's last chance to get in a cautionary word. In other words, to talk them out of it.

None of those things were us. True, we had fallen in love but in our mid-thirties were both old enough to know what we were doing. And neither of us was pregnant.

Although the bishop didn't say the words out loud — he knew, I knew, even Evie knew — a white priest marrying a native woman was a career ender. There'd be no call to a stateside parish, and little chance of ever advancing to dean or rector or bishop of anywhere. Evie and I had discussed this many, many times. As a native Athabascan, it was her chief early objection to our marriage, only put aside when she realized — we both realized — that neither of us could imagine a life that didn't have us together in it.

Would the session be mandatory if the young priest wanted to marry a Caucasian woman from Mason City, Iowa? I doubted it.

Most priests arrived in the Territory married. I would have. Episcopal priests, unlike Roman Catholic, do marry. But my wife died of polio just a few months before I graduated from St. Luke's seminary in Sewanee and departed for Alaska. 'Alaska' had been our dream together. But stricken suddenly, quickly paralyzed, she died in an iron lung just days later. After graduation and ordination, I came on alone.

2

~

For my brothers
Michael and Joel
who not only always
encouraged me
but sometimes
aided and abetted.

~

iii

CHAPTER 1

Where were you when Franklin Rooseve
Or when Pearl Harbor was attacked, or wher
War II ended? I know people who can tell you
where they were and what they were doing.
one of them.

However, I *can* tell you exactly where I v
on Friday, March 29, 1957 when robbers k
over the Alaska Territorial Bank of Fairbanks.

Evie and I were attending our obl
marriage-counseling session, presided over by
other than my boss, the Episcopal bishop
Territory of Alaska.

We'd driven from Chandalar, by crossin
Tanana River on the ice at Nenana then driving
to Fairbanks on snowy highway. It was a warm
day, the temperature near zero, snowing lightly
the sky overcast. We made good time and as
enjoyed each other's company while talking abou
much.

Seated in a pair of gray overstuffed chairs ii
bishop's cozy book-lined study, we sipped co
while talking, dreaming, and planning how we w
be as a married couple and particularly how we w
be as clergy and wife.

The session wasn't my idea or Evie's, or even
bishop's. Rather, it was a provision in the contra
signed three years earlier to come to the small r
village of Chandalar to serve as mission priest.

So here we were, Evie and me, holding our dainty bone china saucers, sipping coffee from matching cups. Back in the village, we'd be selecting from a motley collection of stained, chipped, and thoroughly mismatched event mugs like one from the 1954 Anchorage Fur Rendezvous. While Evie, gamely and demurely answered a question about heading up the altar guild — I knew she'd rather beat on the ends of her fingers with a ball-peen hammer — I retrieved a vision of her from the summer before. We'd been threatened by a rogue CIA agent bent on finding gold he thought we were hiding.

I could still see how the graceful fingers, now gently caressing the fragile china cup handle had grabbed a good-sized kitchen knife by its wooden handle, flipped it — deftly catching the tip — then launched the knife full-force at our assailant. He flung up a defensive hand as anyone would but it didn't help. The blade drove fully through his palm, the haft making a resounding *smack* as it hit flesh. She told me later that knife throwing was a skill she developed as a girl working in the mission school's fish camp.

The bishop cleared his throat, bringing me back into the moment. Fixing us with his deceptively amiable gaze, he asked, "And what about honesty?"

I must have looked puzzled. "Well, sure. Aren't husbands and wives expected to be honest with one another? Isn't that part of the package?"

"Yes," he said, "it is. But *how* honest? *How much* does a partner deserve to know? Is there no privacy left for an individual in a marriage?"

I looked to Evie. Usually she loved to chime in on a pithy topic like this one. But she didn't say anything and in fact, shifted in her chair, as if uncomfortable.

I opened my mouth and might have asked her

about it, but just then the secretary knocked lightly and came in to tell us about the bank robbery.

I'd forget about that uncomfortable look until later.

~

For my brothers
Michael and Joel
who not only always
encouraged me
but sometimes
aided and abetted.

~

CHAPTER 1

Where were you when Franklin Roosevelt died? Or when Pearl Harbor was attacked, or when World War II ended? I know people who can tell you exactly where they were and what they were doing. I'm not one of them.

However, I *can* tell you exactly where I was late on Friday, March 29, 1957 when robbers knocked over the Alaska Territorial Bank of Fairbanks.

Evie and I were attending our obligatory marriage-counseling session, presided over by none other than my boss, the Episcopal bishop of the Territory of Alaska.

We'd driven from Chandalar, by crossing the Tanana River on the ice at Nenana then driving north to Fairbanks on snowy highway. It was a warm spring day, the temperature near zero, snowing lightly with the sky overcast. We made good time and as usual enjoyed each other's company while talking about not much.

Seated in a pair of gray overstuffed chairs in the bishop's cozy book-lined study, we sipped coffee while talking, dreaming, and planning how we would be as a married couple and particularly how we would be as clergy and wife.

The session wasn't my idea or Evie's, or even the bishop's. Rather, it was a provision in the contract I signed three years earlier to come to the small river village of Chandalar to serve as mission priest.

1

I knew why they included the marriage-counseling clause. It was because of the admittedly rare instance of the young unmarried priest who meets someone in the village and falls in love, or maybe lust. In a panic when they end up pregnant, the couple would decide to marry. A proactive session like this one would be the missionary district's last chance to get in a cautionary word. In other words, to talk them out of it.

None of those things were us. True, we had fallen in love but in our mid-thirties were both old enough to know what we were doing. And neither of us was pregnant.

Although the bishop didn't say the words out loud — he knew, I knew, even Evie knew — a white priest marrying a native woman was a career ender. There'd be no call to a stateside parish, and little chance of ever advancing to dean or rector or bishop of anywhere. Evie and I had discussed this many, many times. As a native Athabascan, it was her chief early objection to our marriage, only put aside when she realized — we both realized — that neither of us could imagine a life that didn't have us together in it.

Would the session be mandatory if the young priest wanted to marry a Caucasian woman from Mason City, Iowa? I doubted it.

Most priests arrived in the Territory married. I would have. Episcopal priests, unlike Roman Catholic, do marry. But my wife died of polio just a few months before I graduated from St. Luke's seminary in Sewanee and departed for Alaska. 'Alaska' had been our dream together. But stricken suddenly, quickly paralyzed, she died in an iron lung just days later. After graduation and ordination, I came on alone.

2

So here we were, Evie and me, holding our dainty bone china saucers, sipping coffee from matching cups. Back in the village, we'd be selecting from a motley collection of stained, chipped, and thoroughly mismatched event mugs like one from the 1954 Anchorage Fur Rendezvous. While Evie, gamely and demurely answered a question about heading up the altar guild — I knew she'd rather beat on the ends of her fingers with a ball-peen hammer — I retrieved a vision of her from the summer before. We'd been threatened by a rogue CIA agent bent on finding gold he thought we were hiding.

I could still see how the graceful fingers, now gently caressing the fragile china cup handle had grabbed a good-sized kitchen knife by its wooden handle, flipped it — deftly catching the tip — then launched the knife full-force at our assailant. He flung up a defensive hand as anyone would but it didn't help. The blade drove fully through his palm, the haft making a resounding *smack* as it hit flesh. She told me later that knife throwing was a skill she developed as a girl working in the mission school's fish camp.

The bishop cleared his throat, bringing me back into the moment. Fixing us with his deceptively amiable gaze, he asked, "And what about honesty?"

I must have looked puzzled. "Well, sure. Aren't husbands and wives expected to be honest with one another? Isn't that part of the package?"

"Yes," he said, "it is. But *how* honest? *How much* does a partner deserve to know? Is there no privacy left for an individual in a marriage?"

I looked to Evie. Usually she loved to chime in on a pithy topic like this one. But she didn't say anything and in fact, shifted in her chair, as if uncomfortable.

I opened my mouth and might have asked her

about it, but just then the secretary knocked lightly and came in to tell us about the bank robbery.

I'd forget about that uncomfortable look until later.

CHAPTER 2

Fortunately, police found twelve eyewitnesses to the robbery. Unfortunately, they couldn't agree about anything. They were five bank employees and seven customers. None of them had recognized any of the robbers. They told Fairbanks city police very definitely that the robbers were three men and one woman. Or maybe two men and two women — one of the women dressed like a man — or three men who took a woman bank customer hostage. Nobody seemed to know which, and they absolutely couldn't agree.

After leaving the counseling session, Evie and I were supposed to meet Marshal Frank Jacobs for dinner. He was late because of the bank robbery, we would learn. We had agreed to meet at Andrea's, Central Alaska's first and finest Italian restaurant, owned and operated by native Athabascan and Ligurian wannabe, my good friend Andy Silas, who would also be joining us.

Andy met us at the door and showed us to our table, red and white checkered tablecloth in place, centered by the essential candle-wax-encrusted wicker-bottomed wine bottle. Italian-sounding music of mandolins and accordions played softly in the background. Coffee appeared — the 'good stuff' — Italian roast that Andy imported. It arrived at the table in heavy clear-glass mugs almost before we'd gotten ourselves seated. A waitress came to clear away the armload of our parkas and outerwear.

Evie sighed herself into her chair and leaned back, thumbs kneading tight neck muscles.

"Glad that's behind us," she said, closing her eyes. I sat sipping my coffee, appreciating again the restaurant's pioneer features and wishing the walls could talk.

Andrea's had been a saloon for most of fifty years. There was a pressed-tin ceiling and natural-finish beadboard paneling on the walls. A spectacular hand-carved bar extended along the north wall of the room for a full thirty feet. Local legend had the bar rounding Cape Horn by sailing ship in about 1900 then heading north, finally arriving at the Bering Sea's Port of St. Michael. From there it had been borne upstream on the Yukon, Tanana, and Chena rivers by steamboat, finally arriving in the mostly tent city of Fairbanks to be installed in one of the first permanent buildings. It had moved several times since.

A treasured oil portrait above the bar, itself a popular local landmark, showed a young well-endowed lady dressed in lavender — a *sprig* — leaving little to the imagination. She's a grandma by now, Evie likes to point out, so far failing to dim my appreciation.

There were only a few people in the place this early, and bits of overheard conversation were generally about the robbery. This kind of deliberate crime, as opposed to the routine casual shooting or fistfight-gotten-out-of-hand, was unusual and a big deal in relatively low-crime Alaska. And it shook us. We'd spent far too much time feeling unsettled lately.

In Chandalar we survived a hard winter, heaped and drifted with troubles of our own. One of my parishioners, Molly Joseph, had been kidnapped by someone we called The Prowler. The Prowler had previously kidnapped and killed one local woman, kidnapped a second then taken Molly. Fortunately, we found them in time and The Prowler, caught in the act, was subsequently shot by Molly. A fate richly deserved.

But unexpectedly, this boogeyman turned out to be, not the dark, hairy, scary, stranger of folklore, but someone we all knew and liked, someone mild and funny — a friend. And it left us stunned.

So, it felt good to drive away, if only for part of a day. We traveled to the big city of Fairbanks, population now almost sixteen thousand, and sat with the bishop answering hypothetical questions about how we would or wouldn't 'be' together in this long dream of our future married life.

To be honest, I'd never really thought much about Evie assuming 'the job' of clergy wife. In my imagination, we'd simply be together. I'd be me, she'd be Evie, and we'd be happy. It was a bit of a shock to hear the Bishop reciting the — unpaid — full-time job description for the wife of a mission priest. Suddenly the conversation veered from being happy together, and to what degree we'd be honest with one another, to topics like holding teas for the women parishioners, showing up for choir practice, and chairing the altar guild. For the first time I began to think about what else I was getting her into.

I'd seen her look of dismay and meant to talk about it with her. But at the restaurant, we'd no more than sipped our first coffee and sighed the 'good-coffee sigh' before Andy slid into his chair.

"So, did you get all the answers right? Coupla high achievers like yourselves. Is the wedding still

7

on?" He smiled at us warmly over his own steamy coffee mug. He'd been a sniper with the U.S. Army in Italy during the war, discovering the Ligurian coast, its people, and its cuisine just as the war ended. Thus, sparking his transformation.

Although full-blood Athabascan, born in the mission clinic at Chandalar, he now even looked Italian. With his neatly trimmed black hair all Brylcreemed and shiny, pencil-thin Charles Boyer mustache, and — at work at least — nearly outrageous color choices including yellow slacks, cordovan tassel loafers, white knit polo shirt and sky-blue cardigan. And somehow it all worked, though bright.

When Jacobs finally arrived, clothed in his olive-drab U.S. marshal's uniform, he took one look at Andy and winced.

"Whoa! Explosion at the color factory!" But Andy was used to it.

"Eat your heart out."

Jacobs handed off his parka and ear-flapped fur hat to the hostess and sank gratefully into a chair. His coffee appeared and he smiled at the waitress. "Crazy day, even before the robbery."

Evie, studying her coffee, looked up. "*More* crime?"

Jacobs toasted her with his coffee mug. "You betcha!" He quoted the famous Pinkerton line. "It's why — we never sleep!"

Andy turned from signaling the waitress. "So, what else happened? Serial dognapping?"

Jacobs gave him a look. "Laugh it up, Italian boy." He drew a deep breath, held it, let it go, relaxing. "Those Excelsior snowmobiles? The racing machines they brought up here to film for advertising,

8

the really fast ones? Somebody stole 'em. All three. Gone."

I could tell there was something else he wasn't saying — not unusual for the marshal.

"Oh, man!" Andy sounded genuinely aggrieved. "I seen those running up and down the streets here in town. Passed right by us a couple o' times. And somebody stole 'em?" He looked around for effect. "Wish I'd thought of it."

Evie picked up a black olive and studied it. "I'm surprised there's not a posse." She interrupted herself. "*Not* out hunting for snow machines but out chasing bank robbers. I'm surprised to see you here at all." She nibbled at the olive.

Jacobs nodded and sipped. "Yeah... well, there *is* a posse. But it's a Fairbanks city police case for now. Police Chief Kellar told me to stand down. Even wants me out of the snowmobile thing. Thinks it's amateurs, an easy one and he'll wrap it up quick and nab the headline."

"Is it an easy one?" Evie's doubtful look crinkled the sides of her eyes in an adorable way.

He barked a laugh. "There are no easy ones."

"How'd they get away," Andy asked, "the bank robbers?"

"They stole a Ford, a fast one. You know that green Fairlane 500 with the V8? Belongs to Willie Amory at the Comet Club? That one."

Andy's eyes widened. "Sure, I seen that car. So, they're planning to drive somewhere, a highway getaway."

Jacobs nodded. "That's what Kellar thinks, and I don't. In fact, I'll make a prediction: the car thieves drive less than ten miles."

We had other questions but put them aside when

food arrived, settling down to serious eating. It all tasted wonderful as usual.

"You haven't said what the bank robbers took," I mentioned. He stopped fiddling with his coffee cup and looked up at me, but for a long moment said nothing.

"Funny thing about that. They took *something*, but not cash. They left the cash."

"Maybe they're just robber trainees," said Andy. "Taking the *Bank Robbery by Mail* course. Actually *taking* something is a later lesson."

"Yeah, funny." Jacobs sipped more coffee. "They definitely took something. It's just that nobody's talking about it. Yet."

We puzzled on that for a while until conversation shifted to more typical Alaska topics like snow and ice melting, roads opening or closing. The river ice breakup at Nenana would keep us off the Fairbanks highway for most of a month. We talked about the possibility of statehood, how some people were for or against it, and why.

"It's coming!" Evie had enjoyed a recent brush with politics at the state level, which thrilled her. I was less thrilled about statehood. For one thing, her brush with politics nearly ended up with Andy and me dead.

Now we all had tickets for the coming Nenana Ice Classic, a betting pool based on official breakup of the Tanana River ice at Nenana. My ticket was for May 1. May 5 was the average of days it had gone out since the Ice Pool inception in 1906, but I had convinced myself that it could be earlier this year. The contest was originally started, probably as a bar bet, by six pioneer settlers, all men, with names like Jonesy and Gunnysack Jack. Folklore has the original winner earning enough for a couple of rounds at the trading post bar. The Ice Pool had come a long way since then. This year the pot would be more than $100,000 — about twenty times the average yearly wage, and about *forty* times my wage for the year. Naturally, I hoped to win.

Andy hoped to win, too. "I feel lucky. What do you say I take us all to Hawaii? Fun, huh?" Of course, we all agreed to go. With the temperature outside at just below zero, how could we not?

Later, with Andy consulting in the kitchen and Evie off to the restroom, Jacobs leaned closer. "I've got a guy who comes in, trades me information for a meal. Usually nothing too interesting. But your name came up."

I must have frowned. "*My* name?"

"Yeah, surprised me, too. Have you pissed off anybody new lately?"

It was an odd question. "I don't think so. I've hardly been out of Chandalar lately, and you know how that's been going."

"Boy, don't I? What a mess."

"So, what did you hear?"

"This guy claims there's five thousand out for someone to put a bullet in your head. Not just kill you but shoot you in the head." He sipped his cooling coffee. "Could be just talk. Could be a way to get a meal. I'll follow up where I can, but you keep your head down. Hear?"

"Nobody wants less for me to be shot in the head than me."

"Funny guy," said Jacobs as Evie returned. She looked at me and raised her eyebrows, then at Jacobs. "Talking about you," he said. She laughed, but not much, like maybe she thought we *had* been talking about her.

On the other hand, she hadn't been quite herself since we left the bishop's. I wondered what could be going on and, if something *was* going on, why we hadn't talked about it, though we hadn't had much chance.

We'd almost finished Andy's amazing tiramisu and were lingering over the last of the coffee when a deputy marshal arrived. He made a beeline through the now crowded restaurant to lean down and whisper in the marshal's ear. Jacobs nodded, and the man straightened and turned away. "I'm right behind you," he called after him, rising.

"Hate to eat and run." He paused. "'Course it's better than *not* eating and running."

Andy looked up. "Got 'em cornered?"

"Far from."

"Well, *what* then?" asked Evie. "Come on, we're all curious."

"Remember when I predicted where they'd find the car... less than ten miles?"

"Sure."

"I was right." He smiled, pulling on his parka, accepting his hat from the hostess. "Anybody want to guess?"

I smiled back and told him exactly where they'd driven. "To the snowmobiles."

Jacobs pulled on his hat, aimed his finger at me like a pistol and made a little shooting motion.

"Bullseye," he said.

* * *

My phone began to ring just after three a.m. Whiskey Jack, let out a bark just in case I hadn't heard.

In my dream I got up, exhausted from trying to

12

keep some faceless person from shooting me in the head. I walked into my office to stare at the phone, framed on the desk in a pale rhomboid of blue moonlight.

It looked like a regular Bell telephone — shiny black Bakelite with white finger holes for dialing numbers arranged in a circle like a clock's face.

But it didn't sound like a phone. In my dream it sounded like a siren, actually lots of sirens. Like London during the war. And fire bells, plenty of them, ringing, clanging, making me want to cover my ears.

"Answer it," said a soft voice, one I well recognized — my dead wife, Mary.

"I don't want to," I said. "This is a dream, I don't have to answer it. Because telephones ringing at night are always bad news. And I'd have to get up and do something about whatever it is — someone shot, missing, frightened, frozen, burned — someone cut in half by the train... I can't."

The shape of Mary, now gone these four years, flickered in the dark office air, nothing more than a wink, like car lights passing. I only saw her briefly — a flash — enough to know she was there. Not enough to really see her, not to study her face or her body, not to feel that old wash of love.

I whispered, "You're here!"

"I'm always here."

Another voice — Evie — chimed in. "Answer the phone, Hardy." The faces of the two women I love superimposed — as if the same face — light and dark, though they didn't resemble each other.

"No."

"It's important." Evie urged again as I sensed Mary fading.

"I don't want to."

"I know." Her voice was calm, soothing, making the jangle and sirens fade. Her voice made everything seem okay, though I knew it wasn't.

"But I'll do it for you."

And that's when I saw Evie, as if from a far distance, over a river or a snowy mountain, and I saw a great valley laid out in front of me, and knew I'd have to cross it — maybe alone — to find her.

"Oh, Hardy," she said with that what-are-we-going-to-do-with-you tone of voice. I know that one. I've heard it a lot.

So, I made myself wake up, sit up, and walk out of my bedroom down the short hall and into my office. I held my hand in the air above the telephone like it might stop ringing and I could just go back to sleep, but it didn't stop, and I knew it wouldn't. So finally, I picked up the handset.

"This is Hardy."

CHAPTER 3

As it turned out, Evie and I drove back to Fairbanks in the very early morning, back to meet Jacobs with Andy at the Territorial Bank.

It had been Frank on the phone. No 'Sorry to wake you.' Just 'Need you here at the bank, ASAP. Oh... bring Evie.'

"Can you — ?" The line slammed shut on my question, "...tell me what this is about?" He didn't usually call in Evie and me — and Andy — on his major cases, and especially not in the middle of the night.

Instead of waking her with the telephone, I dressed, slipped on my mukluks and light parka, called Whiskey Jack, and walked the short moon-lit distance to Evie's cabin. The night was warm, near zero, with no wind to speak of and planets and stars beyond counting arching up into a perfectly clear sky. I remember thinking, *It should be a good day.* As if to confirm, a shooting star made a low, bright pass across the entire horizon. I felt lucky.

The street lay empty. No traffic this early and of course, not much traffic later. There weren't that many cars in Chandalar. With this the end of March, a whole winter of snow plowing had buried many of them in six or seven feet of well-compacted snowdrift, narrowing the street to about a lane-and-a-half, all mine now.

So, we strolled along on snow as hardpacked as

concrete, but not slick this early in the morning. Later, with the sun up, there'd be a thin layer of melt that could be treacherous. And slick enough for kids to ice skate. For now, it was all easy going, just a few minutes to Evie's cabin, me yawning, Jack circling, sniffing and peeing on everything.

I knocked on her door, calling out, "It's Hardy." It took a minute or two but she clicked on the porch light and opened the door. She wore a long, cream-colored flannel nighty embellished with tiny rosebuds, her bare toes curled against the cold floor, and one eye closed against the harshness of an unreasonable dawn. She liked it a lot better when a 'reasonable dawn' showed up at about eleven, just before a brunch I'd fix her.

Evie stared at me for a long moment, absently patting Jack's head and ruffling his ears as she tried to figure out why I was knocking on her door at three thirty — whether we'd made a plan she'd forgotten. She shook her head, apparently nothing adding up.

"Come in." She pulled the door wide, turned and walked away, leaving it for me to step in, closing Jack outside where I knew he'd stay. I followed her back through what was essentially a long one-room cabin to see her jump back into bed. Pulling the covers up around her chin, she allowed half a smile.

"You here for sex?"

"Sadly, no."

"Darn."

I sat on the edge of the bed and told her about Jacob's call. She opened her eyes wide, knitting her brows and jerked her head back in a double take of surprise.

"Bring *me*? That's weird."

"Will you come?"

16

"Along with you? Anytime, anywhere." She grabbed the covers, set to give them a fling, difficult with me sitting on them.

"Come on, move it, Hardy. I'm trying to get dressed here." I gave her a kiss, getting up, leaving her to it. Walking back to the rectory, I grabbed the spare gas can and a few supplies while warming up my pickup truck, admittedly still thinking about being 'here for sex.' It had a nice sound.

* * *

We reached the bank at about six, finding the double glass doors unlocked with only Jacobs and Andy visible. They looked up as we came in. Jacobs looked at his watch.

"Made good time."

Andy looked uncomfortable. There was no other way to say it. He looked fidgety, and like he'd rather be somewhere else. I looked at him with raised eyebrows, asking the question, but he just shook his head and shrugged.

The two stood in the middle of the lobby, on a floor of honest-to-god marble, freighted to Seward by steamship and on to Fairbanks by rail, way back in the twenties. This was a bank in the old style, built to inspire confidence, something in short supply back then for banks in gold rush territory. In addition to the marble, the whole place had been trimmed in sturdy, yellow-finished oak — also shipped a very long way — including a stand-up writing desk out in the middle of the lobby, used by customers to prepare deposits.

On the floor beside that desk, the focus of their attention, I saw a small scatter of debris that turned out to be several bulky textbooks, a notebook, and a small purse. Jacobs nodded toward it.

"Apparently they *did* take a hostage... a college

girl. Which puts it in my jurisdiction." He held something out, not to me but to Evie. "Looks like you know her." He extended what appeared to be an ordinary checkbook in a tan leatherette folder.

Evie took it, flipping back her parka hood. Before opening the checkbook, she used her teeth to nip at a glove fingertip and pull it off her hand, pulling off the other glove and stuffing them in her pocket. She pointedly looked at me, a brief unreadable expression shifting across her face. She opened the checkbook, silently reading the names then handed it to me.

"Yes," she said, "I do know her."

I knew her, too. It was a joint checking account with two names listed: Evangeline Williams — Evie — and Roberta Jeanette Moses.

If you'd held a contest to guess what other name would be on the check, Roberta's wouldn't have made even my long list. She'd been a thorn in my, well... butt a couple of years earlier, getting herself involved with a murdered local lowlife known as Frankie Slick. Back then I'd thought she was a victim of Slick's. Later, I wasn't so sure who was the victim, or if there *was* one.

I looked at Evie and she looked at me. Jacobs looked at both of us, from one to the other.

"Somebody tell me something," he said after a silence.

"Roberta's been legally my... foster child, my ward... though she's eighteen now and technically on her own. She's attending the University." Evie chanced a glance at me. "Doing well. Reliable."

Jacobs took a deep breath then exhaled audibly, a long sigh. "Do you have any information about what went down here?"

Evie looked incredulous. "About a bank robbery?

18

No. Nothing. How would I?"

He said it straight, no hemming or hawing. "Some of the witnesses have called her out as a possible accomplice." Evie looked stunned.

"No. That's not possible."

I asked the obvious question. "If she's an accomplice, why are her things left here on the floor? Why a checkbook with her name printed in it? A piece of evidence that takes about ten seconds to identify. From here it looks like she was stretched out on the floor with everybody else." Evie shot me what might have been a grateful look.

"Yeah, that's what we thought. And it still might be so. She might be a hostage. But the thing is, she knew at least one of the robbers — called him by name — Chilt, and when he left, he took her, and she didn't struggle much."

Andy stepped over from where he'd been leaning on the writing desk. He gestured at the pile of Roberta's school things. "Okay to dig through this?"

Jacobs waved his arm. "Yeah, we got fingerprints and photos. Knock yourself out."

Andy began going through each book, deliberately, carefully. After paging through each, he'd turn it upside down, holding it by the spine. A small piece of paper, with handwriting, shook out of the third book, *Fundamentals of Psychology*. He read it, handed it to Jacobs, who read it, handing it to Evie, who didn't read it. She already knew what it said. She handed it to me.

It was Evie's writing. 'Do well today. I have confidence in you. Love, Evie.'

Jacobs looked pensive, standing with thumbs tucked in his black leather gun belt. "I've left her off the APB for now. If she is a victim..."

I finished the sentence for him. "You don't want to make it worse."

Andy finished with the books. Shoving the last one aside, he did a double take at the floor.

"Hey!"

He'd uncovered a nickel-sized spot of bright color, too pink to be blood. We looked around for others. But there was just this one. Once uncovered, it was easy to see from across the room.

I squatted to touch it with a finger. Dry, though it had a wet, fresh quality. I looked up. "What is it?"

Jacobs shrugged.

Evie stepped closer. "It's nail polish. The new hot pink from Revlon. *Persian Melon*."

Jacobs frowned. "And you know this, how? You've memorized all the new colors?"

Evie snorted. "Not hardly." She looked at Jacobs, looked at me. "I know this because I bought it for her."

Andy rubbed his finger on the nail polish again. "So, she is a hostage. And it looks like she's marking her trail."

* * *

Evie and I didn't say much on the way home. We listened to the radio. I remember a Dow Jones average of 465 at Friday's closing bell and something about ten prisoners who walked away from a work detail in Anchorage. Ten? In the middle of winter? Good luck with that. Of course, walking away in the summer was worse and they usually ended up surrendering to get relief from the mosquitos. I told Evie they wouldn't be out long.

On the hour-long drive we got to hear "Young Love" by both Sonny James and Tab Hunter. I liked the James version and Evie liked Tab Hunter. I think

20

it was because Hunter was an actor hunk. I remember accusing her of liking his 'glamour boy' look better than his sound, and she blushed. James, the so-called country gentleman, was an actual singer and musician. Hunter sounded like he was chanting. We agreed to disagree.

In the news, Viet Cong guerillas from North Vietnam had taken to targeting Vietnamese government officials in the south. I admit not getting what all that was about. I remember feeling glad that Vietnam was so far removed from the United States and from things we had to care about and get involved in. Yes, I did know we had CIA and military advisers there but knew Eisenhower would never let us get embroiled in a meaningless overseas conflict. It had 'sinkhole' written all over it.

All the while, I expected Evie would fill me in on this Roberta thing. I kept waiting to learn that it all made sense in some way. Waiting to understand that my knowing absolutely nothing about this other *relationship* was an oversight that would make perfect sense once she explained it to me. Except that she didn't.

If I thought she'd begin talking when we got back to Chandalar, I was wrong. On an ordinary drive home, we'd come back to my place together, do something like fix a meal and maybe spend part of the afternoon or evening together before I'd walk her home. With one thing and another, it was nearly suppertime as we drove into town. I was engrossed in figuring out what to fix for dinner when she put a hand on my shift arm.

"I'm worn out," she said. "Would you just drop me?"

"Your place?"

21

"Yes, please."

"You okay?"

She looked at me, long and slow. "No."

* * *

She told me not to call her, that she'd be going right to bed, something about a headache. I drove home in a funk. A double funk.

Funk One, that she was involved in some way with Roberta — of all people — and Funk Two, that she couldn't have been bothered to mention it. Or maybe that was Funk One. Add to it, I was pretty sure she had fibbed about tonight, saying she was going right to bed, expecting me to believe it. So, make that Funk Three. Whichever, I drove home irritable.

About an hour later, when Andy picked her up in his white-topped sky-blue '53 Chevy — a recent acquisition and his pride and joy — I was standing knee deep in snow in a bit of spruce thicket, close enough that I could see and even hear the two of them. Yes, embarrassed to be skulking around in the bushes, spying on the one I love and claim to trust. To Andy's credit, he was arguing my side.

"I tell ya, it's not right sneaking out on Hardy. He should be in on this. For one thing, we're gonna need him."

"No! I don't want to get him involved if this all turns out badly. I got myself into this and I need to get myself out. If you don't see that then just give me your car keys and stay here. I'll do it myself."

"You're just gonna follow bank robbers on your own?"

"If I have to." Evie loaded out her backpack and bedroll, snowshoes, and her Winchester 30-30, a lever action like my old gun, with no scope. When they'd stowed it all in the Chevy's trunk, they climbed in, slammed the doors, and drove away, a cloud of gas-rich exhaust lingering in the frosty air.

I'd seen this coming and already had my own backpack and bedroll stowed in the truck, also snowshoes and my new Winchester Model 70, chambered as a 30.06 and scoped with the American-made 8x Unertl scope. The Unertl, so William and Andy assured me, had been the sniper-scope-of-choice in both the Pacific Theater of the last European war — what we now call World War II — and in the Korean conflict. The Model 70, my Christmas gift from Evie, even came with a custom stock of highly figured Oregon claro walnut. This was not just your run-of-the-mill grainless hardwood — like alder — but special order, hand carved. I swore it made me a better shooter.

As I watched their taillights move away down the snowy road into dusk, I almost wished I hadn't come over to hide in the bushes and spy. Now I knew too much. And now I'd have to figure out what to do about what I knew. But would I have been better to just stay home and wonder while my two best friends put themselves in danger?

Evie didn't want me along. She'd made it clear. So, I did the only thing I could do under the circumstances. I went home to make myself a pot of coffee. I used my new French press — a gift from Andy — with the good Italian roast, but it didn't help. Since it was well past dinner time, I heated up slices of moose meat and built myself a sandwich with horseradish and mayonnaise. It should have been a good sandwich, but I didn't taste it, and ended up feeding the last of it to Jack, who thumped his heavy tail appreciatively. He'd grown to expect horseradish.

He kept going to the door and sniffing at the

handle. I'd let him out but then in a minute or so, he'd thump to get back in. After about ten minutes, we'd do it all again. I finally got it. *He's looking for Evie, expecting her to show up.* I scratched the top of his head and he settled at my feet with a thud. He didn't just lie down, he dropped. After a few minutes he got up, went to the door and started his whole cycle again.

So, where were we? I was here in Chandalar eating worms — as my mother used to say — miserable, angry, and alone. Meanwhile the one I love, along with my best friend, was out on the trail of armed bank robbers. The girl they were trying to rescue was one of my parishioners. Gradually, I began to see that I was sitting around moping about my girlfriend while others were taking actual risks.

I thought about trying to call Roberta's parents, Teddy and Effie Moses, back in New Hampshire for dogsled races. If my daughter were in trouble or in danger, I'd want someone to call me. But the strong memory of Teddy, distraught, attempting to kill himself here in my office chair, putting a bullet hole through my roof, dissuaded me.

After ten o'clock, well beyond a decent hour for telephoning, it finally occurred to me to call William, my other good friend in the village. I'd first met him as the school custodian, a Russian by birth, and originally believed him to be a Soviet spy, though he turned out to be an agent for the U.S. He'd saved my life several times, and I his. Now I had to wonder why I hadn't called him already! For one thing, he doted on Evie, like a fond older uncle, and she adored him.

I tried him at his cabin first, knowing that Alice Young, his 'lady friend,' had a late shift at the Bide-

A-While. He answered on the first ring.

"Yes." It wasn't a question. It was that spooky spy thing that makes you feel like the agent on the line already knows what you're calling about. But I pushed on.

"It's Hardy."

"Yes," he said again. And then I didn't know what to say. I certainly couldn't tell him my girlfriend ditched me and I was in a snit.

"I'm pretty sure Evie's in trouble." I thought he'd ask for more information. I imagined a conversation where I'd explain all this stuff, and he'd reassure me and say he'd drop by in the morning and we could discuss it over coffee, something we usually did anyway.

"I am on my way," he said, and hung up.

CHAPTER 4

I'd just pushed down the plunger on the French press when William knocked quickly and let himself in. Taking off his parka as he walked back the short hallway to my kitchen, he hung it on a stool.

I don't know what I thought he'd say, maybe that I was behaving childishly. Maybe I was. I told him the whole thing from the beginning. It didn't take long. I left out the parts about me sulking.

Listening intently, he pulled a mug from the rack, filled it, declined canned milk or sugar — as usual — settled himself on one of the tippy stools and fixed me with his steely gaze.

"You should have called sooner."

And in that moment, I knew it. *Damn!*

"Evie didn't want me in. She said it. I heard her."

"You wanted to give her that space," he said. I nodded. "But what if she is injured or killed?"

I stared back. "That's the problem."

He nodded. "She is good. Good on the trail and an excellent shot."

"And she has Andy," I reminded him. He nodded again.

William took a sip and worked the coffee around in his mouth before he swallowed. "So, you are betting that the two of them can catch up to a gang of four armed robbers — four that we know about — safely retrieve the hostage, and make it back alive? That is your bet?"

It didn't sound so reasonable when he said it.

I sucked in a breath through my teeth, the audible hiss revealing the frustration I felt.

"One of your American philosophers — perhaps it was Doc Holliday — said never bet something you cannot afford to lose. So, I must ask..."

"... if I can afford to lose Evie... or Andy." Our eyes met. "No, of course not!"

* * *

William closed his eyes behind rimless spectacles, his thinking pose, tipping his head back. "So, they stole the most obvious snowmobiles in Fairbanks as well as a highly recognizable motor car."

"They stole everything that goes fast. Clearly, they wanted to make a speedy getaway."

He opened his eyes. "But why? Did they really need to *race* through town to get to the snowmobiles? Was anyone chasing them?"

"No. According to Frank Jacobs, the thieves were long gone before any of the city policemen even got there."

"Which is also interesting. It is as though they stole things that would be sure to get them noticed." William took off the glasses and rubbed the bridge of his nose with a thumb and forefinger. He looked tired. I imagined we both did. It was nearing midnight and I'd been up since three. He settled the glasses back on his nose and hooked the bows behind his ears.

"Tell me more about the nail polish."

"There is no more. Except that Evie and Andy think it's a signal from Roberta that she really is a hostage. I think it's why Evie is so determined to follow. The nail polish is a call for help... a personal call for help. So, she's got to go."

William's eyes met mine. "That is one

possibility."

"What's the other?"

"Bait."

* * *

"So, what do we do," I had asked him. In reply, he stood to rinse and rehang his coffee mug then grab his parka.

"We get a good night's sleep." He shot his shirt cuff to squint at his wristwatch. "I assume that you are packed and ready to go." I assured him I was. "Pick me up at six," he said, and went out.

I had already called the CAA to check the twenty-four-hour weather forecast: no snow, no wind, and the temperature hovering overnight at a balmy minus ten. Sleeping in my own bed made sense and we would easily pick up the trail in the morning. At least that was the plan.

But it turns out I couldn't sleep. I tossed and turned, grinding my teeth, not so much about bank robbers and getaways, as about this whole thing with Evie. About me and her. Us. We were supposed to get married in just two more months, and now this. I trusted her and she'd let me down, left me out, and made me feel stupid. Made me *look* stupid! Everybody would know. There were no secrets in a town this size.

The more I thought about it, the worse I felt. Andy knew. Even Frank Jacobs knew there was *something* going on. Why didn't I? Instead of being on the trail with them, I'd been left to rotate like a prize pigeon on the spit of my own anger-fueled fire.

Emerging before dawn with Jack trailing, a Thermos of hot coffee in hand and the snub-nosed police .38 in my parka pocket, I climbed into my truck. Wordlessly I picked up William at his cabin and the two of us drove north toward Fairbanks.

On the lonely snowy road, with William dozing, Jack lay stuffed at his feet, paws and nose up on the transmission hump near my leg where he could keep track of me. I stared out into the silver headlight tunnel, alert for moose. It was then I finally ran out of what my dad used to call 'piss and vinegar.'

I settled back into knowing that Evie loved me, was a good person, was honestly trying to help Roberta, and now felt like somehow she had to make it up to me, maybe even to prove something. Last night, I would have agreed. This morning, just as the sun began to rise, I realized — again — that she had nothing to prove to me. I love her and trust her. An adult like me, she gets to do what she needs to do. Period. My job as someone loving her back was to support her. I would. But yes, it still irritated me that she went off with her cousin and without me.

A random thought: they're chasing dangerous, armed criminals. What if something bad happens before we can get there? I pressed my foot harder on the accelerator pedal, leaning forward to peer out the windshield, picking up speed.

I certainly didn't want to be late for trouble.

CHAPTER 5

Tracking Jacobs presented no problem. We found him behind his desk.

He nodded at us and came around the desk to sit, scratching Jack behind the ears.

"I'm off the case," he said. "Grounded. Told to stay out of it." He looked up. "I know that's like an engraved invitation for you guys, but for me it means stay home if I want to keep my job. I know it won't do any good — it never does — but I suggest you two, and your buddy Andy, also stay home."

"Stay home?" I couldn't help jumping to my feet. "So *Kellar* is in charge? He couldn't find his feet in his *shoes*!"

He stared at me a long moment, as if seeing something he'd missed. "Sit down," he said, "and calm down. Kellar's out too." He looked up from petting the dog, seeing our blank faces. "Federal crime, above both our pay grades, they say. The Army's got it."

William pulled down the zipper on his parka, sliding back in his chair. "It is not above mine," he said. "The Army?" He considered. "What was stolen? *That* is what this is about."

Jacobs nodded. "Yeah, you're right. But they're not telling what was stolen. The bank won't, the Army won't. The only thing I *do* know, it wasn't cash. I managed to talk to a couple of the tellers before the Army showed up and moved all us local

30

lawmen out." He looked at me. "I can see you're upset. Have to tell you, your buddy Kellar wasn't too happy, either."

"At least it's not *all* bad news," I told him.

Fairbanks police chief Kellar and I went back a ways. Why he still had his job was beyond me. He was a thug, known for taking money from politicians and oil companies, and for the severe beatings he would personally dish out whenever he had the chance. According to Jacobs, the last man Kellar beat up still drooled. I didn't want to be the next.

I'd amateur-boxed my way through seminary at St. Luke's, instead of a side job as a waiter, short-order cook, or janitor like my classmates. And I'd done my best to stay in shape in Alaska even in the winter. Kellar stood large, more than six feet, and probably weighed north of two fifty. Though it may have been all muscle once, his best fist-fighting days were behind him. The one altercation we'd had, standing out in the snow with an audience of his deputies, they managed to lure him away before he had a heart attack. So yes, technically I won and he showed no signs of forgiving me for it or forgetting.

"So," said William mildly, "who *is* in charge?"

Jacobs looked at him and pressed his lips together. "You're not going to let this go, are you." It wasn't a question.

William shook his head. "Evie and Andy are already out on the trail."

"What!" Now it was Jacob's turn to look upset. "Already? Shit! And here I was thinking that with you two still in town I had this thing all bottled up. I should have known better." He brightened. "When did they head out? Maybe we can get 'em back."

"Last night," I told him.

31

His face fell.

"So, will you please tell us who is in charge?" asked William again, less mildly.

Jacobs sat up straighter in his chair and looked away for a beat, as if considering. "You've heard of Wild Bill Hanson, commander of the eastern wing of the 10th Mountain Division in the war? He's in charge."

I hadn't heard of him, but apparently William had.

"O-o-oh," he said, as if that explained something.

Which surprised me because I didn't think many people impressed William. I could tell that whoever he was, Wild Bill Hanson held a place on William's short list.

"Okay," I said, "so tell me."

"Colonel 'Wild Bill' Hanson is the man — well, one of the men — credited with crushing the Nazis in Norway," said Jacobs. "The 10th were uniformed all in white and trained to ski down mountain slopes while accurately firing a thirty-caliber rifle."

"Hanson is an American..." added William, "...I believe you would say a 'ski nut' from Colorado who started out training with the Finns. In 1939, when we... when Russia invaded Finland, Hanson served with the Finnish 9th."

"On skis," Frank added, "those Finns annihilated two tank divisions, humiliating the Russians. When America joined the war, they brought Hanson and some others in to create what became the fabled 10th Mountain Division."

"They were," William paused to search for the word, "formidable."

"And now he's in charge?"

Jacobs nodded and shrugged. "He's running a Mountain Division out of the Army base at Ladd

Field. Kind of a demotion, really. With his rank and reputation, he should be running the base. He showed up yesterday, just after you left. Told us all to 'stand down and get out of the way. It's an Army thing.'"

William stood, already zipping his parka. "So, you know nothing of the whereabouts of the bank robbers?"

"Not much. And I don't think the Army does, either. Story is, robbers hit the river on the fast snowmobiles and headed off. Down on the ice like that, with no stoplights and no cars to dodge, they would have been out of town in minutes. It's a pretty good plan."

He had an Alaska map on his wall. It drew me. I used a finger to trace the Chena River out of town. "Not much of a short cut. The Chena winds around too much, especially heading west."

"Yeah." Jacobs came to stand in front of the map. "Dollars to donuts they headed east and got off here." He poked a finger. I squinted to read.

"The Steese Highway?"

"Yep." He traced his finger along the meander of what I knew to be a summer gravel highway headed north. "And then here," he stubbed an index finger. "They've got the old Chatanika trail to get off on. Heck, there are dozens of gold trails or Jeep roads leading to nowhere really, but out of sight. Especially now, while everything's still froze up. The thing I don't get..."

"It is not an escape. It is a feint." William had come up to stand behind us. "This doesn't take them away. They are *pretending*, for some reason. Possibly to draw us out."

"Yeah, that," said Jacobs.

"Whatever they have taken from the bank," said

33

William, "they would need to take, not just out of town, but away. This is not that direction. They need to get whatever it is out of the Territory... go south, east... west. Yet they go north. The Army after them makes it worse." He pointed. "This road just gets them deeper in and seems a distraction. I am not getting it, either," he concluded.

I turned to William. "We need to go. We're not getting anywhere standing here. And they're moving." He nodded. I turned to Jacobs. "Sorry you're out of this thing."

"Out, hell!" he said with feeling. Crossing the room, he took down his parka from the coat rack, unpinned his badge from its front to toss it rattling and sliding across the open field of his desktop. "I've got leave built up, and not much else to do with it. I'm coming along as a private citizen."

"Can you do that?"

"Watch me," he said.

* * *

Courtesy of Frank Jacobs, we knew exactly where the trail began: in the heart of Fairbanks at a place still called The Line, Fourth Avenue between Barnette and Cushman. It was the old red-light district, partly indicated by the remains of its encircling twelve-foot-high board fence.

This street, a literal line of mixed log and frame cabins, some as small as six-by-nine feet, had been the legal home to prostitution in Fairbanks for more than fifty years. In fact, well regulated and taxed prostitution had long been the city's fourth-largest industry. Now closed for some years and officially shut down, only a few of the cabins remained, the rest bulldozed in hopes of attracting new and more respectable business. I'd heard talk of a Woolworth's.

In the yard alongside, a tangle of birch thicket littered with old rusting cars and pickup trucks, sat the metallic green Fairlane 500, gleaming like a gem set among all the rust. Imprints in the snow, and a ragged canvas tarp tossed aside, showed where the stolen Excelsior snowmobiles had been stashed.

As a testament to Fairbanks' low crime, the keys still hung in the Ford's ignition and I slid them free to pop the trunk lid. To be honest, I feared finding Roberta there — imagining her blue and frozen — and what I'd tell her parents.

My fears were the logical result of what felt like a full season of discovering the remains of brutalized young women. Though it would be unlikely even for the Fairbanks police to fail to check the trunk. I found nothing scary, only the usual trunk things plus another of the nickel-sized pink spots of Persian Melon nail polish. I had a vision of Roberta, tossed into the trunk with little but her nail polish, painstakingly applying this little circle of color. Working by the dim inner taillight glow, Roberta marked her trail. She knew Evie, at least, would be coming to find her. I wished she knew *I'd* want to come after her as well.

I wondered why they would hide the snowmobiles right here in the middle of Fairbanks, hidden less than six blocks from where they'd been stolen. I closed the trunk and replaced the keys in the ignition.

Fourth Avenue and The Line lay at the wide side of a V, its point just three blocks distant and aimed at the Chena River, still well frozen. Once on the Chena, the Excelsiors could travel more than sixty miles an hour up or downstream on smooth snow-covered river ice.

But I'd seen the Chena on Jacob's map. It never

flowed straight. Especially heading west, the river looked like a snake from above, arching, curling, even braiding around islands, taking a long time to get clear of Fairbanks proper. West would be no good for a getaway.

Taking the river east, upstream, would have the robbers — and their hostage — out of town in as little as four blocks, and that would be enough. From there they could head out cross-country, going anywhere. Although, as William had pointed out, also headed nowhere.

With Jacobs officially 'on vacation,' we took my truck. Since there wasn't room in the cab, Jacobs said he'd sit in back. William thought he ought not to sit back there alone, so joined him. And then both of them were joined by Jack, who jumped at any excuse to ride outside. I went from feeling overcrowded and claustrophobic in the cab to feeling like I had body odor as they all bailed. I felt like their chauffeur.

At about eight o'clock, with people just beginning to get out and drive around, I parked my pickup in the small lot of a boarded-up eatery. I could easily see the steel lattice of the Cushman Street Bridge, now rose-colored in the early light. From here, a smooth well-used trail — just dogsled- or snowmobile-width — ramped easily down the riverbank to winter ice.

Piling out of the truck, grabbing packs, guns, and snowshoes, we were an easy target for the two canvas-topped military-issue Jeeps that crisscrossed behind us, blocking us in place, just in case we wanted to make a break for it.

Jacobs' eyes met mine and he shrugged. I knew what he was thinking, that our little rescue attempt might now be officially over, before it had begun.

CHAPTER 6

Four military men climbed out of the Jeep. Each carried the standard M1 Garand rifle and wore a Colt semiautomatic sidearm. I recognized one of them as an officer, though showing the bare minimum of insignia.

"Hanson," muttered Jacobs, indicating the officer. Jacobs set down his pack and leaned his rifle against the Ford.

"Colonel," he greeted.

Colonel Hanson made a face. "Bill," he said, correcting Jacobs and shaking his hand. "You're Stoltz, from Clear," he said to William then turning to me, pulled off his mitt and stuck out his bare hand. "I don't know you."

"Hardy," I said, "from Chandalar."

"Oh!" He nodded, his brows knit. "I've heard of you, Father... all good. Impressive, actually." He stood taller than me, about six feet, medium-to-thin build, with a clean, firm handshake.

He wore a closely cropped military mustache, aviator-type sunglasses, which he'd pulled off to greet, and probably a military-issue crewcut back under his olive-drab parka hood. On his feet, instead of mukluks, he wore heavy leather boots, slightly oversized and stiffened with a protruding square sole. Given his reputation, I guessed some kind of ski boot. They all wore them, and now that I noticed, both Jeeps had overhead racks with long narrow skis well secured.

He saw me seeing. "The Army *pays* us to ski," he said, like 'what a crazy idea that was!' Everything about him said 'leader' and 'really likeable guy.' And in spite of any earlier intention, I liked him right away.

Stepping back, he examined the three of us. I felt a little like he'd caught us at the cookie jar, but he didn't act like he cared. He stooped to scratch Jack behind the ears, another good sign.

"What are we doin'?" he asked. And then to Jacobs, pointing to the empty badge flap on his parka. "And what are you doin' out here without your badge?"

"I'm here on my own time."

Hanson waved a mitt at him. "Nah. You should have said something. I wasn't trying to squeeze you out. We can use all the help we can get. Especially yours. I'll clear it." Jacobs nearly smiled. I could tell he was pleased.

Hanson turned to me. "But why are *you* here?"

I explained about Roberta, Evie, and Andy, leaving out the parts about me feeling abandoned, hurt, and angry. He nodded all the while and didn't interrupt.

"Okay," he said when I'd finished. "I didn't know most of this." He put his sunglasses back on. "Having civilian lives on the line raises the stakes. It's a little more critical than... bank stuff."

"What bank stuff?" I took the chance and asked him directly. He pressed his lips together, looked at the ground, and then looked off in the distance, deciding.

"Aw, heck," he said. "I'm not even sure why it's supposed to be a damn secret. But! Keep it under

38

your hats if you can." He looked at each of us.

"They stole bearer bonds. A big stack of 'em."

I could feel myself frowning. "Those are just paper. Aren't bonds registered somewhere? If you lose them, you just check back to your list, cancel them, and issue more?"

He shook his head. "I wish. You're talking about *investment* bonds. And you're right, they leave a paper trail. *Bearer* bonds aren't listed anywhere. They're just like money. They belong to whoever has 'em. And this is a lot of 'em. We haven't seen the accounting yet, but we're told they grabbed a couple million dollars' worth."

Jacobs made a sucking-air sound. "A fortune! What were a couple million dollars' worth of bearer bonds doing in Fairbanks?"

Hanson made a disgusted face. "You mean without local law enforcement having a clue? Excellent question. Something to do with the government buying a big pile of private gold. Anyway..." he looked around. "we're burnin' daylight here. I'm waitin' for helicopters from Anchorage... Elmendorf. You guys have a clue where you're goin'?"

"No clue," Jacobs told him. But then on impulse I filled him in on Persian Melon.

He grimaced. "Okay, I get it. Gutsy girl. But she's takin' a big chance."

For the first time, I thought of Roberta that way. Not as a thorn in my butt, but as a young girl, caught up in something — something dangerous — trying hard to be more than just a victim.

"You guys take off," said Hanson. "See if you can pick up the trail. That way, if nothing else, we can trail you."

Jacobs caught his eye. "You guys coming by chopper?"

Hanson did a face shrug. "We've got 'em coming and they're certainly good for backup. But you can't sneak up on anybody with a chopper. We'll probably use them for scouting, this phase." He turned to his men and, as one, they turned to the Jeeps. In seconds they were gone.

Jacobs turned to William and me. "They say his men will ski through fire for him."

"Yeah," I said, "I just met him, but I can see that."

* * *

So, we started walking, packs on, snowshoes over our shoulders, rifles in hand. Jack cavorted in circles around us, lapping clean dry snow, peeing endlessly, occasionally racing ahead as if to check something then racing back.

We quickly reached the intersection where the sled trail branched, ramping back up the riverbank to meet the snow-covered Steese highway. We paused at the fork, where William spotted the tiny Persian Melon nail polish bottle nearly buried at the trail edge, indicating the Steese route. "She has taken us as far as she can," he said.

"They're not going to see *that* from the helicopter." Jacobs looked skyward as if to see one flying by. "Or even skiing."

We made the turn and in minutes were walking along the firm, snow-packed highway. The highway, dusty gravel in summer, wasn't much used and we could go ten to fifteen minutes without having to move over for a passing vehicle. The sifting of snow we'd had night before last gave us a chance to pick up the faint tread imprint of the Excelsiors on the highway shoulders. At least, that's what we hoped we were following. It was all we had, so on we went.

The nice thing about tracking in deep snow is there's nothing subtle about it. When someone decides to leave the roadway and break trail on snowshoes, or with a sled or snowmobile, there's no question. They leave a clear trail that can't be hidden. The challenge for us would be to figure out which trail.

The sun angled up, higher in this season, but still mostly from the south, brilliantly reflected from a million diamonds on the snow surface. I wore sunglasses from the start. It wasn't long before I partly unzipped my parka, tying my heavy mitts behind me on their woven cord, and flipping back my parka hood.

"It's a warm one," said Jacobs, doing the same.

"It is April first," reminded William.

"April Fools' Day," I added, hoping it wasn't an omen.

Though it still looked a lot like winter, it felt like spring. The air came soft to the nostrils with a bit of scent in it, unlike the usual frosty absence of scent, or the more typical winter overlay of wood smoke and vehicle exhaust. After a long, cold, hard winter, this air smelled nearly like perfume, like leaves, soil, and growing things, though nothing green showed through the drifts. It wouldn't have surprised me at all to hear melt drip.

At noon we paused alongside the steeply plow-thrown snow shoulder to eat. Both Jacobs and William had military rations in cans, which they opened with little twisty openers and offered to share. It was the same old corned beef I remembered, eaten cold with a spoon. Just seeing and smelling it, took me right back to France and the war.

"Stuff still isn't any good," said Jacobs, as though he thought that somehow it might be. Add to everything else, these K rations were five to ten years or more in the can.

I had sticks of Chandalar fishcamp-smoked salmon wrapped in waxed paper, and two pieces of pilot bread smeared liberally with peanut butter, the faces stuck together to keep them neat. All I had to do to eat them was pry the two crackers apart. Sometimes at home I sliced dill pickle on them. *My* lunch, at least, tasted pretty good. We'd already worked up an appetite. We shared cookies, also from a K ration can — chocolate coconut. They weren't bad, especially served with coffee from William's big Thermos, only because he had it out and pouring. We were all carrying.

We neither saw nor heard airplanes. Crunching my pilot bread, I turned to Jacobs. "I thought there was a search on?" He shrugged.

William tipped his Thermos cup back, tapped it to coax the last drops then shook it out. "It is possible *we* have become the search."

We walked five miles along the highway, by my estimation, before a promising snowmobile trail broke away headed west. Unlike others we'd seen, this one hadn't been used much. In fact, probably used twice. Once for planning and again for the getaway. The track we'd been following, the one we believed to be the Excelsior, showed clearly in the dusting of snow. The trail wasn't as well packed or as easy walking as the highway had been, and we didn't go too far before stopping to put on snowshoes. Existing snowshoe tracks offered tangible evidence we were also following Evie and Andy.

"You *do* realize how far ahead of us they are

now?" asked Jacobs as if reading my thoughts.

I did realize, and it took a Herculean effort on my part to not let it make me crazy. At this point, I didn't care a bit about being *the last to know* about whatever Evie and Roberta had going.

I had an odd thought: *It's none of my business, anyway.* At this point, I just wanted to get Evie and Andy back home safely... yes, and Roberta.

I kept thinking about the difference between bank robbers on snowmobiles and us on foot. Of course, they wouldn't be going anywhere near sixty miles an hour, fully loaded, on these hilly twisty back trails. They were probably traveling more like ten miles an hour. Against that, I calculated our pace on snowshoes at about three miles an hour. Every hour we pursued, they gained a probable seven miles.

And there was another larger question. I voiced it. "Where do they think they're going?" We were well out of Fairbanks by now, the brief neighborhoods giving way to larger tracts and scattered rustic log cabins, some abandoned, some collapsed, some possibly dating back to the various gold rushes.

The trail started off flat over what Jacobs called 'the goose fields.' Tens of thousands of Canada geese would gather and feed in these fields spring and fall as they migrated north or south. Through the summer there'd be cattle here from Creamer's — Fairbanks' one big dairy — just a few miles off. If we needed reassuring that this was really the robbers' trail, the carelessly clipped barbwire did it for me.

A few miles farther on, more clipped barbwire let us out of the flat, smooth fields into low, lightly treed rolling hills. It still wasn't bad walking — or snowshoeing — but it did both slow and tire us. Even Jack had given up cavorting and circling, content to walk along behind stepping on the snowshoes of the last man in line, usually me.

We were climbing our third or fourth small hill when we followed the trail around an evergreen thicket to find one of the Excelsiors abandoned.

Jacobs unscrewed the gas cap. He looked at each of us with purpose. "Empty! This'll slow 'em down." He squinted, his face reflecting the question: How can you stage your big escape by snowmobile and not remember to bring fuel?

We didn't have time to answer. From behind us on the trail, what had been a tiny, nagging mosquito of sound, expanded into the full-blown sputtering racket of a laboring two-stroke snow machine engine.

"Hanson?" I asked, but knowing it wouldn't be.

Climbing into view came a Polaris Sno-Traveler, the one with the exposed engine and drive belts at the rear, an actual steering wheel, and an upswept aluminum prow culminating in a flat windscreen.

Looking down the grade, we could see two men aboard. The passenger was a tall fat man wearing high, polished black boots, a black service hat with long ear flaps tied under his chin, and a heavy wool stateside overcoat. He had to partially unbutton and roll the coat up around his waist to straddle the machine. I'd seen both men before. They were Fairbanks city cops and this, the fat man, was none other than the police chief, Kellar, approaching.

Jacobs clutched my arm. "Here comes trouble. Try to not let him shoot you."

"We don't have time for this," I said.

"There's always time to bleed," he replied. "Let me handle it."

The machine pulled right up to us before the driver finally flipped the switch to snuff the engine racket. Silence almost palpably swept back in around us. There were no greetings. We stood watching Kellar and his driver struggle to extricate themselves from their machine. When finally standing up to his boot tops in snow, Kellar smoothed his overcoat down across his legs. Then he pulled off one black leather glove to reach up and release several buttons at the top, making a show of reaching inside for something that turned out to be a shoulder holster. He pulled a Smith & Wesson .38, appropriately the one they call the 'Chief's Special,' with the three-inch barrel. Facing the three of us he aimed the revolver only at me, the blinding sun reflecting off its nickel plating.

Nodding carefully at Jacobs and at William he turned to me. "You," he said, "are under arrest."

CHAPTER 7

Jacobs stepped between us, his back to me. "Fairbanks ended about ten miles back. You're out of your jurisdiction."

Kellar bent his face into what was supposed to be a smile while attempting to wave him aside with the .38. But Jacobs didn't 'wave' easily.

"I'm deputized, like you. Territorial patrol, as you know." He reached around Jacobs to keep the pistol trained in my direction. "Hands up."

I put them up but didn't like it. Each ticking moment Kellar delayed us allowed Evie and Andy to move farther from us but closer to the danger they pursued. Each of those moments felt like a gnawing buzz saw in my gut.

Kellar and I had history. It wasn't just that I'd embarrassed him in front of his men by not allowing him to beat the crap out of me.

More than that, both his sons, while working on the Fairbanks city force, had come to serious grief while tailing me — through no fault of mine. The younger, Tim, had been nearly suffocated by carbon monoxide on a stakeout in front of the rectory. It was later proven that someone — certainly not me — clogged the tailpipe of his idling patrol car. It was only Evie's timely insistence that I go fetch him in out of the cold that allowed us to find and revive him.

Andy, Evie, and I, along with nurse Maxine, had saved his life that night. But it was close, way too close, and he nearly died. Soon after, I heard he quit his job with the force, quit working for his father, and left Alaska. Somehow Kellar managed to forget the saving-his-life part, remembering only that it was my fault he was gone.

And the older son, James, along with a couple of Fairbanks city patrolmen, had been privately hired to tail Evie and me. We were driving home late one night on the Chandalar road. There's a place it extends, arrow straight, for about five miles across a bog. It must have seemed clever, easy, and maybe even fun to switch off the headlights and drive too fast in the dark, guided by our taillights through an inky, moonless night. To be sure, we never knew they'd been following us, or that they'd been injured, until we put it all together from what we heard on the radio.

According to the Territorial Highway Patrol, they'd been traveling way too fast when their patrol car slammed full on into a bull moose. I heard the only reason James Kellar survived was that he'd been stretched out in the back. The moose's forty-pound rack immediately crushed the driver to death even as the impact ejected young Kellar through the windshield and nearly thirty feet up the road into a snow bank. Somehow, he survived.

In Chief Kellar's mind, the more time passed, the more both of those events had become my fault. I can't say seeing him here now with the gun was a surprise. I'd been expecting him.

A formidable fighter in his day, Kellar stood over six feet tall. He had seven or eight inches of head height on me, and a lot of reach. But pushing fifty, he ate too much, drank too much, and had long since quit splitting and stacking his own wood and shoveling snow. Activities that I still do regularly.

Now he shouldered Jacobs aside, menacing, closing the distance between us.

Closer, he didn't look better. I revised my earlier estimate. North of three hundred pounds, he had big, dark, puffy bags under eyes that looked oddly yellow, and a purpling nose. Doing nothing more strenuous than holding a gun, he wheezed. As I looked at him around the gun, he looked old, slow, and out of shape. But somehow, he managed to still look dangerous with his nasty reputation wrapped and tied around him like a butcher's leather apron — thick, scarred, and bloodstained. I knew he'd kill me if I gave him even half a chance and, in spite of witnesses, would insist I attempted to escape. In my mind, I had little to lose.

"Hardy, no!" shouted Jacobs. I swiped my right hand down fast, getting my fingers around the pistol barrel, yanking down then twisting. I peeled the gun right out of his hand before he could fire. By the sound of his grunt of pain, I almost took his trigger finger, too. Rather than turning the gun on him and prolonging the incident, I tossed it, spinning. We all watched it sink and disappear into the snow. But it wasn't over.

"Back me," Kellar barked to his deputy, who thus far had seemed content to watch. The deputy began to paw at the front of his parka like he might sometime get to the service pistol he wore, conspicuously bulging at his beltline.

Jacobs didn't even bother drawing a weapon. He pointed his index finger gun-like at the man. "Don't do it." The deputy froze.

That should have been the end of it, but not with Kellar. His hand dove for his overcoat pocket, for

48

what I had to assume would be one of his backup guns. I knew he carried several, from watching him empty his pockets before our previous fistfight.

I considered shoving my .38 up his nostril to get his attention. Discarding that notion, I stepped forward and pressed the overcoat pocket tight against his gun hand and his thigh. The pressure kept him from drawing the gun. And because of his footing in the deep snow, he couldn't shuffle back to ease the pressure without overbalancing and pitching backward into the drift. I had a sudden vision of the chief stretched out in the snow as if making snow angels. But no, he froze.

"Your play," he muttered. "Maybe your last. Better make it a good one."

I shook my head as I looked up at him, into his piggy eyes while keeping the pressure strong on his wrist. "We don't have time for this, Chief. My friends are chasing bank robbers and trying to save the hostage." I didn't add that it was something he could be doing.

"Someone is coming," interrupted William, as the sound of a distant approaching engine closed fast. This far out of town it could only be another snow machine. But the engine note sounded lower, more like a car or truck and less like the high-pitched whine of a two-stroke motorcycle.

It came up fast, not along the trail but up and over the rounded brow of a low hill just to the north. It was a dual-track all-terrain Weasel, built for the European war by Studebaker. I knew about them in Norway and had heard of their Army use in Alaska, but this was the first I'd seen. Canvas covered and painted white for camouflage in snow country, this Weasel seated four. A ski rack bolted on at the back bristled with white skis and poles.

The machine's arrival had an odd effect on Kellar. Abruptly he relaxed. He quit trying to pull the gun and I let go the pressure on his wrist. As the engine cut and both doors swung wide, I realized he'd raised his hands to shoulder height, now standing as though someone held a gun on him.

"What's going on here?" Two pairs of white-suited soldiers literally sprang from the vehicle. Emerging from the front passenger side — barking the question — was Colonel 'Wild Bill' Hanson. Probably because of Kellar's raised hands, the colonel seemed to be barking at me. It felt like long ago, my father catching me at something. I resisted the urge to stammer.

"You'll have to ask him." I nodded at Kellar.

Hanson stepped up, taking a position at my shoulder — which was interesting — to face Kellar. He looked around to see which of us was holding a weapon on Kellar. Finding none, he pulled off his sunglasses and his brow furrowed.

"Put your hands down," he said to Kellar. And then he asked again, this time more conversationally, "What's going on?"

I could see Kellar expand, feeling like he was back on solid ground. He pointed a finger at me. "I came out here to arrest this man. You got here just in time. He's resisting, took my gun."

Hanson turned to me. "That true? You took his gun?"

"It's true he came out here to arrest me, though I don't know why. And yeah, I took his gun away. It's..." I turned to look for the gun. "over there."

"Uh-huh," he said, turning to me, scarcely suppressing a smile. "You took the weapon from an

50

officer of the law," he looked me up and down, "about twice your size?"

"Look Colonel..." I said.

"Bill," he replied, and he pointedly made eye contact with Jacobs and William.

I plowed ahead. "We don't have time for this, Bill. I'm not sure why the chief is arresting me. If he insists, I can turn myself in later. But right now..."

Bill nodded. "Right now we need you three on the trail, moving." He turned to the chief. "Hear me Kellar. Your arrest can wait. And if you lay a hand on this man, you'll answer to me. And if you do arrest him when he gets back, you better be able to show cause."

Kellar stuck his chin up. "Or what?"

Hanson stepped so close so fast, the chief stumbled back, nearly falling.

"Or you won't like what happens. You won't like answering to me. Nobody does." Hanson turned to the three of us like Kellar had vaporized.

"Tell me something."

We did, though it wasn't much. We recapped finding the nail polish bottle and the abandoned Excelsior.

"So, they're down to two machines. That helps. You have to wonder about bank robbers who don't bring enough fuel for the escape." He paused and glanced around, glanced over his shoulder at Kellar and the deputy still standing by their snow machine. Then he lowered his voice.

"The getaway is on the news and a civilian pilot reported what sounds like them west of you about ten miles with two others following. Those will be your people."

"Evie and Andy," I said.

Jacobs frowned. "West? How does that make sense?"

"Perhaps these robbers are lost," ventured William. His brow furrowed. "They have forgotten also to bring the map?"

Hanson gave a short grim laugh. "I'm thinking we'll stay on this trail with the Weasel, as long as we can. It won't go everywhere. If we get stopped — when we get stopped — we can take to the skis. It gets rougher out here in just a few miles."

"You know this area?" I asked.

He nodded. "Some. We've trained out here before." He rummaged in his deep parka pocket for a section map that had been somehow wrapped in plastic to be completely water resistant.

We followed his gloved finger across the page. "We're here," he said. "They're over here... and see how the trail curves through this long valley? I'm thinking you three can head west from here, over this hill and along through this stream cut — here — in a nearly straight line, to lop off a couple of hours and maybe catch up with your people. Don't bother trying to brace the robbers. Just get them out of harm's way. You're outnumbered and probably outgunned."

Jacobs looked up from the map. "You know something about this that we don't. Might as well tell us."

Hanson nearly hung his head. I could tell it wasn't a posture he was used to. "Some of my men are missing. And one of them, a man called Chilt, was named by the hostage at the scene. Not likely a coincidence. There aren't that many Chilts out there."

"Where do you get a name like Chilt?" I asked.

"Chilton. Walter Chilton Bradbury, the Third. He was a big deal from back east. I met him at Stowe early in the war, liked him and recruited him, I guess you could say. Hell of a skier. Turns out I may not have made the best choice."

"Job doesn't come with a crystal ball," said Jacobs.

Hanson flashed him a grateful look. "I'm usually not *that* wrong," he said. "We've been together for years. He was my right-hand man." Jacobs nodded knowingly.

"We need to be on our way," I said. Every moment we stood talking, the ticking moments of no progress built to a buzzy crescendo in my brain.

Bill turned to flash a look at his men, all smoking. His look was a signal. To a man they tapped cigarette ash into their pant cuffs and stubbed out the smokes on their shoe soles. Pawing handfuls of snow, they deposited the butts and covered them, not to be seen again until the thaw. I wondered, as I often do, why smokers think the whole world is their ash tray.

He turned back to speak, lowering his voice again. "Take no chances with Kellar." He saluted us. After four years in France I had to consciously resist the urge to salute back.

When he moved back to the other side of the Weasel to haul out the map and consult with one of his men, another stepped up to me to offer a casual salute with a handshake.

"Newhouse," he said. "Pleased to meet you."

He extended his cigarette pack. I waved it away and must have looked impatient. "This is crazy," he said.

"Hunting your own team?"

"Yeah." He looked around to see who was listening. "It's really hard on the old man." I must have looked confused. "Colonel Hanson," he said.

"These guys we're looking for were his right-hand men. I'm the new boy. Just transferred in. All of the others were handpicked and personally trained by Hanson. Chilt — Lieutenant Bradbury — would have replaced him in a couple of years. So, Hanson's taking it hard. Like a kick right to the teeth."

I turned to look at Wild Bill. With his sunglasses off, his eyes had a tight, red, glassy look. A muscle ticked and twitched in his jaw. Finishing with the map and jabbing a finger at his driver, he slogged back through the snow to the Weasel, which fired up before he was even properly seated. Newhouse saluted again.

"Nice meeting you." And he jogged to his seat. We could see them all fastening seat belts like they were in an aircraft. In seconds they were moving and in less than a minute they'd gone out of sight over the rise.

Kellar approached, and I noticed both Frank and William edging nearer, ready for trouble.

"You owe me a gun!" he said, petulant. "A good one!" He shook a fist under my nose then turned to wedge himself back onto the Polaris. In seconds, it was headed back down the trail.

Jacobs walked over to a gun-shaped dimple in the snow, plunged in an arm and came up with the service .38. "Guess that fat bastard didn't want to wrinkle his belly," he said, tucking the revolver into his pack as we turned to go.

CHAPTER 8

We headed west, breaking trail on snowshoes. Jack romped and carried on in the drifts like this was all sport. William took the lead, followed by Jacobs then me. Dragging my snowshoes over and through soft powder, sweating lightly, I was unable to stop thinking about and fearing for Evie and Andy.

Topping a rise, we paused. The next valley stretched out before us like a flattened V, about five miles long and three across. We had the sun on our left, still shoulder high in a flawless sky. Back in January the sun would have set at three and we'd be left to break trail by moonlight and stars. This far into spring we'd have light until nearly nine, which was good. We needed it. After that, if we hadn't found them, we'd break trail in the dark.

Small stands of birch, alder, and aspen spread throughout the valley, punctuated with a few smallish evergreens. On our right, too far to take the shot — not that we would out of season — a young bull moose, still carrying his considerable rack, grazed on willow tips unaware.

"He makes a pretty easy target out here," I said.

"Not as easy as us," Frank snorted over his shoulder. He was right. We were set up like yellow tin ducks in a carnival shooting gallery, ripe for a sniper with a scope. And according to Hanson, that was exactly who we were pursuing. I began imagining the bullet hole as it would appear in my chest, first a *zip* sound, unremarkable, and then the small red hole, just where I could bend my neck to see it under my chin. I'd been standing next to a man who was shot like that. He was already on his knees before I heard the shot. Being exposed like this made me want to duck, weave, or find cover until dark, not just keep walking along in a straight line, the tallest, easiest-to-hit targets for a mile.

"According to Newhouse," I told them, "Hanson is pretty stressed about it all. I know I wouldn't want to be tracking my own men!"

"It's a pretty terrible thing," said Jacobs, "to like a man, train him, and then have to go out hunting for him."

"Perhaps," said William. "But Hanson has trained him. He knows the quarry and what to expect. It is all the big surprise for *us*. Only when the bullet comes, will we know we have been shot." He thought for a beat. "Or maybe we will not."

So, he's thinking about it, too.

We made good time, for snowshoes, and within an hour were heading up the far slope. We'd seen no more moose and no people. The sun moving west, now shone much closer to eye level, not an advantage to us at least. According to Hanson's plastic map, we'd cross this rise and head down into a stream cut and deep shadow, which might feel a little safer even if it wasn't. Though as far as we knew, neither the bank robbers nor Evie and Andy would be expecting us to come this way. A short cut, Hanson had said.

Topping still another rise we started down much more steeply into the valley of a good-sized stream. It approached along the curve of the hill beneath us then into its own steep-sided canyon, still headed almost due west. Much less snow had fallen here, or drifted, and the frozen stream made a flat, stable trail almost like a highway through the wilderness. Though we'd still have to snowshoe, I welcomed the quickening pace.

When I *could* stop thinking about being shot, I couldn't stop thinking about Evie. Did I always know she was this headstrong? Well, yes, actually. Was it one of the things I loved about her? Sometimes. Maybe not so much right now. Did the idea of losing her fill me with fear? Even the thought of it makes it hard to breathe.

I tried to walk faster but still had William and Frank in my way, both their heads swiveling from side to side.

They're uneasy!

"Great place for an ambush," said Jacobs, his voice low. As if in answer, William held up a hand and beckoned us to circle up.

"There are no tracks here," he said softly. "Nothing that says people are near. *But...* these robbers, at least some of them, have trained in this area. They may even have the same map. Which raises the question..."

"Why didn't they head this way," I asked, "if it's supposed to be a short cut?"

"Exactly." He considered. "We are either in a very good position, ready to intersect their trail, hopefully just in front of Evie and Andy, or..."

"...we're headed into an ambush," said Jacobs, looking around, listening hard. We all were.

"Let us make it more difficult for snipers," said William. He led us off to the far-right edge of the streambed to walk single file beneath an overhung fringe of small trees. Now a sniper shot from this side of the creek would be difficult or impossible. Of course, shooting from the far side, we were dead yellow ducks.

It was nearly murky at the canyon bottom and I had taken my sunglasses off, glancing skyward, blinking and squinting at the still-brilliant edge of sunlight off the snowy rim. That's when the sniper rose in his white snow suit, outlined in sunset gold, sighting through his scope.

"Sniper at eleven o'clock," I blurted, watching the gun barrel sweep back from William to Frank to me. Knowing I had waited too long, I threw myself to my right. A rifle fired, the blast deafening in this closed, hard-edged place. In midair, I braced myself for the hit, landing, trying unsuccessfully to roll in more than a foot of snow with snowshoes still on. I couldn't.

But I wasn't hit. Not even nearly. William had fired first, either wounding the sniper or startling him so badly that he dropped his weapon. We saw and heard it rattle and clatter, bouncing off the rock ledge until it finally fired on its own about halfway down, the blast echoing and re-echoing.

The sniper ducked and disappeared. By then both Frank and William had a knee with rifles up and shells bolted in, searching through scopes for a target. Picking up my rifle and dusting the snow off, checking the barrel, I joined them, Jack all but glued to my side. But our target had flown, which only made sense since he'd lost his long gun. When the echoes faded and the ringing in our ears began to subside, we stood. I brushed myself off and readjusted my snowshoe bindings, preparing to move forward.

A hundred miles from here the sun slipped behind a mountain rim in the Alaska Range, leaving behind only its glow. For us in the bottom of a canyon, the light simply winked off like a switch thrown. There was no question of losing our way. We could only go ahead or we could go back. We welcomed the anonymity of this sudden twilight and approaching darkness. At least I did. Even though the bank robbers knew we were here, knew we were trailing them, for the first time all day I didn't feel like I had a bullseye on my back.

William waved us up. "We could camp here."

"They know we're here," said Jacobs. "They could line up along the rim there and blow us to pieces. I say we keep going. Not much else we can do."

"Maybe one thing." I told them my idea and we started scrounging through the woody creek fringe for useful materials. Within about an hour, when the attack came, our small fire had burned lower but the three dark shapes encircling it remained easy targets. They fired maybe fifty rounds in all, on and on, more than enough to decimate the three of us. They even shot the fire, leaving scattered embers to glow like cat's eyes in the frosty darkness. Then they went away, probably feeling successful, no doubt feeling safe.

CHAPTER 9

"Bullets to burn," said Jacobs. He pointed at some of the glowing embers. "Looks like they are."

The camp scene was a fake. We had bundled ourselves in our sleeping bags about a hundred feet farther on, nesting in snow, well back under the fringe of trees. Rifles ready — shells in the chambers — we nibbled cold snacks and dozed, me half leaning against a pair of small willow trees. Partly warmed by Jack, who curled up alongside, I wasn't nearly as uncomfortable as I could have been. Fortunately, we didn't have to wait too long. We turned in at ten and they hit us at just about midnight.

Breaking off tree limbs and digging beneath the snow for old leaves and branches had allowed us to construct sleeping bag shapes in the snow. Firing by starlight from the cliff rim, from about a hundred feet, we reasoned they wouldn't know the difference and clearly they hadn't.

I admit I shivered surveying the 'carnage,' a deeper chill than that brought on by the minus-twenty degree temperature. This could have been us — would have been us — had we bedded down in our usual way around the fire, under the stars. We'd be dead now, bleeding out in the snow, not knowing or caring that sometime before dawn wolves would come.

Back on the ice, snowshoes on, with our sleeping bags rolled up and stowed, William gave me an uncharacteristic pat on the back.

"It was a very good plan. Now, we do not have to guess where they are. All we must do is follow their trail."

From the bottom of the canyon, the sky above appeared light, glowing with starlight and the first sliver of moon. We set out again, single file behind William and about twenty feet apart, pushing along through the canyon and still heading mostly west.

Stepping and dragging my snowshoes, feeling the tightness in my lower back, I had plenty of time to wonder why our quarry avoided taking the canyon short cut, but staked it out anyway. My suspicion? That they expected to be tracked by Hanson and the rest of his group, using their same map. They'd all trained out here together, knew where to go and where to shelter. But Hanson had warned us, hadn't he? *Not so much*, I decided.

My thoughts returned to Evie and Andy. Knowing them, they were tracking along through this same darkness, taking advantage of being hard to see and shot at by starlight. Were we near them now? Did they hear the shots? Would we rejoin the trail behind the robbers but in front of Evie and Andy as Hanson had suggested? I hoped so, but without much confidence.

I don't know how to navigate by stars, not that we had to in a canyon. And truthfully, I can't name much of what I see up there. I do know the popular formations and, wrapped in the quilt of darkness and lonely cold, those stars smiled at me brightly, warmly, like old friends — the Big Dipper, the North Star, and Polaris. And I could pick out Orion's belt and the Pleiades. I guessed at planets, Venus, Mars and maybe Jupiter.

I also tried to see something moving up there, the Russian Sputnik II. William had explained that the name Sputnik means 'something with a traveler,' in this case an object traveling with the earth. They say you can see it, but I hadn't yet. It was hard to imagine some manmade thing circling, so far up and so far away from the comforts of the earth.

I thought of the Moscow street dog named Laika that the Soviets had put aboard with no intention of trying to retrieve her. The story I read was that they developed a feeding mechanism, a lever she could push to get food. I imagined her finally flying through space at some ferocious speed, hopefully pushing a lever after the food had all been dispensed.

Here on earth, searching through the night for my lost friends, the plight of that lost dog made me teary and I had to swipe at my cheeks with a sleeve to keep tears from freezing in their tracks.

In a couple of miles and less than an hour of snowshoeing, the steep canyon walls gave way to a broad flat plain. Relieved to be back out in the open, we left the ice and, backtracking, soon found the ambushers' trail. It turned out to be not so easy and obvious as we had imagined. They were on skis not snowshoes, the trail hidden in darkness until we were literally stepping on it. William waved us up.

He shook back his parka hood. "We have their trail," he said, the warm breath of his words forming a moonlit silver cloud. He looked west, at the same time pulling off his wire-rim spectacles to massage the bridge of his nose. "We know which way they are heading."

"Time to camp?" asked Frank.

"Yes," said William, "I am thinking it so."

I turned to look around the snowscape. Off on a

slight rise to our right stood a dark cluster of small trees. The only near shelter. "Over there?" I pointed and we started for it.

From that slight rise, before bedding down, I pulled out binoculars to scan the landscape, hoping to see the smallest flicker of firelight. I saw nothing. Of course, at something like three in the morning, who would be awake feeding a fire? Who but us?

Frank turned from shaking out his army bag. "Come on," he said. "Get some sleep. We're close. We'll find them soon."

I was glad to shed snowshoes. I hated them, really. They played heck with my lower back. *Am I too old for this?* I wondered fleetingly, not that it mattered. But walking with snowshoes was far better than stumbling through deep snow without them. Shedding only mukluks, I augered my way deep into my sleeping bag. Settling back, feeling the bite of those tight, lower back muscles beginning to relax, I turned my eyes to the stars and allowed a quick prayer. *Keep them safe.* Then I pulled the drawstring tight, leaving just the small opening to breathe through, and closed my eyes.

* * *

In the next moment, it was already light, the sun rising. I dug up my sleeve for my Timex. After nine. We'd slept some six hours in that instant.

Our clear skies from the day before had blown away, along with the night's stars, leaving the sky heavily overcast and leaden. A few fat flakes settled like casual afterthoughts. An insistent breeze sighing and *wooing* coldly in crannies lifted and skittered small flurries of snow and icy pellets to about knee high. I shivered, not from cold — still bundled in the depths of my goose-down sleeping bag — but from the expectation of cold and a long day out in it. And then my bladder complaining, I had no choice but to crawl out and start the day.

We three were a dour bunch in the morning and in these moments, I more than missed Andy. I missed his ease on the trail in snow and genuinely lousy conditions, his quick way with a fire and trail food, his really dumb jokes and his willingness to laugh at them again and again. The risk and possible loss of him made a painful fist in my gut.

Within about fifteen minutes, we were packed and ready to head out, snowshoes strapped on. "I'll break," I said. I saw the look exchanged between William and Frank. "What!?" I demanded, imagining myself weighed in the balances and found wanting. "Why not?"

"It is the leader," said William tentatively, "who is most likely to be the target."

"Okay."

"It's not in your job description," said Jacobs. "This is a manhunt. You're not even supposed to be here. And if we find Evie, but you get your ass shot all to pieces..."

"This is our job," said William, cutting in, still delicate. "Let us do it."

I looked at them, annoyance subsiding. I heard what they said, knew they were right, and that it *was* more their job than mine.

"No," I said turning, picking up the ski trail to lead us down a long grade, hopefully to Evie and Andy. Silent, they fell in behind me, again about twenty paces between us.

The trail led down another long valley and then up and over the other side. I kept wondering where was the rest of the manhunt? We neither saw nor heard snow machines, and the occasional airplane droned over without interest.

About an hour on, we found the place the skiers had camped. They left nothing, not even cigarette butts.

"Camp stove." Frank pointed to a six-inch circular snow imprint surrounded by melt. "Must be nice to have all the gear."

"To borrow from the military," added William.

I crouched, flexing my knees to stretch my aching back muscles. Jack saw it as the perfect opportunity for me to pet him and he nuzzled my parka pocket for a bit of moose jerky.

Jacobs pulled a compass out of his parka pocket, focused on it, and turned a slow circle. "Anybody know where we are?" I didn't. William shook his head.

"If I'm right at all," he said, "we're heading toward the Yukon, skirting just along the edge of a big swampy valley. We should cross the road to Manley Hot Springs within a couple of hours. Maybe that's what they're up to. They'll have a truck waiting there to whisk them away, and we'll be stuck afoot way out here in the boonies."

"It's not a bad plan," I said.

He shook his head and put away his compass. "No, it isn't." He looked around. "Sure oughta be crossing their trail soon."

He was right. In about two hundred yards, the ambush trail met up with the snow machine trail. More than that, we found it all overlaid with what looked like Hanson's Weasel tracks. Snowshoe tracks told us we were also still following Andy and Evie. We hadn't gotten here first to intercept them. Hopefully Hanson would.

65

"Damn," I said.

Jacobs squinted off west. "We'll find them. Maybe by the time we do, Hanson will have them all wrapped up for us. We won't need to get shot at... again."

A sift of snow starting to fill in the tracks told us that we weren't as close as we hoped.

William waved a dismissive hand at both of us. "We are walking. The robbers and the army are driving snow machines. It is not likely we would overtake them. But..." His voice trailed off.

Frank gave him the sharp lawman look I'd learned to recognize. "But what?"

William examined the area, walking from point to point, his mitted hand numbering whatever it was he counted. "We were told five. There are too many. Maybe..." he hesitated, "...maybe ten. It is lucky we have the army ahead of us. Otherwise we are badly outnumbered."

Frank also counted. I didn't. The truth being, I didn't care. "Let's move," I said, and they both looked at me.

Jack whined, making his fake let's-get-going moves toward the trail, like he was thinking what I was thinking and wanted us to just get on with it. Or I may have just been looking for anyone who would agree with me.

"We need to get going," I told them and started walking. Again I got no argument. They fell in behind.

But it began to snow shortly, which was troubling. This a springtime snowfall, nothing like a blizzard. Just fat leisurely flakes with plenty of space between them. But at the same time, more wind pushed a steady cloud of the stuff low around us, and it would soon wipe away any but the machine tracks. I made myself walk faster.

For a time, the land became very flat, and I said so.

"Swamp," said Frank. "I've flown over this. There's a thousand ponds here. You can't make it through here in the summer without a canoe. Even then it's rough going. Couple more miles we get some sharp hills. Unless the trail turns north. I'm betting it does."

It did. But not before we found ourselves following along a steep-sided forested valley. That's when I circled us up.

"Too many places to hide around here," muttered Frank. What we were all thinking. Even Whisky Jack looked worried, and instead of roaming forward, had pulled back to walking behind my snowshoes, occasionally stepping on one of them. I hadn't fallen on my face yet, but it was only a matter of time.

"It is a good place to be ambushed," agreed William, speaking very softly. Out of the wind, silence sat heavy here. His eyes met mine. "I am taking the lead." I shrugged. There didn't seem to be anything worth saying.

We followed on, rising out of the valley and steadily up a steep-sided hill. This wasn't just a sled trail. I turned to look back at Frank, the question on my face. "Tractor road," he said. "I've seen it from the air. Forest Service plus hunters and prospectors. The road to Manley is..." he pointed, "just over there... somewhere."

At a wide spot, around a sharp bulge of hill, the tracks went crazy. Both the Excelsior snow machines and The Weasel had sloughed around, tightly circling, munching up tread tracks a blind man could have followed. We stopped, circled up, and tried to read an unreadable trail. I looked at the others.

"Something happened here. But what?"

It was Jack who sniffed out the clue. Something had been dumped over the edge where the hill fell away steeply down through tree trunks and boulders. Jack snuffled and danced sideways from foot to foot. He kept looking at me like, 'This is important, do something!'

They'd rolled something here, something bulky. I could make out its trail down thirty or forty feet to where it lodged against a rock. By now heavily snow dusted, it looked like a gunny sack of something like refuse. Like something not worth carrying and they figured this was as good a place as any to dump it.

Jack started down the steep slope, which was good enough for me. I shed my snowshoes to climb down behind him, wading in two feet of snow, grabbing at branches and trunks to catch myself and keep from rolling down.

But I was wrong. It wasn't refuse, at least to me. And it certainly wasn't something I wanted to throw down, to have freeze solid and disappear forever.

My heart pounding in my throat, I brushed away snow and felt in the parka hood for a pulse. Then I looked up and shouted to the silhouettes of the others watching from the ledge.

"It's Andy! He's alive."

CHAPTER 10

It took all three of us, with Jack lunging and muttering at my side — wanting to help — to drag Andy back up the steep snowy slope to level ground.

About half way up, his eyelids fluttered then opened. His lips moved but I couldn't make it out and leaned closer.

"What kept you?" he mumbled.

Admittedly still pissy about being deceived and left behind, I said, "Next time just take me with you. You can save us all a lot of trouble."

He blinked his eyes open. Making a rueful face, he jerked his head in a kind of snort then winced at the pain of it. "Then you'da been down there with me," he said. "Or worse."

He tried to turn his head and look around. "Where's Evie?" I just shook my head.

Once at the top, we laid him out in the snow and I crouched close. This could be bad. We were miles from anywhere. "Where are you hurt?"

"Everywhere! Feels like they rolled me down a mountain."

"They did."

He thought about that for a beat. "Better roll me down again, I think I missed a tree." He tried to laugh but that hurt, too.

"Are you shot?"

"No, I think I'm mostly okay, except for where I hit the trees. Just feel like shit. If there's any part of me that *doesn't* hurt, I ain't found it yet."

I felt myself start to breathe again. "That's good news. It could have been a lot worse."

"Yeah," he agreed. He lay there a minute more, his eyes rolling up toward the heavy clouds. "Get me up. We gotta go after Evie."

"You sure... about standing, I mean?"

"I think I am. Might as well give it a try."

Jacobs and I each grabbed him by an arm to lever him up. At the same time, I noticed William move off a bit, standing guard, rifle ready.

On his feet, Andy wobbled then steadied. "Sure got a headache." He reached back into his parka hood to feel the back of his skull. "And a goose egg."

"I got aspirin," said Frank, and went to dig in his pack.

Andy looked William. "Got your hanky?" He did, and gave it to him. Andy filled it with snow and used it to ice the back of his head. When Jacobs came with the aspirin, Andy took four and swallowed them with snow. He looked around. "Seen my rifle here anywhere?"

His rifle, a German-made Mauser, had been his sniper rifle from the war, a custom Karabiner 98 with the long barrel and Zeiss scope.

To no one's surprise, the gun was gone.

"Ouch," said Frank. As we all realized that our bad situation had just gotten worse, especially in the hands of a trained shooter.

"Well," said Andy, "we'll just have to get it back." He looked around, eyes clearing. "So, they took Evie…"

I just nodded and swallowed hard. Honestly, I couldn't speak at the thought of it.

He reached out to pat me on the shoulder. "We'll

get her back."

We talked about backtracking to the canyon where the sniper dropped his rifle. But it was too far to go for a rifle that — having fallen a hundred feet and bounced off rocks — might not be worth much, anyway.

"Take mine," I told him. He looked at me and then at the rifle, my new Winchester, a Christmas gift from Evie.

"You sure?"

I handed him the gun. "Can you walk?"

"Oh, yeah," he said. "I'd crawl if I had to. I owe them… at least a big headache."

"Look at this!" Frank, now circling on the edge of the clearing sounded happy, bending to reach for something in the snow, and I imagined — hoped — it would be Andy's rifle. But it wasn't. Instead, Frank straightened with Andy's snowshoes in hand.

This was good. I looked around at the others. "Nothing to stop us now. Let's go." Finding the snowshoes definitely upped the score in our column. Andy bent to strap them on, wobbling a little.

We were still on the tractor road, thanks to the Weasel, a wide trail that allowed me to walk along at Andy's side. "What happened back there?"

"Man, I don't know! We caught up to them… thought we were chasing five. But it was an ambush, like they knew we were coming. Turns out there were ten or twelve in all. They came skiing fast down out of the woods in those white army suits, guns up. We knew we were toast, so we set our rifles down and raised our hands. One of them snagged our guns and then somebody walloped me from behind. The rest you know."

Within a mile or two we found another Excelsior,

the tank dry.

"Why forget gas on your getaway?" Jacobs again said what we were all thinking. About two miles farther on we found the last Excelsior, also bone dry. The trail was a mishmash from here. There were a bunch of skiers, followed by Weasel treads, breaking trail for a snowshoe pair and one set of mukluk tracks.

Andy knelt to sort it all out then looked up. "This patched mukluk sole is probably Roberta's." He didn't have to tell us the snowshoes were Evie's.

"With Roberta walking, we should be catching up with somebody," I said. But we didn't.

About three o'clock, the clouds raised and opened, sunbeams knifing through to find us, the air warming, or maybe just seeming to. We'd been climbing a long, forested hill. Coming up and over the summit, we saw yet another extended dish of smooth treeless valley spread out before us. Near the far side, we could make out a shiny ribbon of something, four or five miles distant on a north-south line.

I pointed and asked, though I should have known. "What's that?"

"The road to Manley," said Frank.

"We need to find a payphone," said Andy. "Call for a ride."

"A payphone? Good luck," muttered Frank, who hadn't yet learned that about half of what Andy said on the trail was for amusement, mostly his own.

We heard a distant gunshot and its echoes. William searched through his scope and then pointed. "Ahead! It is the Weasel, under fire."

At first we hadn't seen the white snow machine, well blended into the snowfield and shifting light, with its black rectangle of windshield angled away.

Peering through his scope — my scope — Andy said, "Heads up. It's Hanson and his men under fire. Which means we will be, too. Soon."

But we weren't. Nearly jogging in our snowshoes, we made it out to the Weasel in record time, without drawing fire. We found Hanson and two of his men covering behind the machine. I looked around. One missing. "Where's Newhouse?"

Hanson made a glum face and jerked his thumb at the Weasel cab. I ducked to look in and saw Newhouse, just sitting in the passenger seat. Moving around the machine to make eye contact, I first saw the bullet hole through the front of the engine cowling then through the windshield, and finally through his chest. His blue eyes were open, but he was gone.

Opening the Weasel door, I crossed myself and then made the sign of the cross on the dead man's already-cooling forehead. After three years in Chandalar, I could say the words in my sleep... and probably did.

"Unto God's gracious mercy and protection we commit you. The Lord bless you and keep you. The Lord make his face to shine upon you, and be gracious unto you. The Lord lift up his countenance upon you, and give you peace, both now and forevermore. Amen."

As soon as I straightened, Colonel Hanson circled us up.

"There are more of them than we thought," he said. "We thought five, but there are at least ten. Some are highly trained for combat in these conditions, and deadly. Men like these on skis, are the ones who stopped *two* Russian armored divisions during the war." He met each of our eyes.

"What I'm saying is that we're in deep trouble. Three of us up against ten of them is nearly suicidal. He sounded cautionary but looked proud. Though according to him, these men would be trying to kill them.

"Seven," I said.

Hanson looked up. "Huh?"

"There are seven of us."

He looked around as if surprised. "You're civilians. Your job is to get down and stay down."

"Civilians?" Frank scowled. "I don't think so." William just *humphed*.

"What about them?" asked Hanson, meaning Andy and me.

Frank shrugged and jerked a thumb in my direction. "People are offering money to get rid of him." Hanson gave him an odd look.

Frank turned to Andy and me. "There isn't anything I could tell you that would convince you to stay out of this, is there?"

Andy shrugged and turned to me. "Nothing I can think of."

I shrugged back and shook my head.

Frank turned to Hanson. "See what I'm up against?"

We heard a *zip* and a hard whack as a round hit the Weasel undercarriage. Then distantly we heard the discharge.

A volley of shots from up the hill, cover shots, drew our attention back to the top just as three skiers came blasting out of the trees, over the brow of the hill and down, picking up speed.

"I'd never seen anything quite like it. They came roaring down the long slope, actually firing their semiautomatic M1s on their way. How accurate could they be? Flattening myself in the snow, I didn't wait to find out.

The M1 clip holds eight rounds. Each shooter would fire as fast as he could pull his trigger and change magazines in seconds, so all together, most of one hundred twenty rounds could be fired in the next minute.

From where I lay, they seemed to be aiming at the Weasel, the large target, which absorbed hit after hit. So many of the slugs hit Newhouse where he sat that he seemed reanimated, shifting and jumping in his seat. It was one of the most horrible sights I've ever seen. We tried to stay low behind the Weasel's metal parts, though many of those weren't stopping the .30 caliber slugs.

About halfway down the hill, the hail of bullets stopped as all three skiers reloaded in the same three or four seconds. Poor planning. I looked at Andy who raised his eyebrows at me, like 'Here goes!'

He stood in an almost leisurely way. From up the hill someone snapped off a shot at him. It zipped by like a flying insect, which was as much attention as he paid. At the same time, he raised my Winchester, sighting through the scope.

"Get down!" shouted Hanson, used to being obeyed. "You don't stand a chance!"

Andy didn't get down. He fired just three times. After each shot he bolted a fresh shell into the chamber in a smooth, nearly continuous motion. I knew he'd had enough of killing in the war, but it didn't stop him from firing arm and leg shots at attackers. It was enough. They went tumbling, rifles falling into snow, skis flying off, some sliding down empty. The world went silent.

Hanson gaped at Andy, back under cover and

fiddling with an adjustment on the scope.

We all fully expected a fresh volley from the shooters remaining on the hill. None came. We waited, crouched in the snow. The minutes felt everlasting. I think we knew what they'd done but we stayed put. Finally, it was Andy who, looking up from his scope — my scope — spoke the words.

"They're gone."

CHAPTER 11

The bank robbers and their hostages just disappeared. Like they fell off a glacier into space. The snow trail ended at the Manley road, and they apparently made it out before the Territorial Police roadblocks went up.

With the exception of Newhouse, the new guy, Hanson's team got to go home unscathed. And in spite of all the bullets aimed in our direction, Andy, William, Frank, me — and Jack — also made it out without getting shot.

Within the hour, a rugged Sikorsky Chickasaw helicopter, all in army drab, came skimming low over the hills. They would pick us up back at the Weasel. They put out four perimeter guards just in case then loaded us in with all our gear, quickly getting us strapped into our jump seats.

At four thousand pounds, the Weasel would be too heavy to haul home, at least with the Chickasaw, so they got Newhouse out of the front seat and into a body bag, with some difficulty as he had already started to freeze sitting up. But they'd done this before and we were loaded and airborne in less than fifteen minutes, headed back for Fairbanks.

After most of two days of snowshoeing, it turned out Fairbanks was only about twenty minutes away.

Jack didn't like the helicopter noise and so he yowled and complained. I didn't like it much myself but resisted yowling. More than being agitated by noise, I felt nearly frantic about losing Evie's trail. Andy looked at me and pressed his lips together, like he could read my mind, and reached over to pat my leg. Frank and William were practicing their inscrutable lawman looks. I couldn't tell what they were thinking.

From Ladd Field, Hanson and Smitty, one of his aides, Jeeped us back to my truck next to the Cushman Street Bridge. They waited, idling, while we made sure the Ford would start. With the temperature at about minus ten, the battery cold, and the oil well thickened, it didn't want to. In fact, hearing the labored growl of the engine as it slowly turned, I thought we'd be walking back to Andy's restaurant where he kept his Chevy plugged in.

But then it coughed once, coughed again, and started. I let it idle slowly to warm the oil and give the surfaces a chance to coat. It was a good truck and I hoped to keep it a long time, well worth waiting a few minutes to let it warm up.

Hanson climbed out of the Jeep with us. I could tell he had something to say.

"I'm sorry we lost the trail, lost your friend." He looked at me directly. "We'll find them. I'm ordering out extra aircraft from right now." He turned his attention to Frank and William.

"I can't order you boys to stay home. I know you'll do what you need to. But I am asking, as your... friend... that you leave this search to us. The people we're after are trained killers." He made an *aw shucks* kind of shrug. "I trained 'em. I can find 'em. And I'll do everything possible to bring the women home safely. You trust me, don't you?" We nodded. What could we say — 'No darn way?'

Nobody said anything. Hanson bent to scratch

Jack behind the ears. "I'm just glad we all — well, most of us — made it home safe. Let's see that we stay that way." He climbed back into his Jeep, the vehicle jumping into motion just about the time his butt hit the seat. I wondered if they practiced that move.

"Okay," said Frank.

I looked at him. "Okay what?"

"Okay, now I know how it feels to have some official big wheel tell you to not be doing what *you* know you *need* to be doing."

"Only now?" I asked, admittedly baiting him. He snorted and waved me off.

"We gotta get Evie and the girl back," he said, cutting to the chase. And I agreed.

* * *

Our Thermos coffee had run out at the end of day one on the trail. Since we hadn't built a fire, we'd had neither coffee nor tea most of two days — nearly an eternity — as Andy was quick to point out. So, when I said, "Where to?" his answer was simple and direct.

"Coffee." So, we headed straight for *Andrea's,* the northern home of high quality, Italian-roasted coffee. We got there at dinner time, but found the place closed and locked up tight.

"What the heck!" said Andy.

"It is Monday," reminded William. "You are closed."

"Oh, yeah." In minutes, Andy had water on to boil, beans ground, and a French press warming. With Andy on coffee duty, Frank, William, and I eased wearily into chairs at a nearby table and Jack sank to the floor with an audible *clunk*. I think he was looking forward to getting home and getting back to his furnace grate.

The conversation didn't start until Andy came bearing a tray with coffee in the clear glass mugs, cream, and sugar.

Frank selected a mug and sipped from it, nodding. "Looks like you're getting the hang of this restaurant business."

Andy smiled at him, but only about half wattage, his mind elsewhere. I knew we were all thinking about her so I said it.

"How are we going to get Evie and Roberta back?"

"We must find them first," said William. "Somehow. I do not think we will be getting much help from the Army."

"We need a map." Frank got up to cross the room and dig in the pocket of his parka where he'd hung it on the rack. He returned with a plastic-laminated, folded map, just like Hanson's. He spread the map across the table, moving the tray to another table and shifting coffee mugs, all the while pretending we weren't all staring at him. Finally, he looked up.

"What?"

"Nice map," said Andy.

"Oh, this? It's just something I picked up... right after one of Hanson's men set it down. Look, you can spill coffee on it!" And he did spill coffee, grinned, and then wiped if off with a napkin.

"Nice going." Andy clapped him on the back. "You stole it. I knew hanging around with criminals would do you good."

"Oh yeah, thanks," said Jacobs, a forefinger already tracing our route out of Fairbanks and around in a westerly loop toward the Manley Hot Springs road. "Somebody tell me why bank robbers would do this? It's not a getaway. It's a..."

"Diversion," said William. He leaned in. "They got us to watch them and chase them while they did something else with the bearer bonds. It was a good plan and it worked."

"Except that none of us give a hoot about bearer bonds," I said. "We were trying to get the women back safely. They took Roberta to help focus our attention. Why did they take Evie? They didn't take you," I said to Andy. He shrugged and raised his eyebrows.

"They already had the Army's attention." Jacobs furrowed his brow. "The bearer bonds made that happen. But why…?"

Andy clunked his already empty mug down on the table top. "And now the Army won't talk to us? They were happy enough to send us out at the front of the pack. What was that about?"

"Cannon fodder," said William. He held his coffee mug in both hands. "I do not think they wanted to be the first to go out searching for their own snipers."

Andy twisted his mouth around, scowled, and said again, "So they sent us out and now they won't talk to us."

That's when it came to me. "But I know who will." And I told them my idea. They agreed right away.

"Might as well," said Frank, fetching his parka and sliding an arm into one sleeve. As Federal marshal, he would be the contact. He said it. "There's not a single other thing we can do." And I told them I'd take care of it.

In Central Alaska, where there aren't many telephones or ways to connect, a program called *Tundra Topics* functions as a kind of radio bulletin board.

People in the villages can write or call in with news they need to communicate. Like 'Celia Jones from Minto had a nine-pound baby boy on Tuesday. Mother and son are doing fine. They'll fly home on Friday.'

I worked on the wording all the way back to Chandalar, Jack curled up on the seat beside me with his chin resting on my thigh, his head handy for petting. By the time I got home, I knew what to say, already anticipating the satisfaction of hearing it read on the air. With any luck, this would be the tiny snowball starting its roll down the mountain. Now, if it just wouldn't get so big that it crushed us.

Two nights later I dragged myself to dinner at the Coffee Cup Café, a 1920s-vintage false-front building next in line on the main street to the larger, false-fronted general store. It was twilight as I approached, and lamplight shining out the two, big plate-glass windows — still frosted halfway up — shone warm and welcoming.

Coming in to the warmth and noise, greeting friends, I worked my way across the room to sit at my regular chair beneath the dusty moose head. Lost in thoughts of Evie, I didn't even taste my usually delicious moose cheeseburger, greasy fries and coffee from the red can.

Rosie had the little Philco tuned to KFAR as she worked the room, clearing tables and refilling the famous bottomless coffee mug. She wore her pink waitress uniform, the one with *Rosie* stitched provocatively over her left breast, her white-framed eyeglasses — the ones that swooped stylishly back at the bows — and on her feet, sporty white U.S. Keds with the little blue emblem at the back.

Guy Mitchell had just finished his hit, "Singing

the Blues" — which seemed appropriate — when *Tundra Topics* came on the air and Rosie went to turn it up.

The noise level in the place subsided as we all paused to listen to the messages. From the kitchen, we heard water running and pans gently clanging, while out front, patrons finished up, sipping last coffee and exhaling silver streams of cigarette smoke that rose like dreams, only to flatten at the ceiling and dissipate.

For me, listening to *Tundra Topics* was a bit like picking up the receiver on the party line, back in the South where I'd been raised. Most of life's essential elements were represented here. Births, deaths, lost and found, back-ordered parts for outboard motors or generators, scheduled meetings...

"Nolan Titus should meet Emerson George at Bishop's Rock on the Yukon, below Galena. Bring the beaver traps."

No surprise, our message came last.

"Finally," read the announcer, "this from U.S. Marshal Frank Jacobs, marked urgent. He says Fairbanks' bank robbers with two female hostages are on the run. There are about a dozen of them, some on skis. If you see them, *do not* approach. They are to be considered armed and very dangerous. Contact Marshal Jacobs in Fairbanks." It finished up with his phone number and the direction, 'Call collect.'

That was it, then. I finished my coffee, not the 'good stuff.' All the while Rosie circled me. She knew from her sweetie, Andy, that Evie was still missing. Knowing how I'd feel about it, she circled back by frequently, patting and fussing over me. But she had stopped bustling when *Tundra Topics* came on, coming to stand with her hand on my shoulder as we listened together. When it was done I looked up, meeting her eyes as she nodded. I didn't say it, but I remember thinking, *Just try to hide now!*

* * *

It happened in the Alaska way. I heard a trapper on snowshoes saw them, as he was headed in with a bundle of stretched-round beaver hides strapped to his pack frame. He told a woodcutter north of Minto what he'd seen, and I could just imagine how it went.

"Just about sundown," he'd said, firing his pipe with a wooden kitchen match, sucking and blowing great clouds of bluish smoke, "I seen skiers — three of 'em — in white suits. "They was tryin' to *not* be seen." He laughed. "*See* 'em? Hell, I *smelled* 'em. Store-bought cigarettes and Old Spice."

Next day the woodcutter told the Minto postmaster about the skiers, what the trapper had seen, where and when. The woodcutter had come in for lesson six in his mail-order course on the ancient art and science of phrenology.

I heard he said, "Yep, won't always be a woodcutter. Someday gonna have an office in Fairbanks, with my own shingle." He was going to have a wife too, as he'd just received the information he mailed in a dollar for. He'd been waiting for a brochure titled, *Japanese Women Make Good Wives.*

And the postmaster told all this to the bush pilot who flew in Friday from Fairbanks, delivering home Celia Jones and her baby, as promised on *Tundra Topics* earlier in the week. Hours later, the pilot, Len Samuels — also known as Petey — landed at Ladd Field in Fairbanks. Then as directed, he dropped a nickel into the payphone just outside the pilot's lounge to call Marshal Frank Jacobs.

And then Petey called me.

CHAPTER 12

"I don't get it," Andy said again, a tight muscle ticking at the side of his jaw. "Somebody picked them up on the Manley road where they might have gone north and looped back around to Fairbanks." He paused to let this sink in. "Instead, they went south about twenty miles — just enough to lose everybody tracking them — and then headed off overland again? Does that make sense?"

It didn't. Late on Saturday we were still stuck in Chandalar watching the weather erode. Through my kitchen window we watched heavy clouds sweep in, blotting out sky, driven by gusty winds. There simply wasn't a single other thing to do but stand in my small kitchen, too wound up to even sit on the tippy stools. William had gone home for fresh clothes and to check in with his security work at Clear's government RADAR station. Jack was pacing. Andy and I were drinking the good Italian coffee but not really tasting it. The caffeine only added to how jangled we already felt.

Our conclusion? That instead of making a clean getaway to somewhere, these bank robbers were just circling, miles and miles cross country. And they still had Evie and Roberta.

"I don't get it," Andy said yet again, as the phone rang. "Maybe they're lost?" he added as I went to answer.

Usually I dread the phone ringing. But now I

nearly jogged to it, Jack surging and clicking along at my heels down the short hall and into my office. Dropping into my office chair, I said, "Hardy."

"Jacobs." And then without preamble, "Found those three skiers that Andy winged."

"Oh!" In that instant he had all my attention. "Are they talking?"

"Not frozen stiff with bullets in their heads. You fellas didn't find them and finish them, did you?"

"No!" I said maybe a bit sharply. "Why would we?"

"Gotta ask."

"Identities?"

"Carrying nothing. Stripped to their skivvies and unidentifiable. Two of them had short-range shotgun wounds to the face and to one arm that all but blasted them off.

"Tattoo removal!"

"That's what we think. Probably the SnoCorps insignia. Pretty messy. Pretty stupid, since they're probably local guys and easy to identify anyway. Dollars to donuts they're military. They have the look. Young and fit, with extra-short hair. Hanson's on his way down to see if he can identify 'em." Jacobs paused as if considering. I waited.

He took a breath. "We got a call," he continued, "about a possible sighting. Not sure if I should tell you."

"Why wouldn't you?"

Jacobs sighed. "Because I don't want you and William and Deadeye headed off into the woods trying to find these yahoos to get Evie back. Especially without me. There's too many of 'em."

"Well, don't tell me then."

"Huh?" he said. "That's not like you."

"Maybe I'm changing, maturing." He considered that.

"No, you're not. You already heard, didn't you? Samuels?"

"Yeah," I admitted.

"*Gaaaa!*" he said, frustrated. "You sure can't keep a secret around here, especially if you're the Law. Everybody knows everybody. Well, look. Don't start without me. I can't fly down in weather like this, but I'll be on the road as soon as this storm blows by. Promise me you'll wait."

"Frank, I can't promise you that."

"Well, try." He hung up.

Dropping the handset into its cradle, I had about one more second to wonder why the bank robbers were out circling in the Bush instead of hightailing it away with what sounded like a lot of loot. Then someone knocked on my front door.

I've learned to recognize the different kinds of knock. Some are timid, like 'I don't really want to bother you.' One of my parishioners, Adele Nielson, doesn't so much knock as scratch at the door, like a small cold bird that wants in.

Others, like emergencies after midnight or Fairbanks police chief Kellar, demand to be let in by pounding the door so hard it rattles an adjacent loose window pane — that I now need to re-putty this spring after the thaw.

But this knock was neither of those and Andy, knowing I'd been on the phone, stuck his head in at the office door. "I'll get that," he said. And Jack jumped around me to follow.

Andy moved out of sight and I heard him turn the knob, heard the complaint of a cold door swinging on frosty hinges. I heard his voice, greeting. "Hey there..." And then I heard the gunshot, impossibly loud in the small, closed space of my cabin.

I fairly blasted out of my office chair, driving it back on its small wheels to clatter against the wall. I made the tight turn through my office door, grabbing the door trim with my fingers, spinning out into the front room, never considering — until I was out there — that I could be the next target.

In the heartbeat it took me to get to the front door, my mind flashed images of what I might find, the final — the worst — being Andy down on my floor, deep red blood pooling on brown squares of linoleum.

But I found Andy on his feet, seemingly intact. With the door swung wide, bitterly cold, visibly-frosty air whirled and tumbled across the floor at knee level, dancing and dispersing a heavy cloud of bluish gun smoke.

Andy had the barrel of a .45 automatic clutched in his left hand and the throat of the apparent shooter in his right. Albert Jensen, who came to the church to borrow money every month or so!

Jensen was splayed against the doorframe, pinned by the throat in an attitude of surrender and of failure, attitudes he'd practiced. Probably in his late thirties, he looked older, with a chapped, weather-worn face and perpetual one-eyed smoker's squint. He wore a blue and orange knit cap pulled low over his ears, a red Sears parka, mismatched mitts, old jeans and thin-soled city boots. He smoked a hand-rolled cigarette and had perfected letting it hang carelessly from the farthest edge of his lip, so that more than anything it just looked stuck there. Even now, after being slammed into the wall, the cigarette still hung, ash building, smoldering, adding to the haze.

"Let him loose," I said.

"Loose?" said Andy. "He just tried to put a big hole in me."

"I thought you was him," wheezed Jensen, not getting much air, as he attempted a nod in my direction. As if that would make it all right.

"Oh, well, then…" said Andy. He pretended to let him go then slammed him back. He turned to meet my eyes. "You're gonna ask him why he came here to kill you, and he's gonna lie about it. I know him. We were at the mission school together. If we was standing out in the snow and I asked him if it was snowing, he'd say it was sunny, just because he likes the way a lie feels dripping out of his mouth."

"So, what are you thinking?" I asked him.

"I take him out back," said Andy. "Ask him once and then when he lies, shoot him between the eyes. We still won't know who put him up to this, but we won't have to look at him or listen to him, either." I must have looked surprised.

"So, how 'bout it? Can I just shoot him?"

"Well…" I said as if considering, hoping Andy really was bluffing.

"Wait!" wheezed Jensen. Andy loosened his grip slightly. "I'll tell. I won't lie. Don't let him shoot me!"

I raised both hands in a what-can-I-do shrug and his eyes widened.

"No, I really will," he said, but then I saw him start to look cagey. "If you let me go."

"You try to kill me and I'm supposed to let you go? I thought you and I were friends."

Something changed in his eyes, a refocusing. "Oh," he said. "Well, yeah. We're friends?"

"I thought we were," I said sadly. Andy let him stand but didn't let go of the throat.

"I... I... only took the job for the money. I needed the money. I didn't *really* want to kill you."

"Well," I said, "that's good. I guess." We looked at each other. "Did they already pay you?"

He shook his head. "Cheap bastards. Said I had to do the job first. Said if I had the money, I'd just go get drunk and not shoot you."

"Is that true?"

"Well..." He considered. "Yeah. Because we're friends."

I looked at Andy, who rolled his eyes, then back at Albert.

"Since we are friends, I guess I could ask Andy to let you go, if you can tell us — honestly — who was going to pay you to kill me? It's a thing I'd like to get to the bottom of."

"Sure." He pushed his mouth sideways in a thinking expression. Not one he was used to.

"Trouble is, I didn't exactly see them."

"He's lyin'!" Andy tightened his throat grip but I waved him back.

"Tell us," I said.

"I was at the Bide-A-While."

"When?" demanded Andy.

"Last night."

"What then?"

"I had to take a piss really bad. I think somebody was having like sex in the Men's, and they wouldn't come out. So, I went out the back door. I heard somebody walking behind me but didn't think nothing. There was two of 'em. Just when I started to unzip, one of them grabbed me and shoved a gun into my back, right here." He struggled to point at his kidney. "It really hurt and I *really* had to piss. Almost pissed myself standing there."

90

"Okay, what next?"

"The other guy — they was both wearing face masks — asked me did I know who you was. I said yeah. He said did I want to make some easy money? I said, sure. He gave me this .45, told me it was loaded, and told me I'd get a grand if I shot you dead. Told me to just knock on your door, blast you, and walk away."

Darn! In just days the bounty on me had slipped from five thousand down to one.

"And you thought this was okay?"

He looked at me and his jaw hung slack while he considered. "Hey, I really needed the money."

Andy and I exchanged a glance. "Let him go," I said.

Andy looked at me like my hair might be smoldering. "Seriously?"

"You won't try this again, will you, Albert?"

"Nah, man, I really learned my lesson this time. You sure won't see me trying this again."

Andy was right, Albert had told at least three lies in that one simple statement.

"Let him go," I said. Andy did let go of Albert's throat but caught him by the shoulders to turn him and make eye contact.

"You know me, right?"

"Sure," said Albert. "Andy." He shrugged and looked proud like, 'That was an easy one, and I nailed it.'

"And you know I can shoot."

"Sure," said Albert again, his expression darkening. I think he knew where this was headed.

"So you know. I see you coming our way again with a gun in your hand, I… will… put… a bullet… between your eyes. Get it?"

He got it. Unexpectedly, a tear rolled out of each of Albert's eyes and down his leathery cheeks. "Sure," he said, and sniffed. I shook Albert's hand and palmed him a ten. He looked at it, surprised. "What's that for?"

"Telling the truth," I told him. He nodded but still looked confused and turned to shuffle out the door into the blowing snow and brittle cold. Even Andy appeared to soften, and clapped him on the back as he went, like they were old friends.

"That was *too* close," he said when we finally got the door closed and locked. He looked down at the inside of the door panel which still had three wooden blocks glued in place at belt buckle level. They were there to keep the cold from seeping through the last set of bullet holes, from someone trying to kill me not that long ago.

"Gotta get you a new door," he said. "Thicker. Maybe plate steel." He examined the .45, ejecting the magazine and clearing the chamber. Holding it up to the ceiling light fixture, he squinted down the barrel. "Hardly been fired," he said. "Next time I'll let you answer your own door." He shivered, which could have been the result of a really close call, or the well-cooled house.

I used my thumb to melt ice on the front room window pane to peer out at the thermometer. Minus twenty-something. With the wind chill, it would be well in the minus forties out there. And after all that time with the front door open, it felt darn near that cold inside.

As I looked at my good friend, considering how very close we'd just come to losing him — again — I shivered, too.

CHAPTER 13

"So," said Andy later, "someone really wants you dead and is willing to pay." He said it thoughtfully and the words seemed to hang in air as we both considered. That's when I told him about Frank Jacob's earlier warning.

"Five thousand dollars? Really?"

"That's the story."

"And they almost bagged me instead. That's not so good."

From the front of the house, we heard a quick knock and distant door rattle and thump as whoever knocked tried to walk in, the usual way we did things around here.

Andy looked at me. "William?"

"That's my guess." And I went to let him in, cautiously.

"Your door is locked?" He pulled his head back in a kind of double take, bunching his eyebrows. Then he sniffed. "Gun smoke! What has happened here?" And I told him. He had already pushed the door closed. Now he reached out to lock the deadbolt. "There is no sense making it easy for them."

As a trained investigator, William's first act, even before filling his coffee mug, was to ask to use my phone. I could hear him dial the four numbers on the rotary, then speak in a way that told me he'd called Alice, his sweetie, bartender at the Bide-A-While. He came back in a few minutes with his lips pressed

93

together.

"Alice did not *see* anyone talk to Albert Jensen," he reported. "She says it was a busy night and admits she had no time to watch the customers. The one thing she does remember…" He hesitated.

Andy and I may have leaned forward.

"Well, what?" demanded Andy, never one for patiently waiting.

"Policemen. Fairbanks city policemen."

"Uniforms?" I asked.

"No, plain clothes. But she knew they were officers because they showed her identification and demanded free drinks."

"That's a Fairbanks city cop," agreed Andy.

I topped off their coffees from the French press. "But why a bounty?" I asked. It was the obvious question. Just two days ago, out on the trail, Kellar had appeared willing to shoot me for free. Gratis.

William shrugged, gestured 'thanks' with a slight uplift of his mug, and shook his head. "This is the mystery."

In the meantime, Andy had risen restlessly from his tippy stool to go stare out the kitchen window into the blown snow and sleet racing at him out of the darkness. It ticked and rattled on the window panes.

He said what we were all thinking. "They're still out there. We need a plan."

"Let's go!" I said.

William turned, raising his free hand and shaking it at me in a gesture for patience. "Going out on the trail at night in a storm is not a plan. And it is needlessly risky. Foolish. These bank robbers are not traveling tonight. They are not *getting away*. They are holed up, as we are. And I am certain Andy will agree." He turned to Andy who nodded slowly, almost as if against his will.

"No," he said.

* * *

Several hours later, about ten miles north of
Chandalar, William signaled a halt. I was ready,
frankly exhausted. Days of not sleeping, or not
sleeping well were catching up to me. And yes, it had
been foolish to start out in the middle of the night in a
blizzard, to find our friends. But Andy had said it,
back in Chandalar in my kitchen.

"We gotta do *something!*"

Snowshoes on, we roped ourselves together and
started out, shuffling down the already drifted
Chandalar streets toward the Tanana River. Light,
cast along the way from several working streetlamps,
danced and jiggled in the wind, as blowing snow
wrapped us in its gauzy veil, obscuring everything.

We were bundled literally to the eyeballs. In fact,
William in the lead, wore ski goggles to be able to
read his compass, though keeping to the frozen river
bound us almost due north and made it difficult to get
too lost.

All the while, the wind roared, sighed, moaned
and whined, rattling ice pellets off my frozen parka
fabric. I was unable to avoid thinking how dangerous
it was to head out in a storm. This is how people died
up here. We all nod knowingly, solemnly agreeing
that they should have known better. *Well, we do know
better,* I thought, *but here we are anyway. This is
another of the stupidest things I've ever done.*

As usual, I brought up the rear, with Jack at hand,
also on a line to keep from being separated from us.
He didn't like it, but his nose probably wouldn't help
him much in this maelstrom.

Zero visibility meant my lifeline to Andy just

disappeared into darkness and driven snow. Since I couldn't see *anything*, I had to practice maintaining just enough tension to guide me without having Andy pull me.

Once we hit river ice heading north though, we got a bit of relief by having the wind mostly at our backs. But constant buffeting, with my feet sometimes gust-blown nearly out from under me, took its toll. By the time William finally called a halt, I was long past ready. Bleary, I made the mistake of trying to roll out my bedroll into the wind, only to have it blow back at me, instantly wrapping around my legs.

I took off nothing, not even mukluks, just dusted off snow and squeezed myself into my sleeping bag, closing the zipper as far as it would go. I meant to peel out of some of it and did get the mukluks off so my feet wouldn't sweat and then freeze on the trail. The last thing I remember was Jack curling up alongside me in the snow, wriggling himself down out of the wind.

* * *

Jack's low growl woke me, along with his abrupt position shift against my side. With difficulty, I resisted my first impulse to jump up.

The wind had fallen off by about half, but not before drifting snow all but buried us and our gear. It was brighter, the sky blown clear, and through the small, ice-rimmed opening in my sleeping bag, I could make out a spray of stars and golden crescent of new moon. Not surprisingly, I felt toasty warm under the insulating snow layer. But what woke Jack?

I didn't have long to wonder. With my ear to the opening, I began to hear a rhythmic *shush-shush*.

Someone coming! I had my .38 in the right-hand

pocket of my parka, but there was absolutely no way to get to it in time. From one second to the next I began to sweat, and without moving much — fearful of dislodging my snow cover — twisted my head around to check on Andy and William. The good news? They were invisible, too. Then I thought of Jack. If he jumped up, or barked...

Almost immediately, a white-suited skier passed us in a hurry, taking long strides, pushing vigorously with the poles. He looked a lot like a man trying to catch up. I had to believe that whoever he was, he had started out last night following our trail then lost it in the storm. Now we could follow him. Of course, he might soon realize he'd passed us and set up an ambush. If we *did* make ten miles last night, we had at least twenty yet to go, to even reach Minto. And according to Petey, our quarry lay some miles north of there.

With the skier safely past, I began breathing again, just as I saw Andy rear up like a whale surfacing, all in olive-drab, his sleeping bag — war surplus like mine — now stark and easy to see against the snow. I heard the heavy *zip* as he extricated himself. I had been thinking of digging up my sleeve to find my watch, with an eye toward realizing I could sleep more. But snapping awake, back into my moment, I imagined Evie somewhere, waiting. And I hoped, *believing* I would come for her and for Roberta. With that I began squirreling around, struggling to get myself out of the bag and into my mukluks. I knew that no matter the hour, as it says in the hymn with the old Scottish tune, 'morning has broken.'

By a little after five we were on our way, the storm gone, no longer roped together, easily following the striding ski tracks, hoping the skier at least, knew where he was going.

Focused forward, parka hoods in place, we didn't hear the drone of the airplane note at first. We all turned at about the same time, finally acknowledging that the sound had been following the river and now lowering, seemed to be headed straight for us.

I knew the plane, a silver de Havilland Beaver, with the sun behind it, wings outlined in gold. I could see the pilot through the split windshield, not recognize him but knew it was Petey.

It had been Petey, a summer ago, following the Yukon at an altitude of about fifty feet, who landed on a sandy river island to save me before I became hypothermic or bear bait. I'd been thrown off the old Nenana on her last voyage, thrown down into the paddle wheel in the middle of the night, with a life expectancy of about zip. And yet I lived, at least partly because Petey came out like a shepherd, tracking the river's myriad bends and braids, to find me and carry me home.

The Beaver ramped lower, nosed into the wind, flaps adjusting as the plane slowed, then dropped more sharply with the nose leveled out. As we watched, it settled gently on its skis, slowing enough — in not more than about fifty feet — to begin a turn in our direction, the radial engine revving with a clattery roar.

I felt Andy at my elbow. "Always glad to see Petey," he said, "but he just told everybody and his husky exactly where we are."

Still squinting I said, "And he's got a passenger."

"Uh-oh. Hope it's not Kellar. It's just about time for him to show up."

The Beaver taxied in our direction, finally shaking

and rocking to a stop about fifty feet from us, on the edge of ice blown almost completely snow free. As the prop flipped over and stopped, the door opened and Petey stepped out, followed by a figure in olive drab — not Kellar — Frank Jacobs.

"Nice you waited for me," he said in greeting. As the others stepped up, he turned to them. "Well, well. Here we are near Minto. I'm fresh as a daisy, not like *I* slept outdoors all night, in all my clothes in the middle of a howling gale."

"I feel great," Andy said, sticking out his chest as he threw his shoulders back. He looked like a rooster.

William took a more conciliatory course. "Your point is taken," he said.

"Yeah, sorry," I added, and meant it. "We had to do *something*."

Jacobs softened and flapped one hand at me in forgiveness. "Yeah, I get it." He turned businesslike. "Where are we? Talk to me."

There wasn't much to tell, just the skier, seemingly trailing us. Jacobs furrowed his eyebrows but said nothing, examining the tracks. "How far ahead?"

"Well," Andy looked at his wrist. He didn't wear a watch. "About twenty minutes. Or at least he was until you signaled him back with your airplane." He looked at Petey. "You better get outta here just in case there's shooting." He waved upriver. "I wanna put some distance between us and the village, too. Don't want nobody in Minto to pick up a stray bullet on our account."

"You're right," said Frank. "Bullets really travel in this flat country." He turned with Petey to go back to the Beaver for his snowshoes, pack, and rifle.

Before leaving, Petey stepped close, stooping to

speak near my ear. "Find her!" was all he said, giving me a rough shoulder thump. Like so many others around here, they had been orphans together at the mission school.

"Count on it."

He nodded and stepped away. The Beaver isn't a quick take-off. Its engine roar, while ever-so-slowly breaking the 'surly bonds of earth,' seemed endless. Way out here in the Bush, miles from anywhere, and nearing the end of a long, monotonous winter, there wouldn't be anybody for miles around not wondering who we were and why we were here.

We left the river almost immediately, or the river left us, turning west as we continued north. Still following the ski trail, we skirted Minto, a tiny, mostly log-cabin village, hard on the banks of the Tanana. As we passed, less than a mile distant, we heard dogs barking and looked back to see narrow columns of silvery smoke rising in the clear bright air.

Even with the sun at our backs, the day was piercingly bright and I squinted, though I wore sunglasses. Along the way, I paused to turn and look behind us and, for the first time in a long time, felt faint warmth on my face. *It's spring!*

We were moving faster today, all feeling a little desperate about where we were going and what we might find. There was so much about this that simply made no sense. Like bank robbers making a getaway in a big circle in the wrong direction. Or taking not one, but a pair of hostages and keeping them long after any apparent need for 'bargaining chips.' And we were still bothered by the notion of crooks going out of their way to steal the fastest snow machines in the Territory but bringing no fuel! None of it made any sense, but here we were.

After struggling up a long grade, we paused on the rim of another of the shallow scooped-out valleys interrupted by just a few stands of small birch and willow trees. According to Andy, beyond this, we'd be back in the Tanana Valley proper, a vast marsh that goes on for hundreds of miles.

We stopped and I was glad for the breather. Taking his turn in the lead, Andy had been moving along at a fairly ferocious pace.

"Too much time behind a desk," muttered Frank. "Not in shape for all this snowshoeing!"

Andy, studying the terrain with his scope, crouched and waved us in.

Even though we were out here all by ourselves, he spoke low and close like he might somehow be overheard.

"It looks like the trail peters out, just about that last little stand of evergreens on the other side." He pointed. "I think he's waitin' for us there. I would be."

William spoke. "So, this fellow has finally figured out we are behind him."

"He had to," said Andy. "He's following no tracks. So, here's what we'll do." And he told us his plan.

Rested, we started out again, twenty feet apart, snowshoeing down the shallow grade with rifles cocked and safeties on. I had put Jack back on his lead, which he didn't like much, but — as if sensing 'crunch time' — settled down to follow in my tracks.

As we reached the shallow valley bottom and started up again, I began to sweat. Not from exertion but from the pervasive sense of dread that goes with being a target waiting for the shot, and wondering if I'd even hear it if it hit me.

But there were no shots fired as we approached the evergreens and slowly climbed past. Sure enough, at a distance the tracks appeared to end here, but didn't. They turned sharply to the right, and the snow had been swept smooth again, probably with an evergreen limb, making them mostly disappear. But the deception only worked at a distance.

William, taking his turn in the lead, stopped here, stared at the tracks, and turned to face the evergreens. We all did.

The man in the white snow uniform stepped out, gun up.

"Set your rifles down easy," he said. Even on this warmish day, he wore his white balaclava so we couldn't see his face. But I recognized his voice just about the time he got a good look at us. "Oh," he said, clearly surprised. "It's you!"

And that's when I jumped out, turned and waved my arms to Andy, back on the ridge, to *not* shoot Wild Bill Hanson.

CHAPTER 14

"I got to Chandalar just as you were leaving," Hanson said. "I knew Frank had intended to arrive in the morning. And he told me you guys had a hard time staying put when he told you to. So, I was coming to join up. When I saw you headed out, I just followed, but I lost you in the storm."

He'd pulled off the balaclava and was now sharing his fresh Thermos around. His coffee wasn't as good as ours, but we didn't complain. Hot and available are still the best parts of trail coffee.

With the coffee poured, he looked around at us. "I think I know where they're holed up." He started to reach back into his pack then said, "Anybody got a map handy?"

"I got one." Frank dug in his parka pocket, pulling out the neatly folded laminated map he'd pilfered from the Army.

Hanson looked at the map then looked back at him. "Nice map."

"Oh, this old thing?" Jacobs unfolded it and jabbed a gloved finger at a spot just north of Minto. "You are here," he said.

"And I think they're over here." Hanson drew his finger across maybe another twenty map miles to a place where a small blue creek line made a visible sharp bend.

Andy peered at it. "Elbow creek! The old Massey-Stillwell dredge. Abandoned, mostly. Though there used to be a watchman."

"Huh?" said Frank. "I've flown over that. Never could figure out why they called it Elbow Creek. But there it is, right on the map. Doesn't look like that from the air. No elbow."

"Because they dredged it." Andy gave him a look. "Duh! Now you could just call it Gravel Pile Creek. Sure made a mess of a pretty spot."

"We need to get going," I said, and Jacobs looked at me.

"Sure we do," he said. Folding up his map he pointed off northwest. "This way. I got lead." He started out and we fell into line behind him, about twenty feet of space between us, Hanson choosing to bring up the rear.

I'd been too many days away from Evie, not knowing where she was or how they were treating her. Walking along and trying to stay alert to surroundings — to not get shot — I kept disappearing into an ache of memories of her. A slide projector mechanism in my brain kept replaying quick glimpses of our life together, as on a screen. As soon as I'd shake one loose, check the dog, scan the terrain, another image would drop into place.

I'm going to find you!

"Oh Hardy," I could hear her reply, sighing — as she often does with me — in a small breeze that spiraled snow away in a low whirlwind.

Late afternoon found us on the south edge of the Massey-Stillwell tailings. Gravel piles stood sixty to eighty feet tall in parallel wormlike tubes. This, according to Frank, who'd seen it all from the air. Whatever had been here, a stream, a low valley, shallow hills, had all been devoured by this 'earth eater,' leaving only wasteland. In my mind, no matter how much gold they took out of here, not a good trade.

Frank raised an arm to point. "Runs more than a mile north from here and maybe a half mile across." He looked around. "No wonder there's no elbow left in Elbow Creek."

I found myself resenting the machine, as yet unseen.

"What d'ya think? Over the top?" Still on snowshoes, Andy stood poised as if ready to jog up the steep berm.

Frank held up a hand. "There's a road up here, a short one... somewhere. I've flown over it. That's how they get supplies and equipment out across the tailings to the dredge." He put a gloved knuckle up to his lip, thinking, remembering. "And you know what? There's a power cable above the road."

Okay, that surprised me. "Power? Out here?"

Frank gave a little snort. "You betcha. He pointed off in the direction of the still-unseen dredge. This sucker is electric. They got a big generator off on the side, probably diesel."

That gave me the notion. I tipped back my parka hood to listen. Distantly, more like a feeling and almost beyond conscious hearing... a *thrumming*.

"And it's running," I said. "This way." I led them up a slight grade, first along the berm edge and finally starting out across the berms themselves. We found what Frank had called a road, bulldozed flat across the top, not so much for vehicles as for dragging the heavy commercial generator, probably on skids, close enough to the dredge to fulfill its line voltage requirements.

The generator would have been tough to spot from the air. They'd taken some care with it. Not only had it been heavily snowdrifted, but someone had cut and stacked large snow blocks around it, as if constructing an igloo, serving to both hide its small shed and to muffle the noise.

We were now within about two hundred feet of the dredge, staying out of view — and rifle shot — approaching with the generator as a barrier between us. I held Jack tightly on his leash. It wouldn't do us any good to hide and have him cavorting out in full view. It was only when we'd reached the generator, standing right behind, that I crouched and peeked out for my first look at the dredge.

It was bigger than I expected, hard to estimate from here — especially in the snow — but approaching one hundred fifty feet long and thirty-five to forty feet across. Bigger than others I'd seen around Fairbanks. Some of these dredges looked nautical, a bit like riverboats. They did float. This one looked like what it was. A big, deep, steel barge, now well frozen into ice. Built on the barge was nothing boat-like, rather a big, square, industrial building, its ends completely open like an airplane hangar. Out of the front extended a long bucket-type conveyer with a lesser one out the back. Above the front conveyor, a two-car, garage-sized box — essentially a pilot house — cantilevered forward about six feet. It had a full window-paned wall where the operator sits consulting his charts and pulling his levers to guide the behemoth. It was all flat-topped and heavily snow-loaded but melted back where just a foot or two of rusted tin chimney stood up. Heat waves and thin smoke from a well-built fire were barely visible through the binoculars.

"Good," said William, sounding for all the world like he was just in the neighborhood for a visit. "We have found them at home."

A wink of light from beyond the dredge drew Frank's binoculars. "Oh swell," he said. "It's a lookout."

"How 'bout I just shoot him?" asked Andy, not completely serious. I looked at him. He did a reflexive head jerk, squinting one eye, looking like a parody of Popeye, the spinach-eating sailor.

"Chance to use this great gun," he said.

"Let's not shoot anybody yet," said Frank. I agreed.

Hanson agreed also, blinking at Andy and doing a kind of double take. He still hadn't known Andy long enough to discount about half of what he said.

"I don't think shooting anyone — yet — is a good idea. For one thing, there are still about twice as many of them as there are of us. Likely most of them are on the dredge with a couple of sentries left outside. These men all had to be qualified at least *sharpshooter* to get into our ski program. Let's hold off on the firefight as long as we can."

Andy grinned at him. "I jokes," he said. It took Hanson a minute but he got it and grinned back.

"Got to admit..." he said, "never been out on the trail with anybody like you."

"There isn't anybody else *like* him," I added.

Andy tried for a modest look. "Aw shucks."

"So," I said, "we surround the place, wait for dark, kill the generator, and move in?"

William turned to look at me. "If we kill the generator, we say 'Hello, we are here.' Then we must discover our way into this thing in the dark while they are in positions to shoot us."

Frank pushed back his parka hood. "He's right. I've never been in one of these."

"I've been in this one," said Hanson. We all turned to look at him. "I was just poking around, sightseeing, so I don't remember a lot of detail. That center section is full of machinery and a big rolling cage that separates and sorts the gravel. I don't think it's a place to try to sneak into at night." He shrugged, as if regretful.

"Okay then, what?" I asked, a little frustrated. "Anybody?"

I had just turned to face them, the quick step probably saving my life. A bullet tore through the fur and fabric of my parka hood, the sound of the shot arriving just after, as a kind of *thud,* with much of its volume and all of its echo lost in the deeply drifted hillocks.

But the *first* thing I knew was Hanson, suddenly aiming his rifle at my head! I ducked and he fired right across the top of where I'd been. It all happened so quickly, I was already in a full crouch reeling Jack in before I realized *I'd* been shot at first, and he was returning fire. A shout from behind me confirmed that Hanson hit his target. Still crouching, I cranked my head around to see a white-uniformed man falling, arms up and out, rifle dropping into the snow.

Our 'plan' abruptly became ducking to avoid the spitting and zipping of a swarm of shots fired. Too many. It had all been a setup. In the moment, it seemed possible and even likely that *none* of the men were waiting on the dredge. The possibly ten... well, nine now... were all out here in the snow waiting, well concealed, shooting at us.

So, assuming the women were really on the dredge, who was left to be with them? Maybe no one.

I looked at Andy. "I'm going in."

He scrunched up his face. A look of pain. "Nah."

"I'm going," I said firmly.

He looked around at the others. "Then I'm goin', too."

"You *can't* go. You've gotta cover me."

"Well," and then exasperated, "shit!"

I was going to leave Jack. But then I didn't. I set him loose. Even Jack knew we were in trouble. Normally when freed, he'd go into puppy mode, tucking his tail, splaying his toes, running around in circles or through my legs in pure doggie joy. He didn't this time. I could almost see him duck and move closer, as if I could stop his bullet. I gave him a scratch behind the ears. "Sorry I got you into this." His blue eyes turned to me and his brows furrowed. His tail gave just half a wag and he turned to face the dredge. Somehow he already knew what we were up to.

I thought about running to the downed man, to scoop up his rifle. But the two hundred feet of extra exposure didn't seem worth it. I had my .38, and tying my heavy mitts at my back, I pulled the handgun out, inserting a sixth cartridge under the hammer.

Frank Jacobs stepped up. "You sure?"

"Got to," I told him.

He nodded, clapping me on the shoulder. "Sure you do," he said. "Keep your head down." As if I wouldn't.

Up here on the so-called road, I figured I could do without my snowshoes, snow only about ankle deep. I untied the bindings and slipped them off. It would make me faster on the road and I wouldn't have to stop to shed them when I made the dredge... if I made the dredge.

William surprised me. "*Dasvedanya*," he said. He

saw the question on my face and smiled. "Until we meet."

CHAPTER 15

"Okay, *this* is really the stupidest thing I've ever done." Something I found myself saying every time I started running to do a really stupid thing. The scary part? Each time, it was true. I'd truly never done anything quite this stupid.

Starting out, I wondered how many of the shooters would be shooting at me. I soon knew. All of them. For as much as I could tell, ducking, dodging, dashing pell-mell toward what I now considered the 'dredge of death,' there was no one returning fire at my friends.

The good part? Each of the shooters had to rise at least a little and make himself just slightly visible to dash off a shot. That was the opening for Andy, William, and Wild Bill to return fire. While running, out of the corners of my eyes I saw shooters ducking and sprawling as they were variously hit or just barely missed. I tried to count them. Definitely nine, maybe ten. Could there possibly be no one left aboard to guard the hostages? Or maybe there were no hostages. An idea I couldn't let myself consider.

Closing on the dredge, I dropped down into a little cut that had been graded to accommodate the gangway. It would be the perfect last place to ambush me. Sure enough, a white-suited figure jumped out from cover raising his M1. I had to wonder about that. Stories of their fabled fighting had them either skiing down mountains shooting or prone in the snow, nearly invisible, but firing from cover. And now this guy wanted to jump up and make a target of himself to shoot me. *Must not have been one of Hanson's men after all.*

I had the .38 clutched in my hand, already out, already up. I didn't want to shoot him. I had the wild notion of just pulling up and yelling, 'Wait! Can't we talk about this?'

But it wasn't to be. I hesitated as long as I could, giving him time to change his mind. It felt like forever, until — with his rifle nearing level — the look in his eye said he'd shoot me. For bearer bonds! I didn't get it and now couldn't afford to wait until I did.

I pointed the .38 at him, center mass, only about ten feet from me. *"Bang!"* I shouted. *"Your life is over!"* It wasn't what he expected. I saw his surprised look as he imagined a bullet to the chest. It looked like his knees might buckle, and his rifle dropped, sinking into the snow. He turned and stumbled away, and I let him. I ran on.

About a foot of untracked snow still covered this gangway. There clearly was another way onto the dredge, probably on the far side. I found myself running up it like a chimp, bent, both feet and my free hand driving for traction. Reaching the top, I ducked through the wide bright opening, as if diving blindly into muddy water, into the murky belly of the beast.

With Jack close on my heels, I dropped behind what turned out to be a good-sized plate-steel buttress, about three feet wide, going all the way up the wall. Bullets from outside *zipped and pinged,* ricocheting from metal to metal until finally falling to rattle, spent on the steel deck. In spite of a nearly desperate urge to move, to get farther away from the bullets and a lot closer to Evie — who had to be in the upstairs room — I forced myself to stay in place to give my vision time to adjust.

One good thing: so far nothing had been aimed at me from the inside. As my vision cleared, I saw a gray-painted steel staircase built against the far wall, extending about sixteen feet to the next floor, presumably to the pilot house I'd seen from outside.

That has to be where they are!

Rising, I clucked at Jack and started across, running crouched low, dodging from steel object to steel object beneath the fifty-foot cylindrical basket that graded and sorted the lode-bearing ore. There was still no shooting inside, and much less noise from outside as well.

At the top of the stairs stood a battered two-panel door, originally varnished, but by now beaten dirty and nearly raw with careless daily use. 'OFFICE' had been stenciled in tall white letters. Below that, also in white but smaller, some dreamer had crookedly stenciled, 'WOMEN WANTED.' Fat chance. Before Evie and Roberta, it was a reasonable bet there hadn't been a woman up these stairs, or any closer than Minto, in at least ten years — or never.

Reaching for the latch, I caught the sound of what I first thought was a distant motor, a thudding rhythmic beat. But when I flipped back my parka hood to listen and try to identify it, I heard only my heart pounding.

A voice from inside the door, maybe to the left side, sounded familiar and beloved. I heard Evie taunting someone.

"He's coming for you." I felt a rush of love. But then she said, "I've seen Andy hit a dime-sized target from a half mile, in a breeze. That's about the size of

113

one of your eyes. Think you'll miss it? He won't."

"Shut up, bitch!" Just one voice, probably to the right of the door. That was helpful. He started to say something else just as I pulled the handle, unlatching the door. The voice stopped abruptly. After a long moment of silence, he said, "Fred? That you?"

Ducking, stretching myself flat on the stairs and catching Jack by his collar, I reached up to give the door a shove hard enough to open it wide and have it swing fully around and thud.

I saw the guard first. He'd shed his parka in the warm, bright, electric-lit room. A big man with a week of whiskers wore a blue-plaid flannel shirt, white snow pants, and ski boots.

Seeing no one, he squinted into the darkness, firing three shots blindly into the stairwell. At least one of the bullets went low and I heard it pinging around the hard surfaces down on the ore floor. He'd been standing to the right, and now with his military-issue Colt in hand, stood in the door looking for me. He had one hand out and up, motioning for Evie to stay put. She's never been good at that.

I had about one heartbeat left before he could look down the stairs, see me, and shoot me point blank. But two things happened.

Jack saw Evie. Ninety pounds of husky went ripping out of my hand up the last few steps and into the brightly lit warm room. The last thing the guard expected to see was a blue-eyed wolf-like creature catapulting at him from out of darkness. Of course, Jack didn't care about him at all and was headed for Evie. But when the guard aimed a boot at Jack, the big dog caught it and yanked. Throwing up his arms for balance, reflexively squeezing the trigger, the guard fired off another round and I heard a window pane break.

Movement on the left caught my eye. For the first time, I saw Evie, hands tied behind her back, clothing disheveled, her face bruised and puffy and one eye nearly closed. It looked like she'd been slapped a lot. Flashing angry at the sight of her, I came charging out of the stairwell behind Jack. I still had my gun in hand, but what I wanted to do was punch him.

It was a ruse. Evie had been waiting for her chance. She'd gotten her hands free and now, from a cabinet topped by a litter of ill-kept tools, Evie grabbed the handle of a large rusty screwdriver — fifteen or sixteen inches long. She flipped it, a move I'd seen before, smoothly catching it by the tip. With the guard fully occupied by Jack, she drew back her arm from the shoulder and pitched the screwdriver at him, hard and fast.

He saw her windup, throw, and I think he even began a smirk, already turning the handgun in her direction. He looked like he knew how this would go. That her screwdriver toss would prove ineffectual and he'd have her. I could tell by the look on his face he'd been wanting to do more to her than just slap.

The screwdriver rotated once in the air and the tip hit him hard, low and left-of-center on his chest with an almost imperceptible sickening *snick*. It could have struck a rib and bounced off, but didn't. It penetrated three or four inches, and shocked him to a standstill. He stopped so suddenly, even Jack let go of his boot to back up and stare at him.

The sight of a screwdriver protruding from a man's chest shocked me, and Evie even more.

I grew up watching Hoot Gibson and Tom Mix, and always felt the most terrible thing that could happen to anyone was to be shot by an arrow. Worse, with the arrow sticking out the front or back, to fall on it, driving it through the body. Just thinking about it still makes me shudder.

The man looked at his .45 like he might do something, but then it just fell out of his hand, too heavy to hold any more.

"A screwdriver?" he gasped, eyes pleading with Evie, as if she might be convinced to take it back, to make it not happen. But it had happened and she couldn't take it back, something she realized now and burst into tears. He began to lose his balance, and knowing what came next, reached out for her. Then he fell forward, driving the screwdriver into his body to its hilt. He let out one long breath, dying on the floor in front of us.

Evie looked at me, eyes pleading. "Bless him," she said. "Please!"

I could have. I would have. Instead, I said, "You know the words." When she looked at me, stricken, I told her, "It might help you later." She sniffed, nodded, and went to kneel by him, reluctantly placing her palm on the back of his head.

"Unto God's mercy..." I prompted.

"Unto God's *gracious* mercy..." she gave me a look, "... and protection, we commit you. The Lord bless you and keep you. The Lord make his face to shine upon you, and be gracious unto you. The Lord lift up his countenance upon you, and give you peace, both now and forevermore. Amen." She remained there in a crouch, whether praying or just overwhelmed, I don't know.

I kicked the door shut and slid the bolt, in case there were others of them around, but also hoping to save some of the heat. It was a good-sized room, with electric heaters all working. At the center stood a large chart table with three tall stools, the nerve center. The last working chart still lay there, defaced with careless coffee-mug circles. Looking around, I realized what was missing.

"Where's Roberta?"

Evie looked up, shaking her head, blinking at me as though just realizing I was here, or still here. "They took her. I ..." And then fell silent.

When she rose, I held out my arms. She came tentatively to me and stood close. For a time, as I held her, she could only weep.

Finally, very softly, she said, "Why are you here? At first, I didn't want you to find me. I made the mess, I should fix it. But then after a while, when I knew I'd really gotten myself into it, I wanted you to find me. I prayed for you to find me, and here you are!"

I grabbed her fiercely, held her tightly, and said the one true thing. "I'll always find you."

CHAPTER 16

"This guy's *not* one of mine." Hanson knelt by the dead man, turning the head to study his face. He also peered under the body. Seeing the screwdriver handle jammed in deep and now angled, he made a face. "Ugh."

They'd come up the stairs, Hanson in the lead, followed by Frank and Andy. Frank cautiously called out a tentative, "Hardy?" from below until I responded with the all-clear. They filed in, thankfully nobody bleeding, looking around, looking at the corpse, curious about the place, and liking the warm room.

"Shot three outside," reported Andy. "Let the others get away. He nodded casually at Evie, like he hadn't been worried sick about her and snowshoeing for days to find her. "Cuz." Then he squinted at her and tipped his head like 'What happened to *you*?'

Hanson stood, nodding at the corpse. "He's wearing our uniform — well, part of it — but these aren't our boots. We had ours specially made in Austria." He shook his head. "But..."

"But he is not your man," said William from the doorway. He had insisted on making a wide circle around the dredge, coming in last. "I think perhaps none of them are."

I noticed Evie wasn't tentative with William. She ran into his arms like a child and he held her, murmuring to her, kissing the top of her head.

Hanson flipped back his parka hood, pulling off a glove to smooth hair stubble with his palm. "But it *was* my men who stuck up the bank. I'm sure of it. What gives?"

"Ringers," said Frank. "It's the really handy thing about being a masked bandit. Somewhere along the line, they handed off masks and uniforms to another bunch." He looked at Evie, who nodded.

"They were waiting for us here," she said, visibly pulling herself together. "There was already a fire — already *had* been a fire for quite a while — and all the heaters turned on. This place was plenty warm."

She rotated, pointing to the chart table. "They had a plastic map spread out there, and — it was crazy — they just started switching hats, parkas, and pants. The whole thing took maybe five minutes, like a shift change. Then the soldiers left, taking Roberta."

Our eyes met. "Who *didn't* want to go along," she continued. "I told them to leave her be, and that's when this one started slapping me." She indicated the dead man. "I think he had bigger plans and thought it was foreplay." She shuddered.

Jacobs stepped between her and the corpse, deliberately blocking her view. "They say where?"

"No, they were deliberately vague with Roberta and me listening, but I watched them with the map."

"Watched?" I asked.

Her eyes flicked to me then away, like she had a hard time looking at me. "Yes, but one of them put his finger down on the map like, 'We're here.' Then he slid it around in a curve and back north and east toward..."

"Fairbanks," said Frank. She nodded. "And the soldiers took the bonds?"

She looked perplexed. "Bonds?"

119

"The loot from the robbery," I said.

She didn't answer for a moment, looking around, making eye contact with each of us, her brow furrowing. "I never saw any bonds," she said.

* * *

Rising from blessing the last victim, I asked, "Are there mice here?"

Andy grimaced. "I hope not!"

We had carried the men from outside to join their friend in the upstairs room. The corpses would 'keep' indefinitely — well, until breakup — and not be available to wild creatures.

Closing and latching the door, we filed down the stairs and Andy went to turn off the generator. Then we headed off a well-tracked gangway on the dredge's far side, back into the snow, stopping to strap on snowshoes. We looped the dredge to begin our journey back to Minto. It was easy to see where the robbers' trail led away north and west — if Evie was right, ultimately toward Fairbanks — which still didn't make sense. We briefly debated following, but feeling like we knew where they were headed, decided to regroup and get Evie back home.

But to my surprise, when we reached Minto, Evie elected to stay, to rest and heal a few days with Pearl, one of her many cousins.

"I'm just worn out," she said, hugging me briefly and scratching Jack behind the ears. He whined a little, like he didn't want to leave her there. I wanted to whine for the same reason but didn't. It was hard to leave her with so many things still unsaid. But finally, I turned to join the others, to begin walking the Tanana ice for the thirty miles back to Chandalar.

Before we left the dredge, Frank had placed himself deliberately in front of Evie. "I have to ask

120

this." She nodded. "Were you raped?"

The room went silent. "I was... assaulted..." she said, glancing at the dead man who had been her guard. "I think rape was his intention, but..."

Andy walked over to the guard's corpse and delivered a vicious kick, half rolling the body, though it sank back in place, not making a bit of difference. I admit it was vicariously cathartic for us all.

Back on the river below Minto, as if prearranged, at just about the same place he delivered Frank Jacobs, we heard the drone of Petey's de Havilland Beaver and watched it lumber into view. Circling into the wind, the silver airplane landed just about fifty feet from us.

"Been watching out for you," said Petey. He looked for Evie. I think he hoped to see her. We told him what had happened. He pulled off his hat to scratch the top of his completely bald head. "Glad you got 'em."

Though the plane would easily haul all of us, I elected to walk home. Andy, who had a restaurant to run, along with Frank, William, and Wild Bill Hanson, who all had actual, on-the-clock jobs, needed to get back. I needed time by myself to think. Okay, to mope.

I watched them load in. Andy went last, handing me back my rifle. Stepping up into the airplane he hesitated then turned to me. "Want company?"

"No, I'm good. I actually need the time to think."

He nodded. "Need any stuff from me? Food? Gear?" I shook my head. Minutes later, the Beaver was just a roaring echo and Jack and I were alone on river ice about twenty miles from home. I thought just briefly, of turning back north to Minto to see Evie and try to say something. But in the end, I trudged south under a bright but hazy blue bowl of sky.

I didn't make it all the way home before dark and didn't see the use of trying. Instead I slept out another night under stars, with Jack curled up along the side of my sleeping bag. It was very still and quiet, a warmer night than any yet. I set up camp behind a drift berm right out at the center of the ice, in a place where the river stretched most of a mile wide. With no wind and not so cold, I lay for a time with my face out in the air, turned up to a million stars in a black sky that stretched uninterrupted from horizon to horizon. The Big and Little Dippers, Polaris, Orion, and the Pleiades shone down like friendly faces. An immense owl with a nearly six-foot wingspan silently swooped me. Then pulling my face back inside the bag, I zipped the opening small, and slept.

* * *

"You found her." It was my greeting the next day from Rosie at the Coffee Cup. She wore her pink waitress uniform — the one with her name stitched in red over her left breast — the black swept-wing glasses, and tall caribou mukluks with the beaver fringe at the top. I put out my cheek and she kissed it, leaving a scarlet lipstick smear I would wipe away with my napkin. But she didn't look behind me to see if I'd brought Evie along. So, I could be pretty sure she'd gotten the whole story from Andy, her sweetie, over the telephone.

"Safe," I said. "Mostly unharmed. Better than it could have been." I threaded my way through the noontime crowd to my solitary seat under the dusty moose head.

With warmer weather, there was ice only halfway up the front plate-glass windows, still enough to make it difficult to see in or out. Rosie came on the run with

122

my coffee mug already poured with just enough room for a bit of canned milk and sugar, which I added and stirred in. Unlike Andy, I drank mine 'adulterated.'

Rosie had the little red Philco turned on and tuned in, with Guy Mitchell, again "Singing the Blues." It was still how I felt, not quite figuring out what had happened with Evie and me out at the dredge. First, she'd been expecting Andy to come for her, not me. How did that happen? And then not even coming home. So, we still hadn't sat down together to talk this through, understand it, and solve it.

I must have looked like I felt. Rosie paused on one of her coffee-pot passes to perch on the front of a chair and put a hand on my shoulder. She didn't say anything. She just sat there sympathetically for a long moment. We both knew there wasn't much to say, and after a minute she jumped up, kissed the top of my head, and charged back into action.

I ordered the mooseburger with cheese, my favorite, with the fries. It was a dollar and a quarter but worth it. Around the room, people were smoking and laughing, eating, settling up, coming in and going out, but I felt isolated from it all. I felt alone in the buzz and rattle of the small, friendly crowd and wasn't sure why.

In the news at noon, Egypt reopened the Suez Canal, the British, French, and Israelis had finally gone home. The Egyptians had sunk ships in the Canal at the height of the conflict and now had to figure out how to raise them to clear the waterway and safely resume shipping. I found myself shaking my head. People died over there for what? Shipping lanes!

I felt pretty tired and depressed about people dying for next to nothing. I'd just seen a man take a fatal screwdriver to the heart in an incident that began with a stolen stack of bearer bonds — that he had never seen and never would. He was just a nameless flunky working for wages. No matter how old or young he was, or how cute he'd been as a child, how well he did in school, or didn't do, he lay dead and frosty out on a dredge in the wilderness, thousands of miles from anyone who ever cared about him.

Also depressing — though on a different level — was the news that the Brooklyn Dodgers, long my favorite team, were deserting Ebbets field and Flatbush for glittery but parched Los Angeles, of all places. Through my life, New York had been the center of the baseball universe with a New York team, Yankees or Dodgers, competing in the World Series every year except one. Nineteen forty-nine, I believe. This would be their last season in New York.

I thought fleetingly of trying to make it back there for one last game, but came to my senses. It would take me two to three days of heavy travel to get there and the same to come home, not to mention a ton of money better spent on something real, like food, clothing, or fuel for people around here who need it. On balance, it would be easier to see them in Los Angeles.

In Territorial news, the Federal trial of the two men in connection with an oil-lease scam ground on. Their attempt to cheat Territorial tribes out of oil leases nearly killed Andy and me, and *did* kill Eskimo statesman Peter Senengatuk. The longer the trial lasted, the more doubtful I became that justice would be served. There had even been talk that I could be called as a witness.

Finally, in Fairbanks, a house believed to be empty had burned to the ground in an early morning fire, arson suspected. Neighbors, though none close, said they hadn't seen lights or vehicles at the house for nearly two weeks before the fire, which wasn't reported until just before three a.m. The owner of record, named Templeton, lived in Surprise, Arizona, but the house was rented locally by a soldier stationed with the Army at Ladd Field in Fairbanks. The soldier, Walter Chilton Bradbury, had been unavailable for comment.

CHAPTER 17

On Sunday I celebrated Holy Communion at eight and the Morning Prayer at eleven. It was my first Sunday back in Chandalar in two weeks. Fortunately, I had backup, sexton Oliver Sam who also had backup. Deacon Edward Johns would drive down from Fairbanks as needed.

At coffee afterward, when others had gone or were cleaning up, I saw Solomon Esau approaching. An older man, slight, in his seventies with silver hair cut short, he had a face like old brown parchment. Arriving at the service late, he slid silently into a back pew making no sound and disturbing nothing. And I was certain, leaving nothing. Some would say 'leaving no tracks, no ripples.'

There is probably an Athabascan word for what Solomon was. Not a shaman, which is actually a Siberian term. Andy had tried to explain this to me.

"He's more like a spirit catcher or a dream seer. He's almost like a spirit himself. Hard to notice, hard to see, always on the fringe. If you took a picture of a whole group with him in it, I'm not sure you'd see him on the print."

Several times a year, Solomon came to *tell* me something. Something he'd seen, or *knew*, in his frankly sort of spooky way.

Sliding up to me, after the service, he extended one finger to touch me. Apparently satisfied he said, "I seen a spirit. One of your spirits."

"A spirit of mine?" I touched my chest. He shook his head.

"One of your *church* spirits." He lowered his voice and leaned in. "I seen Miss Farthing!"

We all knew the story. Annie Craig Farthing, a Canadian Anglican, had come to help run the mission school early in the century. One night a drunk from town came out to the school demanding one of the girls. Miss Farthing wouldn't allow it, of course, deliberately putting herself in the way. She was small and it must have been pretty scary for her, holding him at bay.

At length he sobered enough to feel ashamed and head back home, but she soon collapsed from the strain and died. She was buried across the river from Nenana under a huge Celtic cross, visible for miles from out across the flats. If any spirit would linger at the old mission school, now closed more than five years, it would be hers.

Out there, prowling at dusk — doing whatever it is he does — Solomon had noticed reflections in a pane of old rippled glass. Looking more closely he'd seen first his own face and then that of Miss Farthing inside, whom he had known from earlier days at the school.

"I seen her," he said again, "with a shawl." He pantomimed a shawl wrapped over his head.

"She's dead," I reminded him. He clustered his wrinkles into a look of forbearance.

"To you," he said.

If anybody *had* seen a spirit out there, it would be him. I couldn't imagine who or what he'd seen. From the look on his face, one thing I knew: he'd seen something.

* * *

Monday morning bright and early, I had the 'good' coffee on, hoping for at least a quick drop-in by Evie on her way to teach. It didn't happen.

I did hear a knock just after seven, and a hello from the front door. I looked up from my deep funk on a tippy stool to see William coming down my short hallway. Shaking back his hood, stuffing mitts in his pockets and shrugging out of his parka, he hung it on one of the empty stools.

He paused on his way to select a mug, giving me a cool look of appraisal over the top of his foggy glasses.

"I see she has not returned." And then he said, "Cold out again," blotting his drippy nose on a sleeve.

He was right. I'd already checked. The temperature had fallen back into the mid minus twenties overnight, just when I'd begun to believe the worst might be past and spring on the way. He selected a bright yellow mug with *Goldrush Days in Nome Alaska, 1947* printed on it. Filling it with Andy's rich Italian roast, he ignored the canned milk, sugar, and honey and took his place on a stool by simply stepping over it and settling.

"Is she teaching?"

I held up both hands, also making my I-don't-know face. When it came to Evie, I'd had a lot of practice with that face lately.

"She has been through a great deal," he said.

"Do you think I don't know that?" I sounded testy even to myself. He raised both hands above the tabletop in a calm-yourself gesture. I did. "Sorry."

"You have been through a great deal, also." He paused, sipped, tasted, swallowed. He turned his head in the direction of my small kitchen radio. "I am curious if you have had the news on?"

"You mean the Fairbanks fire? Walter Chilton Bradbury the Third?" He nodded. "It must be our man," I continued. "There can't be two living in Fairbanks by that name."

He sipped and thought for a moment. "Houses *do* burn when people are away."

I nodded, finally tasting the coffee. It was good. "So, you think it's a coincidence?"

"There is not a chance," he said.

I asked him about his job at Clear Station, the DEW line RADAR installation.

"It is quiet now," he said. "Nothing like a month ago."

"What a difference a month makes," I said. We fell silent, but I knew we were both thinking about when saboteurs with a stolen nuclear device threatened to level the entire facility, of course killing everybody in it. William's half-brother, Vadim — the suspected saboteur — had been a key player for our side. He disappeared into the black hole of U.S. Government custody once it was all finished. "Any word from Vadim?" He didn't answer, just pressed his lips together and took another sip of his coffee. I took that for a no.

From the front of the house, I heard a door knock but no one entered. I couldn't help the sudden hope that it was Evie, finally home, finally here. I glanced at the black Kit Kat clock, tail swinging on my kitchen wall, and then out the window. Nine o'clock, sun full up. Too late to see Evie.

William had straightened over his coffee mug. He knew about the recent 'door knock' shooting event that came far too close to finishing Andy. Whoever it was knocked again, with some urgency, not unusual at an Alaskan rectory door. "Be cautious," he said.

Rising, I headed down the hall, stepping into my study to pocket the .38 I'd left laying on my desk. I'd been here for three years. Ninety-nine percent of the door knocks had been unthreatening. I had to believe we'd settled back to our peaceful norm. Still, I felt my heart chug up in my throat, proving that I wasn't ready to 'settle back' just yet.

Standing at the side to turn the knob, hand in pocket, I pulled the door open.

A low fog of icy air fell in and swirled across the floor, followed by an Athabascan woman, not Evie and not from Chandalar, who stepped in quickly with no gun visible and turned to close the door. From the street outside I heard a whistle and a musher cry, "Hike!" along with the *scritch* of sled runners down the frozen street. She'd come by dogsled.

Flipping back her hood, she pulled off mitts and unzipped her parka. "Father, I..." she said then stopped.

She looked familiar, pretty, about thirty, but I couldn't come up with a name. "Do I know you?"

She smiled, ducking her head shyly, and then I knew who she was. I recognized Evie in her smile. "Pearl," I said. "Evie's cousin from Minto."

"Yes."

I remembered my manners in that moment, inviting her out of her parka and drawing her back down the hallway to the kitchen. "Do you know my friend, William Stoltz?" She shook her head and extended a hand to William.

"Coffee?" I asked.

"Yes, please! It smells wonderful." She came around the table, selected a mug from the rack, and I poured it nearly full. She mixed it well with canned milk and added two heaping teaspoons of stiff honey, letting it melt off the spoon into the hot liquid. She sipped, surprised, exclaiming. "This is good!" Score another win for Andy.

"I remember these stools from the mission," she said, moving to the table. "The big boys made them in the shop. When I was little and sat on one, it always tipped over."

As she settled cautiously, I asked her. "Did you come in with Evie?"

She shook her head. "That's what I came about. Evie borrowed gear and a hunting rifle... early this morning."

I admit it took me a minute to catch up. To realize Evie *hadn't* borrowed the gear and gun just to ride home to Chandalar on the sled.

She must have thought me slow. "You mean..." I began.

"Yes. That's what I came to tell you. She left!"

* * *

Standing on the frozen river bank with my dog and gear, I watched the silver Beaver lumber into view, circle into the wind, and finally settle on its skis on the snow-covered river ice just in front of town. It had been an easy walk over, just across the railroad tracks from the church and rectory to where Petey would pick me up.

He left the engine idling with the propeller in a hesitating-then-flipping rhythm. Climbing out he shook my hand then beckoned me to pass him gear, which he quickly stowed. A big man, he snatched up ninety-pound Jack like a parcel, without even a grunt.

In minutes we lifted off the snowpack into the air, the already small town shrinking beneath and behind. A radiantly orange windsock jerked and jiggled in a stiff breeze against an achingly blue sky. The day was nothing but brilliant. We both wore sunglasses against the silver-dagger glare of sun on the windshield and on snow.

We flew northwest toward Minto, roughly shadowing the river as it wound and braided snake-like, sometimes folding back almost over itself in a meander across the frozen plain.

Leaving the river at Minto, we followed our previous snowshoe trail on a more northeasterly course, bound for the dredge, neither seeing Evie nor expecting to. She had a good head start on us.

Because the roar of the engine made talking difficult, Petey handed me a headset. I put it on, hearing his voice, tinny but loud and clear. "So, she walked away from Minto?"

I nodded, which of course he couldn't hear. "Yes."

"Did you two have a big fight or something? Break up?"

I looked over at him. He had the bill of a blue Yankee's baseball cap sticking out the front of his parka hood to help shield his eyes. The question was unusually personal, especially from a man who had always seemed shy.

"If we did, I don't know about it. Near as I can figure, she had become guardian of a girl who may be hostage from the Fairbanks bank robbery."

"Oh, yeah," he said. "Roberta. Good thing her folks are stateside."

"Sounds like you may know more than I do."

He grunted. "I get around. People tell me stuff." We flew along in silence for a few miles until Jack, sitting on the seat behind us, let out a bark. He'd spotted a moose bounding through snow, a solitary wolf trailing, looking hungry and hopeful. With the

132

moose appearing neither lame nor very old or very young, I knew the wolf wouldn't be having moose for dinner and hoped he would stumble on some other food source.

We passed the dredge. No sign of Evie. I couldn't help re-seeing the dead men as we left them, stretched out stiff and frosty on the pilothouse floor. I hoped Evie hadn't gone back in. She had no reason to. But...

Beyond the dredge, the trail grew harder to follow. One set of snowshoe tracks isn't as easy to see from the air as three or four. Ski tracks were worse. The binoculars helped, but I couldn't spot through them for long without getting airsick and wanting to throw up. A little farther along the trail, we finally agreed we'd lost her.

But the trail curved south before finally becoming indistinguishable and by then we knew where they were headed. After about an hour-and-a-half of flying, Fairbanks began. First, we saw just a scatter of solitary cabins, each with its bear-proof cache built up tall on poles. Next came the town proper, stretching and spreading like a patchwork quilt before us, the twisty Chena river stitching its halves into one. We landed on the river just at 'downtown,' taxiing into the lattice shadow of the Cushman Street Bridge where Andy watched and waited. On the riverbank above him, in the lot next to the old restaurant, I saw his blue Chevy running, its thin stream of exhaust silvering in the afternoon sun.

"Be careful," said Petey just as we touched down. And then gear and dog unloaded, he shook my hand, deliberately waving away any question of payment.

"Just find her."

Andy grabbed my pack, hauling it up the steep bank, stopping at the top to ruffle Jack behind his ears.

"We can't keep meeting like this." And I agreed.

"Any news?" I asked him.

"Nah. Nobody knows nothing or they're not telling." We loaded the gear into his trunk, climbed in, and set off for the restaurant. He didn't live there, though it seemed so. He also rented a small place nearby.

We had the place to ourselves, Andrea's closed, locked, and empty on a Monday afternoon. Andy quickly got water boiling in a polished copper kettle atop the big commercial gas range. Then he conjured his dark Italian-roasted coffee from a glass French press pot.

"Invented by an Italian," he reminded, prewarming the restaurant's heavy glass coffee mugs.

Switching on the radio, KFAR swelled into the room as the tubes warmed. We heard most of "Love is Strange," by Mickey and Sylvia — and I had to agree — followed by Harry Belafonte singing "The Banana Boat Song."

Though Andy drank his coffee 'clear', I doctored mine with a splash of the restaurant's real dairy cream. Skipping sugar, I added a teaspoon of cocoa powder and stirred it in. My new passion.

"*What* are you doing to my coffee!" Andy exclaimed, and in his theatrical way, buried his face in his hands. "Where did I go wrong with you?"

We sipped in silence for a time, no sound in the room but an occasional shift or tail thump from Jack. Andy already knew about Evie taking off. I'd told him on the phone. Now I caught him up on the flight with Petey and trying to find her trail.

"What was she thinkin'?"

I shrugged. "You know Evie. Wanna guess?"

134

"No."

"For starters, I'm sure she went back there to pick up the trail. I mean, that's what we were trying to do, too."

"Hope she didn't go into the dredge," he said. "See those dead guys again."

"Yeah, that's what I was thinking."

"Maybe Jacobs got them hauled off."

"This quick? Doubtful." I set down my mug. "I think they wanted us to trail them. Which means they probably set up another ambush and grabbed Evie."

"Or shot her."

I must have winced visibly.

"Sorry."

"No, I don't think they're ready to shoot her. Or at least I hope not. I think in the beginning they wanted her for bait and wanted us to trail them. Maybe they still do. I just don't know why."

"It's not a getaway," he said. "It never was."

"No," I agreed. "By the time we got to the dredge, we weren't even shooting at the real robbers... luckily."

"I don't get it," Andy said, and I agreed.

I slid a salt shaker like a chess piece across the red and white squares on the oilcloth tabletop. "Then what was it?"

Someone tapped at the front door, gave it a pull, and Jack woofed. But Andy had locked the door behind us. We could see one man, tall, not obviously armed, unrecognizable in his parka, and we hesitated. After our last brush together, with people knocking at the door — wanting to shoot us — neither of us jumped up to run to open it.

Jack, on the other hand, ran to the door, woofed again and wagged his tail. And as if reading our thoughts, the man threw back his parka hood. We were both surprised to recognize Wild Bill Hanson.

"What's he doin' here?" Andy scraped back his chair and went to let him in. He came in rubbing his gloved hands, making it's-cold-out-there sounds. His gaze caught on the painted nude, as everyone's did, and his eyebrows shot up.

"Wow!" Pulling his eyes away and unzipping his heavy parka, he sniffed the air like a hound. "Coffee? Is there more?" There was, of course, and Andy went to fetch a mug as Hanson dropped into a chair.

"Frank Jacobs said you two would likely be here. He also said you were flying the route." He glanced around the room. "I'm not seeing your girl here, so guess you didn't find her?"

"No sign," I told him as he shrugged out of the parka and tried to hang it on a chair. The heavy parka tipped the chair so he folded it and flopped it on the seat.

"I'm sorry," he said. I just shook my head. It all felt pretty hopeless. Used to encouraging his men, his voice took on a kind of false heartiness. "We'll find her!"

Andy returned with a steaming mug. Hanson accepted it with a nod and leaned forward in a getting-down-to-business way as he took a sip of his coffee.

"You heard Chilt's place burned... Lieutenant Bradbury from my squad?"

"On the radio."

He nodded and lowered his voice, as if we could be overheard. "They brought out remains. Probably a man," he added quickly, though Andy and I had both seen Evie — who had seen Roberta — since hearing of the fire.

136

Andy sat up straighter. "Chilt?"

"They don't know yet. It's possible. Burned to a crisp. And they won't know for a while. Had to send to Georgia for dental records." He paused to sip more coffee. "Of course, they searched the place. The house is just rubble but there are outbuildings."

"But they didn't find anything," I said. He looked at me.

"How did you know?"

"Because I'm guessing you want to go out there and search again." He laughed a little and ducked his head.

"Affirmative. You guys want in?"

"Sure!" We said it together.

* * *

The burnt-out hulk of Walter Chilton Bradbury's rental cabin lay due west of downtown on a wide bend in the Chena river, conveniently about halfway out to the Ladd Field Army Base. The house had burned all the way to its concrete block foundation. Only the plumbing — the vent stacks of steel and heavy iron — still stood. Footing was treacherous. The fire had been so hot, it melted snow to the ground and out about twenty feet. The melt water had no place to go, except to puddle up and freeze, surrounding the place with a skating rink.

We had come out the next morning, a warmer day — temperature near zero — sunny, with a very blue sky.

Poking at the ashes, I said, "I'm surprised they could even find a body."

Hanson turned from staring at the outbuildings, "Not much left, mostly just bones. Impossible to quickly identify. They found the skull and worked back." He paused and looked off into the barren

137

woods. "He was a good guy. Always had my back."

Andy looked over. "Might not be him."

Hanson hung his head. "At this point, that might not be better. His career is over."

We found a tall cache, a well-kept privy, and a small older garage, probably built before the war for something like a Model A. The place had been completely trampled, tracks everywhere, so no help there. We found the buildings closed but unlocked, empty of anything worth stealing or anything that looked like a clue. We certainly found no bearer bonds and no obvious place to hide them. All three of the buildings were single-wall with no place for a secret panel or hidey-hole and nothing easy to find, like a loose floorboard.

I asked the obvious question. "Did he have time to rob the bank and come out here to hide the bearer bonds before leading us off on a wild goose chase?"

"And dying," added Andy. "Don't forget that part."

With no place left to search, I stopped to look out over the river, wondering why some parts blew clear, right down to glare ice, and some parts drifted. A clear spot, not more than a hundred feet from the river bank, looked smooth and flat. I imagined myself skating there, briefly wondered if Chilt ever did. He certainly wouldn't now.

Something about Jack caught my attention. Nose to the ground, he circled the whole place, ending up at the privy door. *Why?* I wondered. With weather this cold, it didn't have any particular smell. At least not to me. I opened the door. Nothing unusual. Just a single hole, a partially used roll of toilet paper, and a small stack of way-out-of-date magazines. *Who would sit here and read at forty below?* I wondered.

Not me.

Hanson unwrapped a stick of Beemans and offered the pack around. "We don't know we were really chasing *him*. He might have had... what?... three or four days to come out here, hide the bonds, and get killed, while we were out chasing ringers with hostages and stolen snow machines."

"Explains why the getaway didn't go anywhere," said Andy. "It was just supposed to make us look somewhere else."

"A feint," I remembered. "That's what William said right from the beginning."

Hanson sighed. "And it worked."

CHAPTER 18

We drove back to town without saying much. Hanson, for being a military officer and something of a war hero, was easy to be around, though he seemed a little quieter than usual. We headed back to the restaurant where he'd left his Jeep.

He rode in front, mostly gazing out the side window, so I could only see his image in reflection. He looked sad and tired. As we pulled in, he turned to face us, resting his arm on the seat back.

"A soldier gets paid a basic wage... yeah, and chow and a bunk, and not much more, to beat the bad guys and try to keep people safe. We go someplace, usually some not-too-pleasant-place far from home, to wait and train until it's time to risk our lives or be killed. You know this. You were there.

"If we do something good, we come home and," he shrugged, "most people don't remember, at least not for long. If we screw up, people never forget and certainly never forgive." He shrugged again and twisted the chrome handle to open the door. "I got no excuses to make for Chilt. But I get it. He saw one chance at a better life, much better, and he took it." Climbing out, he turned to push the door until it latched, quietly and firmly then he walked away.

We sat, the car idling, until Hanson drove away. Andy twisted himself around to look at me.

"We're here and I notice you're not gettin' out. And you got that *look*." He turned back around to work the column shifter into reverse. "Where we goin'?"

"Back to Chilt's."

"You saw somethin'?"

"Maybe."

"I thought so."

* * *

We found the satchel hanging from two screws, far to the side — out of splashing distance — under the bench seat in the outhouse. I wouldn't want to be sticking my arm into the pit of a working outhouse in the summer, but in the winter with everything frozen, no slop, no smell, no big deal.

"In the shitter!" said Andy. "Okay, I'm impressed. How did you know?"

I shook my head, gesturing with both hands up. "I didn't. Part of it was Jack. I saw him sniffing around. The rest was a lucky guess." I pointed at what was left of the house. "Indoor plumbing that's obviously been here awhile. Yet they still kept the privy in good shape. I figured they had to be using it for something."

"When did you think of it?"

I knew where he was going with this. "When we were out here earlier."

"But you didn't want Wild Bill in on it?" He stepped closer, eyes wide. "Are we keepin' these?" I just looked at him. I knew he was kidding. At least I thought I knew.

"Nope."

"But you didn't want Wild Bill to take 'em and haul 'em back to the Army." I nodded.

"Well, then," he hefted the two bricks of certificates. "Looks like we got..." he calculated, "two stacks of five hundred bonds at..." he checked, "five

141

hundred dollars each. A half a million bucks here." He smiled at me. "More than I ever seen! Bet we're gonna trade these for women."

"Bingo," I said. "We are." And I told him how.

* * *

Fairbanks radio now reported Evie as the female hostage originally taken in the bank robbery. Nobody bothered to correct them.

With the search at another dead end, and not a single useful thing for me to do, I went home. I had sick people to visit and pray over, two services on Sunday, a session of marriage counseling with a pair of love-sick teens, and condensation apparently collecting in the rectory fuel-oil tank. It was all in a day, or two days, in the life of a mission priest.

Molly Joseph called me, shyly, on her new telephone, to say that she would be coming by to search through the mission barrel to find clothing for young Henry. It was a regular ritual with us. I mentioned to Oliver, who had stopped in to bring back a tool, that she was headed over.

"I'll go open the place up," he offered. I would have unlocked it myself when I got there, but since he offered, I just nodded and went back to what I was doing.

I was outside when Molly and Henry came walking up the street, and Jack ran to greet. It was a bright, warm, almost spring-like day with the temperature near zero. It was the kind of day I kept thinking I might hear dripping and things starting to melt. But I didn't.

Molly wore tall caribou mukluks with a beaver fringe around the top. A talented seamstress, I knew she'd made them herself. And they both wore their new parkas made from one large man's parka I'd

142

been able to get for them. She'd worked right around the bullet hole.

Henry was sliding today, following his mother down the slick road. Backing up, running, but getting some good slides and not falling too much. It felt like he hadn't even been walking that long, and now sliding! I knew she'd be trying to find pants that went all the way to his ankles. It was no easy task. Nothing fit for long.

Henry leaned his head all the way back to look up at me. He was never sure what to call me. Many of the village men he would call uncle, and yet he knew most people called me father.

"Hi, Uncle Father," was his solution and it certainly worked for me. I picked him up, spun him — Jack spinning too, and barking — and pretended I was about to throw him in a snowdrift. He loved it and squealed. After a few more spins I set him down on his feet and he and Jack ran off to build snow forts.

Molly put a tentative hand on my forearm. "Is there any sign of her? Any word?"

I shook my head and she gave me a pat. "She is tough and smart. Smarter than bank robbers, I think." I hoped so.

We went into the icy Quonset hut, finding Oliver still there folding clothes. He nodded at Molly, a little shyly, and she at him. He'd turned on the lights but it didn't matter much. The place still seemed dark and somehow felt much colder than outside. Although we always folded and stacked as we sorted, most of the clothing remained roughly organized in piles on the floor, a men's pants pile, men's shirt pile, and so forth. In three years, we'd never managed to get it all stacked up at the same time. These were clothes sent

143

from churches in the lower forty-eight, mostly in the South where I'd lived and gone to seminary. So, most of the clothes had come from old dead people. Too much of it came in summer fabric, like seersucker, and too little of it fit a child. But we managed to find a pair of tan corduroy slacks that mostly fit Henry, cuffs rolled up two turns. "Not for long," I told Molly, and she nodded seriously.

After they'd all gone, I went back to thinking about Evie, something I'd been doing nearly nonstop for the two days I'd been home. I kept seeing her, hearing her, carrying on conversations with her in my brain as I installed a new oil filter, shoveled snow, or carried in firewood.

One conclusion I came to again and again, that whether we agreed about everything or not, we were far better together than apart. And frankly, all this waiting was making me crazy.

As it does in a village, word got around. All day long, people brought me sympathy food. A moose roast, moose stew, a packet of smoked moose trail jerky, even moose stroganoff — a recipe that called for wine — made with the only wine available, very sweet Mogen David.

Even so, at the end of day two, somewhat guiltily, I left Jack on his furnace grate and left all the food in my refrigerator. I walked the several blocks to the Coffee Cup Café for a cheese mooseburger, to enjoy the company of other human beings, and yes, to let Rosie fuss over me.

The bell above the door tinkled as I stepped in, the place about three quarters full. I knew most of the eaters who looked up, smiled, and waved with a hand, a cigarette, or a coffee cup as I threaded through.

I took my accustomed place under the dusty

moose head. It was always the last seat occupied. Once in an earthquake it had fallen, the six-foot rack alone weighing most of fifty pounds, knocking over and pinning the occupant of my chair. He lay there, the story goes, smoking calmly until fellow diners gathered around to lift away the heavy head.

Now, Rosie came on the run, smoothly hip-sliding between close chairs, holding the glass coffee pot and a fistful of mugs aloft and out of contact range with the other eaters. She gave me a sympathetic look and a kiss on the cheek. I knew by now to blot away the lipstick. She poured my mug nearly full, leaving just room for a smidge of canned Carnation and a half teaspoon of sugar.

She wore a mint green waitress dress today. Her white low-cut U.S. Keds were an apparent nod to spring, even if it wasn't exactly melting outside. She owned four identical pairs of fashionable, swept-wing eyeglasses — black, red, teal, and today's color, white.

I felt myself relax in the chatter and occasional laughter. The good smells of meat frying and cigarette smoke layered with the sizzle, spray, and occasional clang from the kitchen blended with the murmur of the little red Philco radio high on its shelf. Johnny Cash singing "I Walk the Line" gave way to Johnnie Ray's "Just Walking In the Rain." Then at six thirty on the dot, what I'd been waiting for: *Tundra Topics*.

A generator part for the Minto school was back-ordered but should be arriving Friday. So, Minto students would be studying by kerosene lamplight another week. Jennie Forslund from Allakaket delivered a six-pound ten-ounce baby boy. Mother and baby were doing fine, and they'd fly home from

Fairbanks tomorrow. And on it went. As usual, the announcer read mine last.

"This goes out to... I don't know! It doesn't say. Father Hardy, in Chandalar, says he 'found the prize in Fairbanks.' He's willing to trade his prize for the two you're holding... in good condition. Call him to connect." And it concluded with my phone number. It would be read again the next night, but these robbers weren't Alaskan if they weren't listening, and I would have bet once would be enough. I should have bet.

* * *

The call came just after three a.m. It seems like they always do. I was asleep, but not much, and dreaming of Evie. The phone rang like a shriek in the dark, and of course, Jack barked. The two continued apace as I stumbled down the dark hall toward my office and the phone, Jack prancing unseen at my feet, toenails clicking on the linoleum.

"Hardy?" asked a voice, artificially low and gruff.

"Speaking."

"Not so smart, taking our bonds." I swallowed the obvious retort... *Not so smart taking my friends.*

"I'm listening," I said.

"You ready to make the switch?"

"Where?"

"Your place."

"I can be. A half hour?"

"Works for me. And Hardy?"

"Yes."

"Don't try anything heroic. We're watching. We *will* kill the girls, kill you, and take the bonds. We don't have to deal. Understood?"

"I got it." He named a time with military precision, exactly thirty minutes, and he hung up.

"I'll be ready," I said to the darkness.

146

CHAPTER 19

The door 'knocked' precisely at three thirty-six. I was as ready as a person can be for what I figured would follow. They didn't disappoint.

I closed Jack into the study. Not what he wanted. Walking to the front door I turned the bolt, turned the frosty doorknob, and swung the door in while raising my hands. It was dark in the wanigan, but room light showed me two figures. The one in front raised her bowed head. Evie! I felt my heart lift.

The other figure, masked, brandishing a semi-automatic, shoved her roughly across the threshold and stepped in behind. He didn't bother closing the door but I didn't think he'd be staying.

"Bonds!" he said, still in the fake voice. I nodded in the direction of the two banded bundles sitting in a chair alongside. "Hand 'em over!"

I did. He gave each a cursory glance before shoving them into his parka pocket.

I reached for Evie, pulling her close, holding her tight with my left arm around her, my right hand reaching behind me for the .38 in my belt.

"I'm so sorry," she whispered.

"It's okay."

"Good news, bad news," said the masked man. "It's actually *not* okay. Good news is you got your girl back, bad news is now you're both gonna die. *You* were gonna die anyway," he said to me. "She didn't have to. You should have left the bonds where they were."

"Where's Roberta? The deal was for two."

He laughed a little, without humor. "You're a special kind of sucker, aren't you!" He thumbed back the hammer, Evie's face cringing down against my neck at the sound.

"I love you," she said.

"I love *you*." Those would be our last words. At least the last before Andy pressed his shotgun barrel into the base of the masked man's skull.

"You can kill 'em if you want, but it'll be the last thing you do. Except that I'll be shooting off as many of your arms and legs as it takes to find out where Roberta is... before I finish you. Or you can just set down the shooter really easy." He jabbed with the shotgun barrel, the man's head deflecting forward in an involuntary nod.

"I..." he said, lowering the hammer. "Don't shoot." He bent very slowly to set the gun down 'easy.'

I pulled Evie farther into the room as Andy shoved the man forward. We got the door closed and the lights switched off. A soft sheen of blue moonlight flooded in.

"Didn't see anybody else out there," said Andy, "but you never know. This clown didn't see me." He gave the man another rough shove with the shotgun barrel. "Down on your knees, hands clasped behind your neck." Pulling back the man's hood, Andy yanked off the balaclava.

We knew him! He was one of Hanson's men from the first meeting, down by the Cushman Street Bridge in Fairbanks. Not one of the robbers, but one of the searchers. Hanson had more to be troubled about than he even knew.

Leaving him, I turned Evie to get at her tied hands, the leather lacing thoroughly knotted. The only room in the house with no window to show light out of, was the bathroom. I led her down the hall and through the door, closing it behind us, switching on the mirror lamp.

Using a pocket knife to cut through the lacing, I freed her arms which, when I stood, she flung around my neck.

"I was *so* stupid. Stupid, stupid, stupid! And I nearly got both of us killed."

I pushed her back to arm's length to face her. Fatigued, her face still a bit swollen with bruises going to a sick green, she'd never looked so lovely.

"It's done," I said, starting to kiss her, never wanting to stop.

Andy must have been timing us. "Okay, you two. Bet you got those laces untied by now."

I switched off the light and let us out, seeing nothing until my eyes adjusted.

"You guys are making a big mistake," said the gunman, now in a more normal voice. "You don't know what you're up against. Trained killers," he added, just in case we really were out of the loop.

"Uh-huh," said Andy. "What do you think *I* am? Courtesy of the U.S. Army. And by the way, you're the one on your knees."

I retrieved the bundles from the man's parka pockets. Andy smiled. He liked the look of big stacks of any kind of cash.

"We could still keep 'em," he said, a little wistfully. "Half a million bucks…"

"Not really," I told him.

"Not keep 'em or not a half million?"

"Not a half million… anymore. I syphoned off a

149

hundred thousand and re-glued the bundles. I figured with all the excitement he wouldn't notice. And he didn't."

"So, we're splittin' the hundred Gs?"

"Seed money," I told him. "Just in case something like this," I gestured at the kneeling man, "happened."

Our captive managed to look defiant. "You guys are gonna die." Andy whacked him along the side of his head with his own pistol barrel, probably just hard enough to leave a bruise.

"Ow! *Damn!* That hurts!"

"That's a down payment," promised Andy.

"Do you have a plan?" I asked.

"How 'bout we open the door and this guy tells his friends to drop their guns and come in slowly, hands up."

"That's your plan?"

"I think it's a pretty good one. Want to try it?" He seemed so gung ho, and I didn't know what else to do.

"Okay."

Andy handed me the shotgun and I gave Evie the .38. He opened the front door and knee-walked our prisoner to the threshold, giving him a jab with the pistol.

"Invite 'em in!"

The man drew a breath then shouted, "There's only two of..."

Andy shot him in the head.

Or at least that's what it sounded like. He'd actually clapped a hand over the man's mouth while shooting low out the door. He yanked the prisoner back and down, slamming the door as we all dropped, expecting a fusillade through the front windows.

Nothing. Well, nothing but the sound of Jack

barking in my study, scratching at the door. Evie crawled across the floor and opened the study door to quiet him.

Andy leaned over his captive. "I think that's the sound of your buddies running in to avenge you." He put his hand behind his ear, pretending to listen. "I'm not hearin' much. I think you been written off."

A shot fired, not far away. The man quit nursing his sore head to look smug, even by moonlight.

"Here they come."

But they didn't. In another minute or two, someone — a familiar voice — called out, "Hardy, Andy, coming in. All is clear." The captive's face fell.

We got up off the floor and I flipped on the light switch, all of us blinking and squinting as I opened the door. Another masked man came, hands in the air, encouraged along by the muzzle of one of William's service Colts.

"I found this one lurking about. There were no others. They arrived alone with Evie and were not followed."

Gun still trained, William sidled to Evie, wrapping a long arm around her, pulling her close. "My dear," he said.

* * *

They were both Hanson's men. Men who had been part of the search party! We called Frank Jacobs, who called Hanson, who insisted he would put them into Army custody. Within two hours — just about dawn — a Ford wagon, olive drab with 'Military Police' in big letters along the side, showed up with Hanson at the wheel and an armed MP riding shotgun. The MP handcuffed the two and, with a protective hand on their parka hoods, folded them into the vehicle's back seat. Hanson could only shake his head. His world had not only crumbled, there were men, formerly his trusted men, stomping on the leftover bits.

As we watched them drive away, red taillights disappearing into the dawn, Andy said what we were all thinking.

"So much for his men skiing through fire."

Walking back into the rectory, I took Evie's hand and she took mine. When we'd taken off our parkas and mitts, I put my arms around her to hold her, and she held me. I could feel my life, which had felt unsettled and drifty, ease back and settle to earth. I began to breathe again, and it felt like I hadn't been. William and Andy left us like that, moving off down the short hall where I heard sounds of coffee grinding and the kettle filling.

Soon we'd be sitting around the kitchen table on our tippy stools, favorite mugs in hand, drinking Andy's Italian roast and making the good-coffee sounds, as though all had been made right again in the world.

Except that it hadn't. Sipping, looking across into Evie's eyes, I thought of Roberta, as I think Evie probably was. For the first time, I wondered if we would find her. If we *could* find her. In time.

Could it get worse? Sure. Frank Jacobs called about noon. When the wagon didn't make it back to base and didn't answer radio calls, they went hunting. They found it bullet riddled and mostly buried in snow, deliberately covered. It had been run off the road into a snow bank. The prisoners were long gone. Inside, they found the MP shot dead and Hanson badly beaten and marginally conscious.

CHAPTER 20

Andy and I drove to Fairbanks, met up with Frank Jacobs, and the three of us went to visit Hanson in his private room at St. Joseph's. We found him in bed, propped up on pillows with a nun fussing over him. He had a gauze wrap all the way around his head and a purpling bruise across his left cheekbone, roughly the shape of a gun barrel.

"You were lucky," I told him, thinking of the MP.

Hanson gingerly reached up with both hands to hold what had to be an aching head. "Just right now," he said, "it doesn't feel like luck."

"What happened, anyway?" Frank asked.

"They were staked out, waiting. Knew we were coming. We saw a car on the shoulder, hood up, with two men leaning in over the engine. I slowed to ask if they needed help. When one of them turned, he was masked, but I think it was Chilt — with a gun. It all happened pretty quickly. He said, 'Hands up!' but the MP went for his sidearm and that's when the shooting started. They riddled the car, killing the MP, then dragged me out and whacked me."

"Ahead of us all the way," Frank said.

He was right. It made more sense now. Hanson's own men had been working against him, against us. Somehow feeding information to their friends. Small wonder the men we were chasing always knew where we were going, what we were doing, and were set up and ready for us when we got there.

"Hardy's right," said Frank. "You could have been just as dead as the other guy."

* * *

Frank drove us back to Andrea's in his government car and then came in for coffee.

"So, what aren't you telling me?"

We were all seated, steamy glass mugs in hand. Andy started to reply, to deny, but Frank held up his hand.

"Let's just pretend I'm not an employee of the federal government, charged with enforcing the law and keeping people safe. Let's pretend I'm one of you." He looked at both of us. "Vigilante scofflaws who do whatever they damn please." He sipped his black coffee and made an approving face. "What aren't you telling me?"

So we told him about finding the bonds, about baiting the robbers with the *Tundra Topics* notice, and about setting the trap with Andy and William as backup.

"I can't believe you recovered a half million bucks of government money, 'forgot' to tell me — or anyone — and then used it for your own purposes." He paused. "No, cancel that. With you two, it's not that hard to believe." He sipped again. We all did. Then he looked up. "So, you gave the money to Hanson, with the prisoners, and now it's gone, too?" He looked from Andy to me. "No," he said, "you didn't tell Hanson, either. You kept the money, didn't you? You still have it and you're *still* not telling me about it."

Andy gave him a smirk. "Well, we would, or we could if you'd ever shut up."

Frank turned to me. "I'm asking you," he jerked a face in Andy's direction, "the sensible one, to turn

154

that money in... to me... or to Hanson. You just can't be walking around with a half million dollars of stolen government money. If somehow you do lose it, the Feds will come after you for it. *You'll* turn out to be the ones in jail."

"That's why you don't know we have it," I reminded him.

He pressed his lips together. "Oh."

For a time, we sipped on in near silence but for Jack's occasional tail thump or scratching an itch. Then Frank looked up from his coffee.

"Those two you had, Dave and his buddy. They know what you got, and they know where you live and where Evie lives. What are you hoping to accomplish?"

"I'm still hoping to trade the cash for Roberta."

"Roberta's dead," he said. The words stunned me, like a face slap.

"You know that?"

"I don't have a body, if that's what you mean."

"So, you're just guessing?"

"Ask yourself, if you were the robbers and you have *most* of the money... why would you keep her alive? Even if she cooperates, they have to feed her, bunk her, keep her warm, move her around. Why would they?"

I thought about that, realizing he was probably right. "There's only one reason," I told him.

"Yeah? What's that?"

"She's worth a half million bucks. Cash."

He made a face, a grimace of realization. "That would do it," he said.

* * *

Jack and I drove home in time to pick up Evie after school. We made a stop at her cabin where all

155

seemed secure. She grabbed a few necessities and a change of clothing then we headed home to the rectory. 'Home.' Even with all the trouble, I liked the idea of us going there together.

The door was intact, but we went in cautiously, Jack first and me following, .38 in hand. All was as it should be. We set guns where we could grab them, pulled all the curtains, even angled chairs under the front and back doorknobs.

Fixing dinner, squinting and teary while chopping onions for spaghetti, Evie looked over at me. "You really think they'll come after us here?"

"They're not after us. It's the half-million bucks. I read somewhere the average American, certainly not me, makes about $3,500 a year. So that's about — I had to grab a pencil and paper — one hundred forty-two years' worth of wages. More than that for a military stiff."

She scraped onions into an iron skillet of sizzling mooseburger. "I may keep it, myself!"

"That's what Andy keeps saying."

She laughed. "But, except for you — okay, and William and Frank — Andy is the one guy I know who *wouldn't* keep the money. He'd rather be honest. He's funny that way."

"That honesty thing is always good for a laugh," I said. But she didn't.

"I'm sorry I wasn't honest with you about Roberta. I was so sure you'd be angry about it."

"I don't think I would have been angry. I might have tried to talk you out of it." I took a breath. "We're adults. Marriage shouldn't make us smaller than we are. It should make us bigger, stronger, more sure, more daring. It should make us better. I don't want you to stop being you, to stop doing the things that are important to you. I don't always have to agree, and I'm sure I won't. And I'm sure, in our life together, I'll do things you think are stupid or not worth it. And you'll tell me that — or I'll tell you — and then we'll do what we need to do. Mostly together."

She began to weep.

"Is that still the onions?" I asked her.

She put her arms around me. "Oh, Hardy."

* * *

I don't like carrying a gun all the time. A priest shouldn't. I've always felt that a gun changes everything. It frames every problem for a *gun* solution, when many could be a *punch-in-the-nose* solution, or just angry venting. Still, if you get to a gunfight with no gun, where are you? Probably dead. So, I continued to carry my .38. Everywhere.

What to do with the bearer bonds? There's a cubby behind the altar in the church, that I've used to hide things for nearly as long as I've been here. By now, I'm pretty sure nobody else knows about it or thinks about it. I put the two wrapped bundles of bonds there. The one hundred thousand I had already removed, I placed in a heavy envelope and thumbtacked up inside Jack's mostly unused doghouse out behind the rectory. I did it late on a windy night, by starlight, knowing by morning my tracks would be blown away.

Evie slept on the sofa. She'd done it before. We were getting pretty used to sharing a small place, taking turns in the bathroom in the morning, roommate-like, cooking and eating breakfast together and then I'd drive her to work. With Andy and Frank in Fairbanks, and William often staying with Alice, we felt private and unobserved. But we'd both lived in a small town long enough to know someone always saw something, knew something, said something. And we didn't want to give gossips any extra fat to chew. Every now and then, since we'd been *an item*, I'd hear something back about what we were or weren't doing. Pretty amazing stuff. Sometimes I wished we *were* doing some of those things. But we weren't sharing anything more intimate than a roof.

On Saturday morning, after a full week, Evie looked up from coffee with an expression I recognized. I knew what she'd say before she said it and didn't disagree.

"This has been great. Wonderful, really. Almost like a vacation. But I need to go home. I think people — my co-workers, for example — believe we've started living together. It's bad for both of us."

I swallowed my mouthful of coffee. "But if you go home now, they'll think we're fighting. You wouldn't want that."

"Funny! I'll risk it."

She leaned on one elbow, looking more serious. "I think Roberta might be..." she hesitated, "dead."

I blew out a long breath. I'd been dreading this part of the conversation. "That's what Frank thinks."

She pressed her lips together, looking less stricken than I might have imagined. "I pray about it every night, and I think you do, too."

She was right. It had been part of the fabric of my daily prayers since this whole thing began. 'Please, God, deliver Roberta.' But there were different methods of deliverance. Does it make sense to dread death, dread that terrible loss while believing in the Kingdom of Heaven?

I chose my words. "Even if she is dead, and I don't feel like she is, we're still in danger."

"The bonds."

"Yeah."

She sipped, swallowed, thinking. "Maybe you *should* turn them over to Frank or to Colonel Hanson and make a big deal about it. Make it public. It would make a great headline — U.S. marshal recovers five hundred thousand dollars." She had a point.

Andy turned up later for lunch, seeing it differently, shaking his head. "You give the bonds back, you got nothing left to trade for Roberta, if we do find her. I say keep 'em. If nothing else works we can still split 'em!"

With water boiling for fresh coffee, I sawed slices off a moose roast, cautioning Andy about the perils of too much horseradish while he assembled the sandwiches. He had a tendency to overdo, leaving me with tears in my eyes and what felt like a hot poker burrowing through my brain to the back of my skull. It never seemed to bother him.

We both heard the knock on my front door. Jack yipped and Andy and I exchanged a glance.

"Somebody else here to kill you?"

I laughed. "Probably. It's been a week since the last one." And he laughed.

I think I might still have been chuckling to myself all the way down the hall and across the front room, right up until I swung the front door wide and saw the gun.

CHAPTER 21

Again, I knew the man. Walter George, originally from Minto. He stood a little shorter than me, his parka hood thrown back revealing salt-and-pepper hair, cut long on the top with the sides thin, heavy black-framed glasses, and a wispy mustache. I'd done his taxes, lent him money from time to time, and helped with the paperwork to send his daughter south to school.

Now he extended both hands, one holding a .45 semiautomatic — butt first — and the other, a sheaf of five one-hundred-dollar bills.

"Father," he said. "We need to talk."

I let him in, quickly closed the door, bolted it, and accepted both the gun and the cash, which he seemed anxious to get rid of. His face took a grateful set. Jack greeted him like they were old buddies.

"Don't like guns," he said.

The setup had been the same as the last time. He went out of the Bide-A-While to take a leak, was standing there, hands occupied, when someone shoved a muzzle into his kidney and demanded to know if he knew me. When he said he did, the man offered him a thousand dollars, with five hundred in advance — that was different — to come and shoot me in the face. He'd get the other five hundred when he completed the job.

Personally, I doubted he'd ever see that other five hundred, which meant the bounty on me had now

160

fallen from its original high of five thousand to this. A fact that Andy was quick to point out. Most likely, if he shot me — or if he didn't — they'd shoot him. Something Walter had figured out.

Andy knew Walter from the mission school, greeted him, and offered fresh, hot coffee, which he gratefully accepted. The temperature hovered at about minus twenty and he looked chilled in his Sears parka.

"Don't 'spose you got a look at him?" Andy asked.

"Not real good."

Andy made a frustrated face in my direction.

"But I knew one of 'em anyway. Well, not his name, but I seen him last time I was in jail in Fairbanks."

"He was in jail with you?" I asked. "What for?"

"Not *in* jail," insisted Walter. "He was the jailer, the one that locked me in the cell. A Fairbanks cop."

* * *

Walter needed money to get out of town and I was happy to pay for his ticket. He had a brother in Anchorage and planned to stay there until things blew over. Andy and I escorted him to the train. I bought his ticket while Andy sat with him in the truck. When the whistle blew and, bell clanging, the bright blue-and-gold locomotive began to creak and tremble, wheels just starting to turn, slipping and squealing, we hurried Walter to the steps, handed up his ticket to the conductor, and pushed him aboard. We waved him away as he moved off down the line to safety.

Andy asked the question we were both thinking, unanswerable for the moment. "Okay, is this deputies moonlighting or does it go all the way to Kellar?"

I shook my head. "No clue." And we drove back

161

to the rectory.

On Sunday I celebrated Holy Communion at eight, Morning Prayer at eleven then stood around drinking coffee and chatting with parishioners until nearly one. Since I'd been up early polishing my sermon, I caught a nap in the afternoon, and approaching evening was more than ready to kick up my heels with Evie, Chandalar style.

Just before five I left Jack on his furnace grate and walked over to Evie's cabin to pick her up. Arm in arm, the two of us strolled the snow-shouldered streets, talking about not much, just enjoying being back together. Streaming silvery trails of our breath through the frosty air, we made our way to the Coffee Cup Café for Sunday dinner out.

On the way, I told her about Walter, whom she'd also known from childhood at the mission school. She pressed her lips together, bunching her cheeks.

"He wouldn't hurt a flea."

"Fortunately," I said, and she agreed.

"He used to carry spiders outside instead of smashing them, even in winter. I remember telling him they'd freeze. That they didn't have a prayer. He said as long as they're alive, their life is their prayer, and at least they'll have a chance."

The bell at the door tinkled as we stepped into the café. We were a little early, the place about half full. Rosie paused in her gallop, coffee pot and mugs in hand, to carefully hug Evie. I stuck out my cheek to be grazed by a high-speed lipstick-y kiss as she streaked by.

She wore a new waitress outfit, a little more formal for evening. It was a soft gray with black sleeve cuffs and collar, *Rosie* stitched provocatively in hot pink. She accessorized with black swept-wing eyeglasses. She wore the tall caribou mukluks with a beaver fringe around her shapely calves, and long underwear hiked up her legs, mostly out of sight. Just the thing for nearly spring.

We knew everybody, greeting them with a wave or a word, slowly working our way across the floor to 'our' table under the dusty moose head. Before we sat, Evie dragged a thumb across my cheek to remove the hot-pink smear.

Rosie came back around with menus, not that we needed them. I'd had everything on the menu and it was all good, but kept coming back to the house special. The moose cheeseburger with big wedges of golden french fries and a cup of not-terrible coffee. I could get the whole meal for a dollar and seventy-five cents.

"Same," said Evie after I'd ordered.

The little red Philco, high on its shelf, was tuned to KFAR, Fairbanks' station with the great Sam Cooke singing "You Send Me." I nudged Evie and pointed at the radio.

"What he says."

She smiled and squeezed my arm. "You're such a romantic!"

After all the days I'd spent searching for her, worrying about her, having her safe and right here next to me seemed almost unbelievable. Of course, that thought took me to the next — Roberta still unaccounted for.

The news arrived with our burgers at the top of the hour. It was all Roberta, now that they'd acknowledged that she was the one missing — still missing — correcting the earlier story that it had been Evie. It ended with a plea for information.

"They've got nothing new," I said. We listened

163

through the weather, more of the same. Okay, a *bit* warmer, but still no melt in sight. At six-fifteen came the program I'd been waiting for. *Tundra Topics*.

Most people in the Interior make it a point to tune in. Since contacting the robbers that way, it seemed at least possible they would try doing the same. As I said to Andy, they had five hundred thousand reasons to want to reconnect. Sure enough, the final item went out 'to Father Hardy, Chandalar.'

It was simple. They still had what I wanted and still wanted to trade. I was to reply via this program as soon as possible.

Our eyes met. "So, she's still alive," said Evie.

"A good possibility."

"You think she's not?"

It had been most of a month. A whole bunch of the other players had been killed. Why would *she*, the incidental hostage, still be living? They had to move her, feed her, keep her warm, keep her from getting away or causing a fuss. In truth, I imagined her somewhere along the trail, deep under a drift, with a bullet in her brain.

"I think she's alive," I tried to say convincingly.

Evie looked at me carefully. "You're dear," she said, "but not a very good liar."

* * *

On the following Tuesday morning Frank Jacobs called me at about eight. Evie and I had finished breakfast and were enjoying our coffee together before she had to hustle off to work.

"He's been spotted," said Jacobs. "Can you get here?"

I paused, trying to figure out what this referred to. I couldn't. "Who's been spotted?"

He huffed like it should be obvious and why was I

164

wasting time. "Chilt."

"I'm on my way."

Evie looked up as I returned from the phone in a hurry. I reached for my coffee cup to give it a rinse.

"I'll get that," she said. "What's going on?"

"Turns out Chilt's not dead."

She made a face and said, "You thought he was dead?"

I told her about the remains discovered in the ashes of Chilt's rental.

"I could have told you it wasn't Chilt. He has an unmistakable voice. He was the one calling the shots the whole time they had me. I never saw his face, but several times Roberta just called him Chilt right out."

"Really!"

"Yes, and he slapped her for it. So, I wasn't surprised when she stopped. Though she carried on with it for a while, I think just to irritate him. And it did. You know how she is."

"Yes, that sounds like Roberta," I said.

She swallowed a last sip of coffee and rose to rinse the mugs, stretching across the table corner to kiss me.

"Gotta go. See you tonight?"

"Count on it."

Evie went off to teach, and within ten minutes Jack and I were driving north on the Fairbanks road with all my gear.

* * *

We met the others about twenty miles south of Fairbanks, the old gang back together again, except for Evie. Frank had also called William and brought Andy.

"What? No Evie?" said Andy.

"Yeah, I know," I said. "She'll be thoroughly

frosted…but safe."

"Well, like they say — hell hath no fury like Evie left *safely* behind!" said Andy.

"Better safe than sorry."

The road runs northeast there, intersected at that point by a sled trail heading northwest. In response to a telephone tip, a Territorial highway patrol officer had seen a man answering Chilt's description here — one of three — thought he recognized him and called it in.

Andy quickly picked up the trail — three men on skis — but he looked puzzled, shaking his head.

"This don't go nowhere," he told us. "At least it never did. If they stay on this trail, it's gonna curve around here and cross the road again, up a couple of miles. It's a loop. Mushers just use it to work the dogs."

They used it a lot. The trail was so well packed we carried our snowshoes. We expected at any time to see the ski trail break away from the main trail but it never did. After about a half hour of easy walking, we were back on the Fairbanks highway.

"What the heck!" said Frank, frustrated after we'd hiked the highway back to our vehicles, Jack bounding and peeing.

Again, it was William who called it. "It is a… diversion," he said and then turned to me. "Probably intended for you."

He was right, of course, and I knew why. If they could find the bearer bonds on their own, they had no need to trade with me.

Jack and I jumped into the truck, now prepared to head south in a hurry. To my surprise and pleasure, Andy yanked open the passenger door.

"Wait for me." He tossed his gear into the pickup

bed, sliding Jack to the center to sit between us and keep an eye on the road. I'd no more than jammed the shifter into gear, easing out the clutch on the snow-covered highway, when I noticed William in his government car falling in behind us. True, he had to go this way anyway to get back to his office at Clear Station, but I also surmised he didn't want to be left out if Andy and I ran into trouble back in Chandalar.

I made one unscheduled stop at the 40-Mile Trading Post.

"Use the phone?" I asked the clerk. He was a man in his fifties, unshaven this week — and worse, unshowered — with thinning hair and what looked like a perpetual glower.

He eyed me suspiciously, cigarette stuck to his lip, smoke wreathing his head. "Where you calling?"

"Just down the road. Chandalar."

He handed over the phone. "I'll be watching you dial," he warned. "Fellow came in here last week, called Anchorage when I wasn't lookin'. Cost me a buck and a quarter."

"I'll be good." I dialed the Chandalar school, a number I knew by heart, checking just to make certain Evie had made it in. She had. Breathing a little easier, I climbed back in the truck and our little convoy buzzed away south, making good time on a well-plowed road with little traffic.

In less than an hour, we'd made it back to the river, crossed on the ice, and were pulling into the rectory driveway. Andy went out the passenger door fast, with Jack at his heels, and William, .45 in hand, followed me to the front door.

I hadn't left it locked, a good thing since I'm certain we'd have found it kicked in. At first glance all seemed well. At second glance, the whole place had been turned over by practiced hands, left only slightly disarranged. My closet, my dresser drawers, my office desk and filing cabinet — even the toilet tank lid left ajar. At least it was better than the last time my place had been tossed.

As William holstered the .45, I gave Andy the 'all clear.' His eyebrows asked the question.

"Looks like they turned over the whole place," I said.

"Swell." Andy looked around, his eyes narrowing. "Hope they didn't take the coffee." He went down the hall to the kitchen to discover the coffee undisturbed and put water on to boil.

William took off his wire rims, polishing the lenses on a clean and pressed handkerchief. "I am assuming this is about bonds? Did they get them? Were they here?"

"The bonds were here... and probably are here, but I can't check until after dark in case they're watching."

He nodded in his wise way, like he knew what I was talking about. Like he knew I'd hidden the bonds behind the altar in the church. Of course, he had been a spy, a really good one. Maybe he did know.

Finishing with his glasses, he pulled the ear pieces into place behind his ears and, unzipping his heavy parka, went off toward the kitchen to select his coffee mug and get in line.

They were right. Time for coffee. I hurried to follow.

168

CHAPTER 22

Andy spent the night on my sofa, rising early to put on the Italian roast and start frying up bacon he'd brought. Two good smells guaranteed to get me up and dressed quickly. Even Jack came along from his furnace grate, toenails clicking down the hall on the linoleum. He didn't hurry. He knew Andy always saved him some bacon.

Evie showed up a little later. She knocked but we had the door bolted.

"It's me," she called, and I let her in to kiss me nicely and then sniff the air like a hound dog. "Coffee *and* bacon? And you didn't call me?"

We knew the perils of trying to get her out of bed early, so had simply saved her some. Another knock about ten minutes later brought William sniffing in from the cold, his eyeglasses not too fogged-up to keep him from selecting a coffee mug and taking his place on a tippy stool. So, we had a quorum, or I thought we did.

One more knock tensed us all, and we froze for a moment, looking at each other across the kitchen table.

"Open up! U.S. marshal. Give me coffee and nobody gets hurt!"

We let him in and gave him coffee. And nobody got hurt.

"What're you doin' here?" asked Andy.

"Flying to Denali. Somebody joyriding out there

169

in a government snowplow. Evie made a face at him.

"Seriously? And you're flying out?"

"Gotta investigate. Besides, I knew Andy would be here with the good stuff."

Andy grinned. "Shoulda called for a ride," imagining him walking in from the air strip.

"Nah, I just landed out here on the river, tied the plane down, and walked over."

"Any more Chilt sightings?" I asked. He already knew the rectory had been tossed.

"No. If I hadn't seen the ski tracks out there, I'd wonder about the sighting we had." He gestured in William's direction with his coffee mug. "I agree with William. They just wanted you out of the way. At this point, I think anybody in a white army suit, or for that matter, nearly anybody on skis is gonna get reported as the infamous Chilt. He's sure all over the news." He froze. "They didn't get... anything... did they?"

He meant the bonds, of course, and they hadn't. We'd gone out the door last night after turning out all the lights, as if turning in. There'd been little-to-no visibility and I had to braille myself over by staying in the shoveled foot path — not too difficult. I risked a very small penlight at the back of the altar, which Andy reported *not* being able to see from outside through the stained-glass side windows. I found all as I'd left it.

Frank visibly relaxed at the news. Even though he didn't *officially* know we had them, still he *did* know and expected to be held accountable if something went wrong.

Evie, holding the blue mug in both hands, raised her eyes. "But still no sign of Roberta?"

He shook his head. "None at all... which isn't

necessarily bad," he rushed to add.

She smiled but without much wattage. "I know."

"Who was it saw Chilt?" asked Andy. "Or whoever it was."

Frank shook his head. "No clue. Word came from Hanson. They called the Army, too, which is a little strange." He stopped talking to sip and look thoughtful.

Later, after Evie and William had gone, he said it again to Andy and me. "I didn't want to say this to Evie, but Roberta? I'd say not a single chance she's still alive."

* * *

Roberta's parents, Teddy and Effie Moses got back from dog-sled racing in New Hampshire. He'd done well, a surprise third place overall, making a good show for Alaska in the New England-dominated dogsled world. With Roberta all over the news, Teddy came to see me within an hour of climbing down from the train.

Nearing fifty, his hair still dark, face lean, he stepped in the door and removed a pair of expensive aviator sunglasses. He looked prosperous, wearing a commercially made orange goose-down parka. Slick-looking commercial mukluks, with a molded sole, extended nearly to his knees. He still moved like he had a wound spring inside him. He knew the drill and followed me into my office where he took a seat in the customer chair. I saw his eyes flick to the bullet hole he'd made in my ceiling a couple of years earlier, totally overwrought, trying to shoot himself. He was calmer today.

"We knew about the Army guy," said Teddy, "but never knew his name. She just said she was datin' an Army officer." He hesitated. "She said 'dating' like goin' to movies, but I think they were sleepin' together. Makin' big plans. Wantin' things none of us ever had in the village. She says we don't understand how things are these days. We're dinosaurs. And since we aren't payin' for her college, she's on her own and can do as she damn well pleases — sorry, Father — which she pretty much done all her life, anyway." He looked up, meeting my eyes. "We love 'er. Tried to give 'er a good life... yeah, made mistakes, but..." He sat a minute more before making a hopeless gesture. "I know in your job you gotta think every person can turn out okay and every story can have a happy ending. They don't."

* * *

Wild Bill Hanson came to see me. I was expecting him. Frank Jacobs called me that morning, first thing.

"Hanson asked me directly if you had any of the bonds. Lying isn't in my job description so I had to tell him. Sorry."

"Nothing to be sorry about," I told him. "Thanks for letting me know."

So now I had to decide how much truth I needed to tell. Yes, I know how that sounds. But if he demanded the whole pile — and I gave it to him — then I had nothing left to trade for Roberta. I decided to bluff it if I could and retrieved the two packets of bonds from the altar stash, leaving the hundred thousand in the doghouse.

Hanson showed up about ten in another military car, no MP this time. He came in easy, friendly. Dropping his parka in the front room he followed me back the short hall to the kitchen.

His cheekbone bruise had faded to a pale, sickly yellow-green and the gauze head wrap had been discarded, revealing the fine line where the impact had split his head open, and the five neat stitches that pulled it closed. He saw me looking and rolled his eyes up, as if looking, too.

I warned him about the tippy stools as I set about boiling water for coffee.

"Why don't you just get new stools?" It was a reasonable question.

"They were made here," and I told him about the mission school, started in about 1907 and run by the Episcopal church until about five years ago. The stools were made in the shop out there, by some of my existing parishioners. I like to think that it gave them a measure of satisfaction to know the stools were still here and still in use. Even if tippy.

"Makes sense," he said, nodding. Knowing why he was really here, it was one more thing about him that made him hard to not like.

"I'm going to assume that Jacobs called you," he said when I'd handed him coffee and he had doctored it to his liking. I nodded. The notion didn't seem to bother him.

"I'm still hoping to trade for Roberta," I told him.

"Yeah, I figured." He sipped his coffee and made a happy coffee sound. "You realize... it goes missing on your watch, we'll all be in a heap of trouble. You, me, and Jacobs?"

"I do."

"Okay," he said, and nothing more about bonds.

We talked about snow and skiing, clearly a passion for him, and about the continued cold snap, which was okay with him. He told me he still skied every day, unlike other officers of his rank who sat behind desks and ate donuts. "And they look like it."

He didn't. Probably fifty, he had the physique and moves of a man in his twenties, the skiing regimen

173

clearly paid off.

Though hale and hearty, I sensed an underlying sadness, and said so.

"Yeah, maybe. I hadn't thought of it that way. Truth is — and I know how bad this sounds — I miss the war. Not the killing. I miss the adventure, the camaraderie, the sense that we were all in the thing together, all equal in a way. Soldiers were important then. When the war ends, Congress doesn't need us anymore, we're like this embarrassing thing left over that they still have to pay for. I'm not a hero anymore. I'm not this amazing guy who defeated Nazis when I should have been slaughtered on the mountain with my men. I'm not saying I miss being a hero. I'm saying, I wasn't ready to come home and be treated like..." he thought a minute and laughed without humor, "like an old dinosaur."

"Yes," I agreed, "that would be tiresome."

"I want to go back to feeling like there's excitement in front of me in my life, and value. That's not so bad, is it?"

I shook my head. I got it. I'd experienced some of those same things in France, with maybe a bit of letdown coming home. Except that happiness at being home quickly overcame whatever it was I'd felt over there.

"You realize she may be dead?" he asked, abruptly changing the subject, and I nodded.

"Yeah. Sure. But I need to keep pushing until I know it for certain."

"I get it," he said. "That's what I'd do." And I knew he would.

* * *

Normally, snow would be melting by now. It wasn't. At Nenana they'd put up the tripod for the

174

Nenana Ice Pool more than a month ago. But the ice out there still measured more than three feet thick and wouldn't be breaking up any time soon. People had been buying tickets, guessing the day, hour, and minute of ice breakup since January — the pot, said to be more than one hundred thousand dollars this year.

Typically, mid-April saw icicles four and five feet long, a few daytime puddles, a bit of dirt showing through the bladed thin spots on the road, skeins of northbound geese overhead, and the sound of dripping everywhere.

I used my thumb to melt a hole in the frost layer on the inside of my front window and peered out at the thermometer. Minus nine degrees. That was a little better, but I felt more than ready to quit wearing my winter parka. And minus nine wasn't going to get it.

I'd been awake at sunrise, now about six fifteen this far north, saying my morning prayers while still horizontal in my warm bed. I finished with what had become my *mantra* — what Hindus and Buddhists call a verse repeated like a theme — 'Keep Roberta warm and safe, and bring her home.'

The floor furnace came on. Though Jack hated to leave his warm grate, he came to stare at me just at eye level, smiling, tongue out, accepting his morning scratch behind the ears. He knew it was time for me to get up and put him out to pee, but more than that, time for a dog's breakfast. His stomach kept time like a railroad conductor's watch.

With Jack's encouragement, I did finally get up, let him out, and put water on for coffee. The cool house encouraged me to dress quickly — standing on Jack's furnace grate — then let him back in when he

175

thumped at the door. I pondered twisting the bolt and locking it, but felt I'd been locking too many doors lately, and carrying a gun so often it was wearing a hole in my pants pocket. So, I left it on the small table at my bedside.

I had just pushed the plunger on my French press when I heard the knock at my front door. Though I wasn't expecting anybody, William, Andy, or Evie often showed up for morning coffee, so I wasn't surprised. But no one entered, and I heard the knock again. I followed Jack into the front room as he barked and carried on. I guess I was thinking that the door had been locked so often recently that whichever friend this was just hadn't thought to give the knob a twist and walk right in.

So, I grabbed the door and swung it wide. But This wasn't a friend.

CHAPTER 23

Jack growled. I wanted to but resisted.

"Chief," I said. Stepping aside I gestured for him to enter quickly so I could get the door shut. The spring thaw hadn't started yet, and a tide of ice fog and blown bits of snow flakes and frozen pellets came rolling in ahead of him.

He didn't look good. I might have said there was no way for a big hearty fat man to look gaunt and sickly, but he did. In the week or so since I'd seen him on the trail, the yellow of his eyes and skin tone had gone from a suggestion to a statement.

He saw me seeing him. "Liver," he said. "Doc says too much booze." He hesitated then said what I was thinking. "I'm a goner." He dropped his fur hat on a chair, scratched Jack behind the ears and climbed out of his woolen overcoat. He made every move slowly, as if weary. "Coffee smells good."

"Come on back. I'll pour you some." He nodded and followed.

I got him a mug, got it poured and waved him to a stool. "Careful, they're tippy."

"Sturdy, though." Kellar eased himself to a sit. "You weigh up over three hundred pounds, you think about things like 'sturdy.'"

He sipped, jerked his head as if surprised, and smiled. "This is *good*!"

"My friend Andy imports it from Italy."

"Wow!" He sipped again. "Great coffee for a

homo."

I let the comment slide by. "I can put you on the prayer list."

He smiled again, rueful this time. "Think it'll help?"

"Yes."

"You have to think that."

"No more than you."

"I'm gonna burn in hell for eternity. I've *earned* it."

"It's not what I believe," I told him.

"Really?" The question seemed genuine.

"Change. Make good choices. That's what God wants."

He sighed. "It's too late."

"Not while you're breathing." I remembered Evie's spider story about Walter George. "Make whatever is left of your life your prayer."

Conversation stopped as he seemed to think about it and we sat quiet for a time, hearing only the hum and click of my Kit Kat clock and an occasional squirm and scratch from Jack. I watched sunbeams slide silently through frost-decorated windows, silver motes glittering.

"I hear," he said, "somebody wants you dead... enough to pay."

"I've heard that, too."

"And that they been trying."

"Yeah." I took a sip of my coffee. "Without luck so far."

"It ain't me."

It's true, I'd thought about him behind it. But in this moment, I could see clearly it wouldn't be. "I guess I know that." It seemed to cheer him.

"If *I* wanted you dead, I'd just shoot you my own

self."

"Good to know."

* * *

Evie came by after school. "Do you believe him?" she asked when I told her about Kellar's visit.

"He's dying. I think this is when most people tell the truth."

"Yeah, but this is Kellar."

She was right, of course. He did not have a reputation for being trustworthy. More like the opposite.

We worked up an appetite talking about it, decided that we needed to get out, and walked the several blocks to the Coffee Cup Café for dinner. Winter had blown back in with a vengeance, the temperature pegged at minus twenty, a stiff wind driving the wind-chill number far lower.

"This is spring?" The wind blew Evie's words from her lips and scattered them along the snow-drifted street.

The restaurant's bright lights shone warm and beckoning through plate-glass windows refrosted nearly to the top by the cold snap. They drew us on, like a vision of some holy place where we'd be blessed with hot coffee, moose cheeseburgers, and someone lovely to bring them to us, greeting us as we came in the door and anointing us with lipstick.

Rosie had KFAR tuned in, Rusty Draper singing "The Railroad Runs Through the Middle of the House." It would be in my head for days.

Clad in mint green, with the teal swept-wing glasses, she'd pulled back her lustrous dark hair with a coordinated scarf, something she'd likely seen in *Life, Look,* or a fashion magazine. She subscribed to quite a few and studied them. Fashion ended at her skirt hem tonight, with long johns pulled down into her high caribou mukluks. Every time the door opened, a cloud of sub-zero air came sweeping in, far too cold for bare calves.

She came on the run with coffee and warmed mugs, not so much taking the orders, as reciting what she already knew we wanted.

"Moose cheeseburgers, fries, and coffee." All we had to do was nod. She raced away. It wasn't a big crowd tonight but we all must have come in at about the same time, so the place generally — and Rosie, particularly — had a bustling feel. We sat under our moose head, even though other seats were empty. I chose, saying, "*Our* seats," and led the way.

"You romantic fool," Evie murmured, but followed as I threaded my way across the room, her palm flat and fond on the back of my shoulder.

Nearly news time, Rosie turned up the Philco to hear cartoon personalities, Fred Flintstone and Barney Rubble, shilling for Winston cigarettes.

"No wonder my third-graders want to smoke," was Evie's comment.

No amount of mental concentration from either of us could change the weather forecast to anything we wanted to hear. It would be more of the same at least through week's end.

"Have they cancelled spring?" I asked Evie and she patted my arm.

"It's baseball season in Arizona," she reminded me. "Teams are playing."

"Swell."

In national news, a test pilot named John Glenn had set an air-speed record flying across the country, something that interested Evie.

"I wonder if he'll look back on these as the best

days of his life," she said.

"Well, it'll be hard to top that!"

"I wonder if these are the best days of *our* lives."

"You mean before marriage?"

"Ha-ardy!" She gave me a mock slap on the arm then grew rueful thinking of her secret arrangement with Roberta. "But I can see why you might think that."

I shook my head. "I don't."

She took a sip of coffee. "I just wanted to help her. She was already off to a rough start and I thought with help, she could learn to aim higher. Roberta's bright. She was doing well at the U... getting decent grades, meeting new people. She introduced me to Chilt. He was a little older than I would have liked but seemed like a nice guy — *then* — upbeat, a good influence. And now this. He was like a different person out on the dredge. Shouting, slapping us."

I patted her arm and sipped my 'coffee from the red can.' "I'm sorry I wasn't more positive about her and more supportive. I didn't give you any reason to think I'd help."

"Oh, Hardy," she said, as the cheeseburgers touched down and the radio news returned after a couple of commercials.

At the top, the oil lease trial had hit a snag. Several of the witnesses now 'failed to remember' and one had actually failed to appear, which didn't sound good.

Evie finished chewing a bite of cheeseburger and dabbed at her lips with the napkin. "If everybody else disappears, you and I may turn out to be the star witnesses."

"Frank says we're way down at the bottom of the list," I reminded her.

"Not for long," she said. "The list keeps getting shorter. And in case you've forgotten, someone keeps trying to *kill* you."

In South Vietnam, the terrorist bombing campaign continued, so far killing several hundred South Vietnamese officials. The technique was simple but effective. They'd park a vehicle filled with explosives where the targeted official worked or walked and then detonate it, often killing or maiming scores of others who just happened to be there.

"I'll sure be glad when that all blows over," I said.

Evie stopped chewing to give me a look. "You think it will? Be over?"

"Don't you think they'll get tired of killing each other?"

She shook her head. "They want independence, just like we did. Ho Chi Minh was our ally against the Japanese. Roosevelt was willing to support him... them, but in the end, we didn't want to irritate the French." She paused to chew and her gaze grew distant. "Truth is, I think as a nation we didn't want to side with 'little brown people.'"

Back to the news in America, truck driver turned rock star, Elvis Presley, had purchased an estate in Memphis Tennessee called Graceland, a Civil War-era property named after the original owner's daughter. The actual home was much newer, a ten-thousand-square-foot mansion built in 1939. Elvis' mother, Gladys Presley, picked out the curtains. Andy was right. No more truck driving for Elvis!

A Northern Commercial Company ad for beaver trap dye came on. "Huh?" I said.

"The dye keeps the traps from rusting," Evie explained, "and makes them dark and harder to see."

She finished her cheeseburger and nibbled fries

while keeping an eye on what was left of mine. I'm a slower eater.

"You going to eat all that?" I gave her the remaining quarter.

"You *do* love me," she said, like this had been a test. Glad I passed.

Tundra Topics came on next and though we listened carefully, heard nothing further about our 'trade.' Evie drew a long slow breath then blew it out in frustration.

"Damn!" she said. Contrary to the old saying, 'no news...' didn't feel like good news.

It was still windy on the way home, drifting snow leveling tire marks and nearly wiping clean our footprints from the walk over.

"Lucky we don't have to follow our tracks home," Evie said.

We walked arm-in-arm, with my right mitt dangling, my gloved hand in my parka on the .38. Yes, there was something about having a bounty on my head and random people trying to shoot me in the face that made it hard to relax.

Back at the rectory, locked in, pulling off our parkas, Evie stopped and looked at me significantly. "Maybe *that's* what this is about." By now I had no idea what she was talking about.

"We've been thinking — at least I've been — that trying to kill you had something to do with Chilt and the stolen bonds — that he somehow had it in for you."

"He doesn't even know me!"

She waved me off. "But you *have* been after him this whole time."

I could see that he might take it personally. At

183

first, he was supposed to be in love with Roberta. Would do anything for her. Then later, not so much.

"But, what if," she gestured dramatically with both hands, "trying to kill you doesn't have anything to do with the bank robbery? Which makes more sense to me. What if trying to kill you is old business, all about the oil leases? After all, it was you and Andy who turned the whole thing upside down, and then managed to track them down and see them arrested. You'd have a lot less to contribute at the trial if you were out under some snowdrift with a bullet in your face." It wasn't a good image and she shuddered.

"I thought it was Kellar trying to kill you," she said, "but now I'm not so sure. And then I thought it was Chilt, though I really couldn't figure out why, since you two had never even met."

I began to think she might be right, that finally this was beginning to make sense.

It made even better sense in the morning when my subpoena arrived.

CHAPTER 24

A full twenty-four hours of snowing and blowing buried us — again. I gave myself over to office cleaning and then catching up on my magazines. Magazines take most of a month to get here, and then another month or two for me to get around to reading them. In April I was reading *Life* magazine from December. The cover featured a color picture of an American adviser in a red flannel shirt talking to monks in Laos, the country just north on the peninsula from Vietnam. Again, I found myself shaking my head. *Why? What are we doing over there?* Oh, well, how wrong can it go?

Evie came over after school. Never mind all the blowing snow, the school won't cancel classes until the temperature reaches minus-fifty degrees. Then often as not, kids go outside to play! Actually, they only close school at that temperature because they can no longer heat the building.

After dinner we sat like old married people. Drinking coffee, commenting on articles, and sharing the pictures, we whiled away another very pleasant snowed-in evening together.

I asked her if she wanted to stay over and she said yes. She looked around herself at the couch she would sleep on.

"I'm getting pretty used to this," she said. A more serious look crossed her face and we both fell silent, listening to the wind sigh and moan outside.

"I can't help thinking about Roberta out there. If she's alive, she's not comfortable."

"They've got to be inside somewhere," I said. *But where?* Where could that many people, apparently four or five remaining — plus their hostage — hole up for this long? And I began to wonder if they'd just left the area. Maybe they made it to Anchorage, the one place in the territory they might mingle and go unnoticed. They would be obvious strangers in any of the villages and word would come back immediately.

And the larger question, would they drive away from five hundred thousand dollars' worth of their hard-earned gains? I didn't think so.

At length we kissed each other, and kissed each other, and... until Evie said, "Go to bed, Hardy, while you can." And I did, though I admit thinking of not going right to bed and what that might be like. *Soon enough*, I promised myself.

Even though I'd spent the day indoors reading and sitting around, and had no legitimate reason to be worn out, I climbed into bed gratefully and must have gone right to sleep. I remember nothing more than the act of stretching out and pulling my blankets up under my chin.

Until Jack woofed, just once. My eyes popped open. The bedside clock read just after three, and I'd managed to sleep four hours in that instant. I lay listening. Beside my bed, the small wind-up alarm clock ticked faintly, and outside, wind still muttered and whistled, driving flakes and bits of sleet against the already frosted panes.

Truthfully, I began to relax again, like the old Baptist hymn sung as a lullaby: "Throw out the lifeline, throw out the lifeline, someone is drifting away." And I began to drift.

186

Jack woofed again. Was he dreaming? Was I? Awake again, I sat up in bed, hunting for his darker shape in the dim room. I found him lying by his furnace grate, not rolled over sleeping, not dreaming, but on his belly and up on his elbows with head erect and ears forward, listening.

Turning back the covers I climbed out of bed, stuffing my feet into a pair of beaded moose-hide moccasins that Grandma Susie, one of my parishioners, made for me. Pulling a flannel robe on over my waffle long johns, I tiptoed softly out into the hall, Jack at my side. Pausing again, I heard only Evie in the living room softly snoring.

Still without lights, we eased into my study, so far avoiding contact with large potentially painful objects. Outside, about twenty feet beyond my office windows, loomed the large blackness of the old log church.

With the bottoms of the office window panes frosted white, I could only see out of the tops. Blinking, I saw a flash. It happened so quickly, and so well timed to my blink, that I blinked again, just to see if my blinking would cause the flash again. It didn't.

I forced my eyes to not blink, staring out at the church's stained-glass windows. That's where and when I saw the flash again. It wasn't just me. There was someone with a flashlight in the church!

I thought about waking Evie. Thought about grabbing the .38 off my nightstand. In the end I didn't do either. The idea of picking up a gun to go to the church bothered me. What if I'd seen some lonely, miserable soul stealing into the empty church late at night to be alone with his God, or hers, and I came busting in with a revolver? That seemed too wrong.

Also, the idea of walking in on that prayerful someone, with Evie in tow, also felt wrong. I managed to push back the obvious admission to this parishioner that the mission priest had his girlfriend sleeping over. Yes, I was aware how that would get around.

So, for a variety of reasons, both good and silly, I didn't pick up the gun and I went out alone.

I traded the low moccasins for a pair of high, caribou mukluks. Shrugging my warm parka over my long underwear top and bottom, I dropped the cord to my heavy mitts over my head and slid them on. Just heading out the door I grabbed a penlight.

I eased out, also leaving Jack. "Stay," I whispered. He did, not that he had much choice without opposable thumbs to manage the doorknob.

If snow wasn't still falling, it was still blowing around, and I could hear the last tiny ticks of sleet hitting my parka fabric as the wind died and all became still. With the heavy overcast and snow clouds now gradually, grudgingly dispersing, a pathetic glow no more than oozed from a distant smear of stars.

Even though I'd shoveled the church path just before dinnertime, snow had fallen and drifted since, already reaching nearly to the top of my mukluks. Sure enough, my footprints converged at the church front steps with a fresh set that headed up the front entry path from the street. One set in, no sets out. Whoever made the tracks was still in the church. The prints had an indistinct quality to them that at first I attributed to the wind.

Our sexton, Oliver, insists on oiling the church door hinges, especially the one on the outer door. To him, the squeak on that door sounds like a horse

188

laughing. "Don't want no horse laugh during the sermon," he told me.

So, I crept up the steps and went silently into the entryway. From there I could see that one of the interior doors had been left ajar. Beyond, a dark figure wielded a flashlight that shone a compact crisp beam of blue-white light like a biblical sword. I admit I thought of angels, wondering just for an instant if I was about to witness some kind of miracle.

The only miracle was nobody got shot. Whoever this was had come to search the place, not to bring a divine message. I stepped into the nave unseen, into the scents of old wood, candle wax, smoky moose hide — from the bleached and beaded altar cloth — and lingering frankincense and myrrh. Beyond the prowler, I could make out glints of bright altar brass, the central cross and a candelabra on each side. Reaching out to the light switch, clicking it on, left me squinting and blinking at the sudden glare.

"Can I help you?"

In that same second, I realized what I'd missed about the tracks outside with their indistinct quality. A second person had been stepping in the imprint of the first. Now, with the first person masked, in front of me, the one behind hit me hard.

CHAPTER 25

He knocked me down but not out, though I saw definite stars and teetered for just a heartbeat on the fine line between here and gone.

'Here' won out, and still marginally conscious, I was able to get my arms up and not break my fall with my face. I sensed movement and felt the painful jab of what I took to be a pistol barrel on my already aching skull.

"This time I kill him," came the hoarse whisper.

"Not without the bonds," the other person — the hitter — whispered back. "He's worth a half-million bucks to us as long as he can tell us where he hid them."

"So, what are we going to do? We can't take him. We can't... work on him here."

We all heard the distinct metallic slide and click of a lever-action carbine cocking, and then Evie's voice from the shadows.

"What you're going to do," she said in a remarkably even tone, "is set down your gun and walk out of here alive."

"You'd shoot us in a church?" said the one standing over me.

"In a heartbeat," she said convincingly. I felt the pressure of the pistol barrel leave my skull, heard the thunk on the wood floor as he set the weapon down. I rolled over and grunted myself into a sitting position. My head wanted to burst into pieces and fall on the floor. I managed to secure the handgun, easily identifying another of the military Colts they seemed to have such easy access to.

"Okay. You win this one," rasped the one standing over me, the other having fallen silent. "You know, if you'd just give us the bonds, you'd be done with us."

Evie sniffed. "Hand over Roberta and you're on your way." It was an impasse. They couldn't very well produce her out of a pocket.

"You'll see us again," he said, no longer whispering. His voice had a raspy tone, as if forced from his throat. "And you won't like it."

"One of us won't like it." It was hard to out-tough Evie, especially holding a firearm. They moved cautiously around her and out the door. She watched them away into the night, headed back down the main walkway to the street.

"Hardy?" she asked, no longer sounding so tough. "Say something."

I tried to think of something clever but my head throbbed and I had nothing. "My head aches," I muttered.

"I'm not surprised. The short guy gave you quite a whack." Still training the .30-30 on the door, she extended an arm to help me up. I got my other hand on one of the church pews to steady myself and took a minute standing erect to stop wobbling.

With Evie still covering, I moved forward to the altar, to check that the two fat stacks of bonds were still in their hidey hole. They were.

Crossing back in front of the altar, out of pure habit, I bowed my head to the cross, grunting in pain.

"You okay?"

"Except for what's left of my head," I told her.

We eased out, closing the doors, and found our way back down the path to the rectory.

When we'd made it back and out of our parkas Evie pulled the shell out of the chamber and leaned the Winchester back in its corner. I stepped gingerly into her arms. We held each other for long moments, sharing heartbeats, and thinking of all of the things that might have gone wrong.

"Go sit down," she said, finally pulling away. "I'll get aspirin and ice. You're going to have one heck of a headache."

"I have it already."

"That's good," she said. "Means you're not as dead as you could have been."

"Good point."

* * *

"So, you were sleepin' here, in the *rectory*?" asked Andy again, as though we might have defiled a holy place. He was seemingly more interested in sleeping arrangements than my narrow brush with death.

"On the sofa," Evie replied... again.

"Here?"

"Shut up!" she said with only a bit of a smile.

He put up his hands in faux surrender. "I was just askin'"

"Yeah," she said, "repeatedly."

We were all in our places on a sunny morning, clouds and storm gone, and the sky a brilliant cloudless blue. With the temperature hovering at a balmy zero, the whole world had a springish quality it had been distinctly lacking for the past few weeks, although nothing dripped.

Andy showed up first, followed in minutes by William, both having snowshoed over. Evie had at least the morning off, until plows could come through. She wouldn't see kids today but would need to spend at least half the day in her classroom.

With some twenty inches of new snow, blown into drifts five and six feet tall, it would be several hours before anyone could go anywhere. Even the train would be as much as two hours late, reported Andy, who had driven from Fairbanks earlier yesterday to have dinner and spend the evening with Rosie.

"So, you heard these guys in the church?" Andy looked doubtful.

"Jack heard them, or saw the light, or something."

"And you just decided to stroll over and give them a chance to put a bullet hole in you?"

"I went to check it out. What would you have done?"

"I woulda woke up Evie. Maybe taken Jack. I also woulda seen it was two tracks." He hesitated. "Maybe."

"Thanks for that," I said, and he toasted me with his coffee mug.

I turned to Evie, leaning on her elbows, coffee mug in both hands. "What woke you?" She shrugged a raised thumb in Jack's direction.

"He woke me. I looked for you... saw the light in the church window and guessed trouble. So, I brought along your .30-30."

"Lucky thing," I said.

"You need to stop doing these things by yourself."

She was right, of course. But most of the time, myself was all I had. Well, and Jack. I guess, bottom line, I should have taken him along, or maybe sent him by himself and gone back to sleep.

"I don't 'spose," said Andy, "we have any idea who they were?"

I shook my head at the same time Evie spoke. "One of them."

That surprised me. "Which one?"

"The one who wanted to shoot you."

"We know who he was?"

"Sure. Easy voice to recognize. That was Chilt. I thought you knew."

I shook my head. "Chilt. Here."

* * *

It took all of us with snow shovels — well, not Evie — to dig out the truck and clear the driveway. She left before the shoveling started, walking home to change clothes and to organize herself for work. She had to snowshoe to the road.

Andy, William, and I started shoveling from my front porch, snow waist high against my outer door, around the truck and on out the driveway. About a hundred feet in all. We hadn't been at it too long before we heard happy shoveling sounds from the street. Big Butch and Oliver had arrived to start digging their way in. The plow pile stood so tall, all I could see was the shiny dome of Butch's stubbled head with its sheen of sweat.

No matter the temperature, he didn't wear a hat, didn't even wear a parka when he was shoveling snow. And I wouldn't be surprised when we finally got a look at him to find his sleeves rolled up. It's true I switched to a lighter parka, but otherwise managed to keep myself covered.

Clearing the driveway took most of the morning. Out by the street we were running out of places to throw snow. When it melted, if it ever did, I knew we'd be soggy around here for quite a while. Mud season. Even so, I was ready.

At about noon I proposed cheeseburgers at the Coffee Cup, but Butch and Oliver had other snowy worlds to conquer, and William said he probably ought to make the drive to Clear RADAR station and show his face at work. I tried to pay Butch and Oliver but they wouldn't accept more than a dollar each.

When they left, Andy and I walked the several blocks to downtown Chandalar, the place people around here called 'uptown.' Like, "I'm goin' uptown. Need anything? So, we went 'uptown' for burgers, and glad to go! We were both ravenous from all the shoveling.

Sidewalks at the store and The Coffee Cup were as yet unshoveled. "Uh-oh," said Andy. "Looks like more shoveling in my life."

"I'll help."

"Nah, I got this. Married guys do this to get points. This'll be good practice. I'll get me some in advance." We laughed about the 'married guys' reference. "Sure never thought I'd be saying that about me," he said as we headed in.

"The little bell tinkled above the door and Rosie came on the run to greet, glass pot and mugs in hand, kissing Andy on the lips and leaving a quick fond smear of lipstick across my cheek.

"Didn't kiss *me* when I came in," someone said.

"Yeah," Rosie fired back, "you're lucky I let you in."

"A guy can dream," he said. But she went around behind him, leaned over and kissed his cheek. This was a guy who lived alone, worked alone, and probably hadn't been kissed this decade. To say he was stunned would be an understatement. He grinned happily then dropped his gaze to his plate, blushing.

One of his friends looked up at Rosie and pointed to his own cheek.

"Ha!" she said, already speeding away.

Seated under the moose head, parkas hung on chairs and coffee poured, we had only about two minutes of Elvis singing "Jailhouse Rock" before the bell tinkled again and Frank Jacobs appeared. Waving to Rosie, he threaded his way through the noisy, smoky, lunchtime crowd. She showed up to pour his coffee before he even got his parka off.

She looked at us, her gnawed yellow pencil poised by pad. "I'm gonna go out on a limb with you three and guess the cheeseburgers and fries." It wasn't a tough question and we performed a kind of nodding chorus. She made a show of counting to three with pencil stub in hand then whirled and was gone.

"She's just a peach," said Frank. Andy nodded happily. The marshal looked at him. "No taste in men, though."

"That sounds like jealousy," I said to Andy.

"Damn straight," said Frank. Then his expression shifted and I could tell we were getting down to business. "Got the lab report back from East. Body in Chilt's cabin?"

"Not Chilt," I said. He looked at me. "You been reading my mail again? How did you know that?"

Andy chimed in. "Chilt was here last night, wantin' to put a bullet in Hardy's head."

Frank's eyebrows knit. "Here? Really?" And we told him about the late-night encounter.

"Still got the knot to prove it." I ran my hand, too hard, over the back of my head, wincing.

Frank winced too, sympathetically. "Once again, lucky you're not dead. You've *got* to be more careful.

You're not always going to be so lucky, or so surrounded by friends with firearms. Anyway..." he went back to his medical report, which he had unfolded and was holding in his hand. "Would you like to guess who this burned-up guy was? Turned out he was in the system, too, near the top of the pile."

"Someone who escaped from the Anchorage jail not long ago," I ventured. Frank jerked his head around to look at me, mouth and eyes round. He whacked the paper down on the tabletop and nearly spilled his coffee.

"How do you do that?"

"Elementary," I told him, savoring my moment. "The only people I've heard of recently, unaccounted for, are Anchorage jailbirds."

"Yep," he said. "Exactly. You're brighter than you look."

"That's lucky," added Andy. Then he grew serious. "So, what's an escaped jailbird from Anchorage doin' burned up?"

"And shot in the back of the head," added Frank.

"...burned up and shot..." Andy continued, "in the ashes of Lieutenant Chilt's cabin?"

"Ringers?" I ventured.

Frank nodded, sitting up straighter as his cheeseburger plate came sliding in. "That's what I think. The guys who took over for Hanson's mountain ranger bank robbers. Expendable. The four dead guys on the dredge were escaped prisoners, too."

"Which is why they didn't ski or shoot as well as advertised. Hanson told us out on the dredge those dead men weren't his. Now we know why."

"But get this." Frank held up an index finger. "They *were* soldiers. A mix of deserters and drunk-and-disorderly. An overflow from the military stockades in Fairbanks and Anchorage. It looks pretty certain that some of them already knew Chilt."

CHAPTER 26

I dreamed of spring. I dreamed of skeins of geese overhead, hundreds of geese stretched out in giant Vs across the sky, and I heard the joy in their voices, finally headed north. I dreamed of a warm breeze against my face, of *not* having to go outside in my heavy parka, of being able to walk easily on smooth hard ground — not slippery ice or shifting snow. I dreamed of scents: of good old dirt, leaves, grass, the whole order of that world that seemed so lost to us for so long, but now would return.

Then I woke. Winter still had us in its cold hard fist. Snow had drifted halfway up my bedroom window and it was the first thing I saw when I opened my eyes. I listened for drips. None. It all made me feel heavy and old... tired... blue. It certainly didn't make me feel like hopping out of bed.

Snagging my Book of Common Prayer, I lay snug under my blankets while adding my heart's voice to millions of others around the world, asking God for grace. And finally for the safekeeping and return of Roberta, though in truth it seemed less and less likely.

At length I got up and poured water into the kettle for coffee. I was running low on Andy's good Italian roast and almost grabbed the red can, relenting at the last second. I needed the good stuff today.

Andy arrived just minutes after seven and Evie blew in soon after, bearing her armload of school books and supplies. School was open, on time today, but she didn't have to be there for most of another hour. I left the door unlocked after letting Andy in, hoping she might pop by.

"It's not spring," she said, accentuating the obvious, grabbing a coffee mug, kissing Andy on the top of his head and me on the lips.

"I dreamed it was," I told them. "Vivid."

"I done that before," said Andy. "Woke up and it wasn't. It didn't make me want to get up."

I nodded agreement and sipped.

"Soon," I said, though I had begun to believe maybe never. No wonder the Territory of Alaska led the nation in drinkers.

"You hear the radio this morning?" Andy asked.

I looked at my radio as if checking. It was off. "Nope."

"Funny. Well, you *mighta* had it on earlier. I always turn mine on when I shave."

"Good to know. Are you just taking a radio survey?"

He wrinkled his brow at me. "Another Chilt sighting. Territorial patrol out trying to chase skiers through deep snow. Didn't work out, I guess. So, they called out Hanson and his men from the base, but still no luck."

"Think it's on the level?" I asked him.

"Pretty sure. And not good news. They hit the Denali sport shop, you know, downtown near the hospital. Took some guns and *lots* of ammo."

He was right. Not good news.

* * *

Teddy Moses came to see me that morning. "I had a dream about Roberta. She came to say goodbye." Apparently it had been a night for dreaming.

"Goodbye?"

200

"Yeah, said she was going away. She thanked me." He made a rueful face. "Not much like Roberta. She never thanked me for nothing."

The last few years with Roberta had been hard ones. She went from being merely willful to getting involved with a local loan shark and thug, the late Frankie Slick. 'Not late enough,' had been the local line since someone put a bullet up through his chin and into his brain. Slick had opened Roberta up to a whole new line of possibilities, including posing for child pornography. She took to it all, a natural, and thrived for a time. I had started out thinking she was Frankie's victim, but in the end it may have been the other way around. I was pretty sure it had been hardest on her father.

Evie's kindness to her — getting her in at the U, paying her incidentals, and taking a personal interest — had appeared to be turning her around. And now this.

"In your dream, what did you say to her?" I asked.

"Goodbye."

* * *

In the next few days, the weather did warm — and during bright sunny days did even drip a little — though still well short of a thaw. The wind began to blow, and midway through April it seemed March had blown back in. Under clear bright skies, snow blew sideways, drifting and shaping huge cornices on roofs and around parked cars and cabin corners. It made walking difficult. Going out to the edges of town to visit old or sick people, I had to snowshoe, Jack bounding along beside me peeing on everything.

When Andy needed to head back to Fairbanks, he asked if I wanted to ride along. As an inducement, not that I really needed one, he promised dinner at

Andrea's. Spending time with Andy was always easy. Smart, funny, often irreverent, much of what he said was upbeat and goofy. A dose of even mild humor sounded good right now.

"Cheer up," he told me. "Spring always comes."

"But when?"

I dropped Jack at Evie's, then leaving Chandalar, we headed out on the plowed ice road across the Tanana. In the summer, a small sternwheel ferry would carry us across here. My first few times driving out on the ice had been a bit unsettling. But now, having done it repeatedly, and knowing that more than three feet of ice would hold up even a gravel-loaded dump truck, I managed to lean back and enjoy the ride.

Out here on the river, with nothing to block the wind, snow settled in ripples and whirls. Sometimes for no visible reason, some even curled over like an ocean wave. On the other hand, there were places that blew completely clear, right down to the ice. We stopped on one of those to examine the air bubbles, cracks — the big ones sometimes three or four inches across — and other imperfections.

Kids came out from town to these large blown-clear areas to ice skate. It was far too windy to just skate around in circles so skating often consisted of clawing along into the wind until the smooth ice ended. Then unzipping and holding their parka sides out, sail-like, they picked up speed and blew back across the slick patch like an ice boat.

Arriving in Fairbanks and very much on a hunch, we drove by Denali Sporting Goods. Seeing Frank Jacob's official U.S. Marshal Ford still in the lot next to a military jeep bearing a loaded ski rack, we parked and walked in.

We saw Jacobs there with Wild Bill Hanson and his right-hand man, Smitty. They were clustered near a smashed glass handgun-display counter at the back. Most of the guns were still in the case, with only three missing that I could spot quickly.

"Three men?" I asked. Jacobs eyed me suspiciously.

"Who you been talking to now?" I pointed to the three empty display mounts. He pressed his lips tightly together, pouching out his cheeks and furrowing his brow. To say he looked frustrated would be an understatement.

"Do you know what they took?" I asked.

"From this cabinet? Yeah." He read from a list. "Two service-style Colts, .45-caliber, and one similar in a .22-caliber. Mostly they took ammo."

"How much?" asked Andy.

Jacobs raised his eyebrows. "As much as they could ski away with. Not really sure yet." A store clerk appeared with a scrap of paper and handed it to him. Jacobs looked up from it. "About a thousand rounds."

"How much does that weigh?" I asked. Jacobs shrugged.

"About twenty-five pounds," said Andy. "I lugged plenty of it in the war."

Neither Hanson nor Smitty had said anything. The further insult of their old friend and comrade now on his campaign of bank-robbery, killing, kidnapping, and general lawlessness had to hurt. They'd trained with him for some of this.

"We know it was Chilt who did this?" I asked.

"All masked," said Jacobs.

Hanson sighed. "But the clerk described his voice. Rough, raspy. It was an injury from the war. The

Nazis stretched steel wire, like braided picture wire, along downhill ski trails in Norway. They were set just at neck height, and when a skier hit one traveling forty-five or fifty miles an hour... I've seen them just about take the head off."

"Chilt hit one of those and survived?"

"Yeah... badly injured. The Nazis figured us all for about five-foot ten, but Chilt was over six feet and the force of the wire caught him at chest height, then slipped up to hit his throat and jaw as he fell over backward. He couldn't make a sound for quite a while. Then whispered. Finally, his voice came back but never smooth, and never very loud. He used to be really loud. No more. He wore a whistle on a lanyard around his neck for maneuvers."

I said to Smitty, "Did you get along with Chilt?"

Smitty just looked sad. "We all did. He was my hero."

Frank overheard. "And now he's a crime wave. Well... we *will* find him."

Driving back to Andrea's, Andy asked the question. "Will we find him, really? Not doin' so well so far."

"It's more likely he'll find us."

"You mean to get the bonds back?"

"Yes," I said. "And we keep hearing someone wants me dead. Although I don't know why it would be Chilt. I never even met him."

"Maybe it's somebody else."

"Who? Kellar says it's not him, and I mostly believe him."

Andy pulled back as if to better see me. "Wow."

* * *

I took the evening train home, arriving hungry just a little after seven, and walked up the snowy street to the Coffee Cup Café. This was later than I usually got there. Rosie had finished up and gone home, leaving waitress Shirley Kitka on duty. Shirley greeted me with a smile and told me to sit anywhere, and I headed across to my usual table under the dusty moose head, wishing I had dinner company and frankly, missing Rosie.

Not as sleek or agile as Rosie, Shirley didn't so much slide or glide between the tables and chairs as ricochet. Watching her progress toward me with pot and coffee mug was a little like watching a well-padded ball bearing in a pinball machine as it bounced and bounded off the bumpers.

When she finally reached my table and poured the coffee, she struck a pose with the pencil and pad for my order. This wasn't the automatic process, as with Rosie. I had to specify cheese, mayo, and "... did I want lettuce?"

"Do you actually have lettuce?" That stopped her.

"Bobby?" she shouted to the cook in the back, "Do we have lettuce?"

"Not 'til July," said Bobby.

"Hold the lettuce," I told her. She gave me a warm smile.

"You need something green," she offered. "How 'bout a pickle?"

"Sure," I told her. "Hit me with the pickle." She looked confused.

"Just on the sandwich."

"Oh!" Big nod. At length, she went off with my order to make the magic happen and I sat alone trying to make sense of... anything.

We had a getaway that wasn't a getaway and trained, dedicated soldiers who had somehow thrown over their previous dedication and service to turn to crime. And they weren't that good at it. They had taken hostages where none were required in the first place. And though the whole thing should have gone quiet when they escaped several weeks ago, it seemed to go on and on.

On top of all that, someone pointedly wanted me dead. Not just dead but shot in the head. Who didn't like me *that* much? And why? Bank robbers? How did that make sense?

My burger arrived before I'd solved any of the problems. I admit I didn't taste much of it. Sitting, chewing, thinking in a room softly buzzing with conversation, I smelled the good smells of frying food mingled with overtones of coffee and cigarettes. Without coming to any conclusion, I finished up, paid the check, tipped Shirley, and walked the several snowy blocks to my cabin. I thought about checking in on Evie and picking up Jack but it was late and I was tired, and figured she'd be settling in. I was wrong.

When I got to my cabin I found Evie blindfolded, sitting on the sofa in my front room with her hands tied. Also Roberta, though not blindfolded. Her hands were bound and knotted to a length of rope. Jack, barking, had been confined to my study. Across the room were two masked men. One leaned against the wall and held a pistol near his thigh. The other perched on a wooden chair turned backward training a Colt semi-automatic at my nose.

"You wanted Roberta, you got her," he said in his ruined voice. "And I want bonds now. *All of them!* I'm willing to leave you all here alive if I get 'em. And if I don't..." He thumbed back the gun's hammer.

CHAPTER 27

I raised my hands, looking at the women. So far everybody looked okay. "I'll get them," I said. "Please... lower the hammer." He did. He looked at me.

"Well?"

"I'm going to have to leave here."

"Okay. I assumed you might."

"And I'll need about five minutes."

He made a what-the-heck face. "Take as long as you like. Just know, if you try anything..."

He rose from his chair, crossing the room to where Evie sat. He pulled down her blindfold on one side, revealing one brown eye which closed as he gently nuzzled it with the muzzle. He looked at me significantly.

"We clear?"

"Crystal," I said, suppressing a shiver. I flipped up my hood, heading back out the door into gathering dusk.

What to do? I could see them in the warmth of the lit room, the lamp light radiating gold through frosted windows, just as I could still hear Jack barking. Oddly, I'd been in exactly this situation before. It didn't help. I thought about all the same things. I could run to Evie's for a gun or a phone. And then what? The chance of shooting both men before one of them got off a shot at Evie or Roberta was not good, even assuming I'd want to try. I wasn't a sniper in the war, like Andy. I was a medic.

I'd left Andy in Fairbanks, so that was no help. I thought of trying to find William. That could be difficult on a good day. I quickly ran down the list and *out* of people who might help me turn this tide. There was no one. It was just me.

In the end, I did the one thing, the only thing I could do. I reminded myself that what we wanted was Roberta back alive. Now we had her. And that I wanted Evie to remain alive, too. So far so good. Of course, I was relying on Chilt taking the bonds and leaving us alive. Convincing myself I had no other choice, I fetched the bundles from behind the altar, and the envelope from Jack's dog house. I carried them in raised hands, back into the rectory, handing them over.

"Good choice," he rasped. He turned to the other man, jerking a thumb in my direction. "Tie him." When that had been accomplished, he told him to take us one at a time and put us in the bathroom — the only room in the house without a window. He took Evie first then me, and went back for Roberta. I looked at Evie, still blindfolded, standing, waiting, listening. This seemed to be working. They hadn't shot us, and it didn't feel like they would. But I was so busy feeling relieved that I didn't get what else they had done. Then Jack stopped barking.

Evie reached out to me from her darkness.

"Hardy?"

"I'm here," I told her.

That's when she told me what I should have figured out on my own. "They took Roberta. They're gone."

* * *

I thought there'd be more fuss about losing the

208

bonds. In the end, both Jacobs and Hanson shrugged it off.

"So far, everybody's still alive," Frank said. "That's job one."

It was midmorning the following day. I'd called Frank with trepidation.

"I'm on my way," he said, and showed up with Hanson in tow in just about an hour. A fast trip.

I had coffee ready when they got there and we gathered, as always, at the kitchen table with warm mugs in hand, balanced on the tippy stools.

They'd both warned me about the responsibility of holding on to that money and now it was gone.

"How much trouble are we in?" I asked.

"We?" Frank laughed. "I don't know... I don't care. What else could you do? I'm definitely going to call this a win."

Hanson agreed. "Sometimes, you just have to roll the dice. You do everything you can, and then there you are. It's just like any other game of chance. Sometimes you win, sometimes you don't. In this case, you lost the money, but you're alive. Even Roberta is alive, though I wish she were here.

"You guys are lying," said Evie shrewdly, rousing herself. Way short of sleep, she'd called in for a substitute for the day. "But you're doing it really well." She smiled at them.

"Aw, shucks, ma'am," said Frank, feigning modesty. Then he looked up with his official expression back in place. "But, I really don't care about money as long as we're saving lives."

"But you're sure this was Chilt?" Hanson asked.

"Absolutely!" said Evie.

"A tall man," I said, "about six feet with a seriously raspy voice."

209

After they'd gone and Evie and I were alone, I said, "I just wish..." She put a finger on my lips.

"Hush." Removing her finger, she kissed me. "Frank's right. In the end, it's not about the money. We're all still alive."

* * *

That night I got a phone call just after ten. Alice Young called from the Bide-A-While.

"Those Fairbanks city cops you were asking about? They're back. They still expect free drinks," she added.

Evie and I had spent the evening together, she grading papers, and I catching up on my magazines. With May approaching — not that we could tell by the weather — I dug into an unread February *Life* magazine with an article about Sunday school as the most wasted hour of the week. As often happened, an article about Sunday school in suburbia didn't include much that would be helpful in Chandalar.

"That was Alice," I told Evie as I hung up the phone. "I've gotta go uptown. I'll drop you." She had followed me into my office, both of us knowing the anxiety of late night calls that almost always meant something amiss.

"The heck you will," she said in Evie fashion. "I'm going with you."

We emerged into a surprisingly warm, starlit night, the temperature likely about zero.

"Is this spring?" Evie asked. I hoped so. Though only going a couple of blocks, we took the truck, the two of us climbing into the cab while Jack did his running-jump trick to get into the pickup bed unaided. As we drove, he shifted from side to side to make sure he didn't miss seeing or smelling anything.

I angle-parked on the main street, in a clutch of

five other vehicles, one of them a dark Ford, unmarked, but with a chrome driver's-side spotlight mounted ahead of the wing window and a long whip antenna. No trouble telling which was the cop car.

We couldn't hear the jukebox in the street, though we felt the thumping bass. The full impact of Little Richard singing "Long Tall Sally" hit us like a hammer when we pulled open the heavy door.

The Bide-A-While wasn't a big place, about thirty-five feet long with a big part of the end wall taken up by the brightly lit altar-like Wurlitzer juke box.

The varnished knotty-pine walls, now dulled by time and cigarette smoke, were decorated with various beer posters. A lit Schlitz clock permanently indicated five o'clock, quitting time, or 'beer o'clock,' as they say around here, even though darn few of the locals held actual time-clock jobs.

From the bar on the left, a door led down a short hallway past two tiny toilet-and-sink enclosures, a small storeroom — almost completely stacked with cardboard beer cases — and then outside.

We found Alice behind the bar, hands in the bar sink, washing glasses. A slim, strawberry blond — scarcely five feet tall — she was celebrated throughout the valley for a pair of large and shapely breasts she kept on display, nestled in her low-cut sweater. I'd heard of people in Fairbanks driving sixty miles to drink a beer while staring at Alice. For quite a few of her customers, grizzled old bachelor miners and trappers, this was more of a real live woman than they'd seen in decades. She took it in stride.

"It's good for business," she said, and it clearly was.

Alice jerked a sudsy thumb toward the back door. "They went that-a-way."

"You wait here," I said to Evie. I don't know why I bother. She gave me one of her 'looks' and kept coming. "Or come along," I added.

She smiled at me. "Good idea."

Sure enough, out behind the bar in the dim light of a sixty-watt bulb under a heavily snow-shrouded light shade, we found the two Fairbanks city cops. They were pressing a Colt and a bundle of bills on a man I didn't know. When we stepped out, startling all of them, the man hustled away into darkness.

"Who are you?" asked the one with the gun. His buddy, whom I'd last seen with Kellar on the snow machine, knew me and elbowed him. The first cop brushed him off impatiently.

"You don't know me?" I asked.

"No, and I don't want to. This..." he looked around, "was police business that you came poking your nose into. I could run you in."

"Even though you're sixty miles out of your jurisdiction?"

His eyes shifted. "I'm the one holding the gun."

"Backwards!" I pointed out, since he held it by the barrel. Then just as with Kellar, I swiped it out of his grip before he could move and handed it behind me to Evie.

"Hold this, honey," I said.

She stepped forward. "Love to!"

I turned to the cop I knew. "How you doing?"

"Pretty good." He side-eyed his buddy. "This is him... the one..." he said, nearly under his breath, as if we might not hear him.

"Huh?" The first cop, obviously a slow-mover, turned on him peevishly. "Which one?"

"The one you're trying to pay somebody to shoot in the head," I said. "Hardy. H.A.R.D.Y."

"Oh," he said, suddenly more restrained.

He wore another gun, a parka bulge on his hip, and his shifting eyes betrayed his intention.

"Don't do it," I warned. "She always aims for someplace sensitive."

"What?" he asked, feigning innocence poorly. He held his hands out slightly from his hips. I could see him pondering what 'someplace sensitive' might mean.

"I can arrest you," he blustered. I noticed his partner had stepped back, hands clearly in view. He saw me noticing and shook his head. He was out of this and wanted me clear about it. I nodded.

"I need to know who put you up to this."

"Fuck you!"

I grabbed him by the nose, hard. He bleated, nasally, but couldn't break free without leaving the nose. When he tried to grab my hand I just squeezed harder, so he had both hands up around my hand, but not actually touching me, at the same time, sort of prancing on his toe tips as I lifted. I shifted my gaze to his buddy who fought to not grin. When I let the man go he rubbed his reddened schnoz vigorously.

"You know that's assault!"

"And..." I asked him, "you know that hiring a man to shoot me is conspiracy to commit murder?"

He didn't have many thoughts, maybe two, and I could hear them rubbing together. "I'm just following orders."

"So, you're saying Kellar *ordered* you out here... what, three times to try to get me killed?"

"I... um... yeah. He told me to do it."

"Now that's funny." I turned my head slightly, as

213

if talking to Evie. "Chief Kellar came to my house last week to tell me that he *wasn't* getting people to do this."

"Wow!" said Evie, playing along. "Won't he be surprised when you tell him about this guy."

"No, wait," said the cop. "Did you think I meant Kellar?"

"Yeah. That's what I thought."

Evie raised her eyebrows and shoulders in a that's-what-I-thought-too shrug.

"Oh..." blustered the cop, "what I actually meant..."

I put the palm of my hand flat on his chest. He flinched then tried to pretend he hadn't. "You're not a good liar," I said. "Just tell me the truth."

I think he'd heard that before. He looked down, glowering. "I'm not sure but it looked like a woman." He turned to his buddy, who nodded. "About this tall." He held up his hand, flat, indicating someone not quite my height.

"You're not sure if it was a woman?"

"We never saw her face and she like... whispered. But she talked good! Like not from around here."

"So, you're not sure if it's a woman, and she was masked? But you're willing to contract a kill for her?"

"I knew the face on the hundred-dollar bills she gave us for doing the deal. Alexander Hamilton," he said, using up his one remaining flash of panache.

"Benjamin Franklin," corrected Evie.

"Yeah," he said, glum again. "Whatever."

"And you're telling the truth about this?" He nodded, and his partner nodded, too. They looked like a pair of bobble heads in the back window of a Chevy.

"Leave," I told them, stepping back. "Never come back, or you know what will happen."

"Yeah, what?" demanded the cop. I shot my finger and thumb up near his nose, startling him so he fell back a step.

His partner grabbed him by the arm and urged him away, leaving Evie and me alone under stars, out back of a tavern.

"That was productive... sort of..." I told her. She took my arm, handing me another .45 to add to my collection.

"I liked what you said."

I had a quick flash of me facing-off the two thugs, in her eyes, strong, capable, maybe even heroic.

"You called me *honey*." She squeezed my arm. "I like that."

CHAPTER 28

"I seen her again. Yesterday at dawn." Solomon Esau eyed me over his chipped coffee cup. We were in the parish hall on Sunday, after the eleven o'clock service. Once again he'd gone through his ritual of reaching out a finger to touch me.

"Where," I asked, though I thought I knew.

"At the old mission. There was colors of the sky reflected in the old rippled glass. I stepped closer to look, and I seen her lookin' out at me — just like before — with a... you know... a shawl wrapped around her head."

"You're sure it was a woman?" He looked at me like, 'well, duh.'

"You remember her that well from all those years ago? That was..." I calculated, "nearly fifty years ago. This woman looked just like her?"

"Yep."

Later I told Evie, "I think old Solomon is starting to lose it. He's been seeing the Deaconess out at the mission school."

Evie snorted. "She's been dead... how long?"

"Since 1910. That's my point."

"It *is* a spooky place."

I had to agree. I'd been out there several times by myself, wandering the halls, climbing the creaky old stairs, and always felt the presence of people I couldn't quite see, sounds I could almost hear, children laughing or crying, the buzz and clatter of life in an orphanage. The place was empty, unused since before I got here. Fifty years of Athabascan kids went there, Evie and Andy among them — many who went there, dead by now — but the echoes remain.

"People around here *do* see dead people," she reminded me. "You, for example."

It was true. I'd seen, also heard and talked to my dead wife, Mary, through my whole first year here. One night while sleeping over, Evie had seen her, too.

"We see what we're open to seeing," she said. "We believe in the Holy *Spirit*. Deaconess Farthing was a holy spirit. She was as holy as they come."

* * *

I woke the next morning, too warm. I tried to think when was the last time *that* happened? Last spring! I listened, and sure enough, I heard drips from the eaves. Climbing out from under my pile of blankets, I peered out my bedroom window at a dandy row of icicles, already about six inches long, dripping to beat the band.

I went out to my front room, set to melt window ice to check the outside thermometer, and at my touch the ice just fell off the window and melted on the sill. Thirty-one degrees! Spring! I felt elation rising in me. I went to the front door, threw it wide, and stood in the open doorway deeply breathing in the soft, warm, almost fragrant air. As if to certify, an extended V of geese flew over, their cries echoing my elation. It all made me smile, and still smiling, padded down the hall to the kitchen to make morning coffee.

"It's over," I said to my empty kitchen. "Winter is over!" And I felt joyful.

* * *

I got names for the two cops: Burton, the big one, and Schilling. They were known bad actors and had worked hard to make it to the bottom of their heap. They had a reputation for taking 'muscle jobs' on the side. Neither of them had paid for a drink or a meal this decade.

"One thing," Andy said when I told him about the two, "they don't do nothin' on their own. Somebody hired 'em."

"But a woman? What woman? And why?" I asked.

He shook his head. "No clue." He had come down for the day from Fairbanks, taking advantage of still being able to drive across the frozen river. Reportedly, the ice still measured more than two feet thick, though at the current melt rate we didn't have long. Breakup typically fell between April twentieth and May twentieth, with the average falling on May fifth. Already the streets were mostly puddle and slush from being driven on, but it now looked like a later breakup and I'd wasted my ticket dollar.

Sunshine flooded my kitchen as we sat on the tippy stools drinking good coffee. There'd been another Chilt sighting with the marshal and the Territorial patrol out racing around.

"Chasing their tails," Andy said, and I agreed. "Something I don't get," he went on. I looked at him. "Bank robbery happened, when? End of March?"

"March twenty-ninth," I said, the date of Evie's and my marriage-counseling appointment with the Bishop — and a day my life went severely sideways — forever fixed in memory. "Nearly a month ago."

"Right! But the bank robbers *still* haven't gotten away. They finally got their missing half-million from you. They should be on a warm beach somewhere, set up for life. But no. Every few days there's a fresh 'Chilt' sighting. What's that about?"

I shook my head. "Don't know."

"I got an idea," Andy said. "I think they might be back out at the dredge. It's big enough, well off the beaten track. Warm enough. Who'd imagine they'd go back there once the bodies were cleared out?"

"Not me!"

"So..." Andy leaned forward. "You wanna do it? Go out there?"

"You mean with Frank and the others?"

"No, just you and me — and maybe Hanson. It'll be our little secret."

"But why secret?" I asked, though I had a hunch I knew.

"I think somebody in the marshal's service or with the Territorial patrol is tipping Chilt off. Frank gets these reports and they race out, but by the time they get there... nobody!"

"It's a long way to walk," I pointed out, "especially in the thaw."

He looked at his wrist, which was a joke since he never wore a watch. "Which is why I got Petey landing out here on the river tomorrow morning. I figured you'd wanna check it out."

We agreed that I'd call Hanson, which I did, cautioning him to keep it to himself.

"Roger that," he said. "Good idea," and he promised to show up bright and early. I smiled as I hung up. I continued to like him.

"I want to go," was Evie's comment.

When I pointed out that she had to work, she reminded me that she had 'personal days' of leave she could take. Although I didn't really want her out where she could be a target, I didn't really have — or want — the authority to tell her she couldn't go. I wanted to be her husband and lover, not her keeper.

When Petey arrived in the morning, banking the sturdy silver Beaver into the river wind for another graceful landing, there were four of us and Jack waiting. We wouldn't be out long, so carried lighter packs than usual, though we'd each included a bedroll just in case. We also carried food, a few extra clothes, snowshoes, and plenty of ammunition. Again, I lent Andy my Winchester with the scope and carried my father's old scopeless deer rifle, a Winchester lever action. Evie brought along a similar lever action, though newer than mine, and Wild Bill had chosen an M1.

When Petey saw Evie, he threw his arms around her, lifting and turning her, actually holding her up in the air for a long happy moment. She kissed him on the cheek, and beaming, he set her gently down.

Taking off from the riverfront at Chandalar just after seven, it took us about a half hour to reach the dredge vicinity, as opposed to a full day of snowshoeing.

"Good idea, flying," I told Andy. He grinned.

We did a wide fly-by, as though just another disinterested airplane headed for somewhere, while examining the place with binoculars, and seeing no clue there was anybody around. Petey dropped us in a clearing, two shallow valleys distant then flew away at tree-top level until he reached the river. Anybody watching from the dredge would be hard put to know we had arrived. We hoped.

It took about an hour to snowshoe back to the dredge, longer than I had imagined. It looked so close from the airplane. I let Jack run, planning to get him back on the leash as we neared the dredge. He ran, jumped, peed, burrowed his face in the snow, and walked or ran across the backs of my snowshoes multiple times, each time nearly throwing me on my face in a drift.

Drifts were still deep around here, but we heard snow-melt dripping all around. The snow felt heavier — made a good snowball — unlike the usual powdery stuff that refused to pack into a throwable ball.

As before, we came to the tailings first. About fifty feet tall, the undulating piles of discarded rock and gravel looked like giant worm trails from the air. They were steep and not for snowshoeing, so again we followed the bulldozed access road that would take us across the tops directly to the dredge.

We huddled up behind the silent generator, removing snowshoes, checking rifle loads, and leashing Jack.

"I'll go first," said Andy. "Be sure to keep at least twenty paces between us." He looked at each of us in turn. "Nobody else knows we're out here, right?" We all nodded, assured him we'd told nobody, not even Frank Jacobs. "Good." He turned and stepped out of cover. Nobody shot at him. It seemed a good sign.

With temperatures in the high teens and balmy twenties, I'd worn my lighter parka, and in the wetter snow, my first boots of the season. Instead of porous mukluks or leather to soak through, I'd worn snowpacs — rubber bottoms sewn to a good-quality leather top — invented back east by a man named Leon Leonwood Bean, and available from his catalog. I had two pairs, high and low. With the snow still deep, this pair laced all the way up over my calves with my pant cuffs tucked in. My first pair had leaked, and I sent them back, but these, already in their second season, kept my feet warm and dry.

Evie followed Andy, with Jack and me following

her. Wild Bill brought up the rear. Under a bright sky with high overcast, filtered sun and no wind, all lay silent, save Jack's huffing and muttering and the gentle crunch of wetter snow underfoot. I heard a woodpecker, the first one of the season, a distant muffled tapping.

No Roberta, no nothing. I'd been cautiously hopeful. Though the longer this went on, the less likely it seemed we'd find her alive, or find her at all. For some reason still unclear, this had all gone on much longer than made any sense. It now qualified as the slowest, most circuitous getaway in history.

Abruptly, the day exploded. There's just no other way to say it. From all around came the shattering roar of big guns fired rapidly. One of the first shots ripped through my parka, scoring a burning line of fire along my side. I realized the shout of pain I heard was mine. I dodged, stumbled, staggered, slipped, and fell off the side of the road into a ditch that turned out to have several inches of water under the snow. I didn't care. I had kept hold of the leash and dragged Jack down with me. He didn't care, either. We huddled together, out of the line of fire.

I thought I counted six guns firing, all rifles, literally from all around us. Judging by the rhythm, none of them were military semi-automatic M1s — a small blessing. They'd have to reload manually or slide in a new clip every five shots. The first time they fell silent, all reloading, I heard shots from our side. In front of me and behind along the ditch, both Andy and Wild Bill had popped up shooting. Andy had his own shoot-and-work-the-bolt rhythm that enabled three shots, and I heard a distant shout. He'd hit or startled someone. Behind me, Wild Bill with his M1, got off eight shots in the same four or five seconds, with the semiautomatic firing as fast as he could pull the trigger — before the ambushers could muster their next barrage. Then we all kept our heads down as incoming rounds began again.

They couldn't see us, but it didn't seem to matter. Why did they shoot with no targets? Because they could, I guessed. They had us pinned. The next barrage masked the sound Evie must have made crawling down the ditch to reach me, actually startling me when she put a hand on my shoulder, anxious.

"Are you hit? I heard you shout."

I had a vision of Gabby Hayes in an old-west oater, replying, "Shucks, ma'am, it's only a scratch." But I didn't.

"Nicked me. Wrecked my parka, but I'm okay."

I could see the relief on her face. "I can mend the parka," she said, her face close, speaking under the roar. "But I can't mend you."

There was another silence and I almost jumped up to shoot. "Stay down!" Andy hissed. He shoved his day pack up, just slightly, and at least three shots rang out — although none hit the pack. They had already figured out our fire-during-the-reload strategy.

Evie said what I was thinking. "They've got us. All they have to do now is move in to pick us off."

She didn't say the other part. That we'd been ambushed. That they were all set up and waiting. That they knew we were coming.

223

CHAPTER 29

Somehow Andy hit one of them. Or hit another one, if he had winged one earlier. Even though they'd begun to stagger their reloading, he was able to keep track of which shooter had him targeted. He counted the shots then popped up and nailed his shooter when he had to pause to reload.

They must have been feeling invincible before the bleeding started. Now they fired less confidently, more sporadically, as if only half of them were still shooting, and without much enthusiasm. After a few more minutes, they fell silent altogether. Were they waiting for someone to show? Andy tried his pack trick again. Nothing. He finally chanced a look.

"They're gone!"

There had been six, the story clear in the snow. They'd carefully approached and set up from outside their circle of fire, so as to not let their tracks tip us they were there. They'd brought tarps to lay on, stretched out in the snow, and each used snowshoes to stomp out a comfortable shooting nest. We found candy wrappers and abandoned Thermos bottles. They'd been here awhile.

Blood sign showed us two had been hit. One of them, winged, left a spot of blood every few paces in his trail leading away. The other was true blood spatter, a solid, serious hit. He had been carried away, an easy trail.

We huddled up. Andy made eye contact.

"Go after them?"

"Go home," said Evie, without having to think about it.

Wild Bill made a thinking face. "Two wounded," he said. "They don't have much of a start and it's a clear trail. I think we can catch them."

"Do we want to?" I asked. "It's clear they don't have Roberta with them. It's not worth it if they set up one sniper to cover their retreat and one of us gets nailed. I vote we quit while none of us are bleeding."

"Bleeding much?" Evie reminded me.

"Okay," Andy agreed, for the first time noticing I'd been grazed. "You're right." He looked at the parka damage. "How bad?"

"A scratch," I said.

"Been there. Hurts like heck, though, don't it!"

It did.

It took about an hour to get back to the pickup site and then we waited another hour for Petey, arriving back on river ice in front of Chandalar just after lunch time. Wild Bill said he had to get back to base so we waved him away. By then the bleeding stopped and my wound subsided into a dull, burning ache. In spite of that, hungry, I suggested cheeseburgers but was overruled by Evie in favor of a visit to Nurse Maxine and an even more painful patch-up.

"You again!" she said, opening her front door, seeing Evie guiding me. "Are you accident prone?" Then she saw I'd been shot again. The last time she treated me was also a shooting incident, though fortunately with a very small caliber slug. It had still hurt like heck.

"You realize how lucky you were? Again?"

"Lucky? I got shot!"

She humphed. "Could have been *so* much worse."

225

I felt like we'd been out in the woods for days, an extended campaign, instead of one relatively short day with lots of being shot at. When we finally got back to the rectory, it was after three. By then I was still hungry but thinking only one thing: bed. The morphine helped. I just wanted to lie down.

It wasn't to be. Within minutes, Andy showed up with a pair of takeout cheeseburgers from the Coffee Cup that smelled pretty wonderful. Feeling woozy from the morphine, I let Evie guide me to a tippy stool in the kitchen while Andy put water on to boil for coffee from the French press.

"How do you feel?" he asked.

"Pretty darn good," I told him. He made a puzzled face.

"Morphine," said Evie.

"Aaah." He nodded. He'd been there, too.

Nobody said it until we were all seated around the table, several bites into our delicious moose cheeseburgers with aromatic, steamy mugs of Italian roast in front of us.

Evie looked up from her burger, finally saying what we all knew. "You realize we were set up for an ambush."

"No kidding," mumbled Andy, around his cheeseburger.

"I didn't tell anyone," she continued, "and I doubt either of you did."

"Which leaves Wild Bill," I said, the obvious conclusion.

She nodded and took a sip of her coffee. "Which leaves Wild Bill."

* * *

Frank Jacobs looked at us like we'd just blown in from Mars. We found him in his office on the second

226

floor of the Federal Building. Though we usually took the stairs, today, in deference to the bullet-cut groove in my side — still very sore — we took the elevator, an Otis with lots of brass.

"First elevator in Fairbanks," said Andy. "Everybody in town stood in line to ride up and down in it."

"An *elevator*?"

Andy shrugged. "You're forgetting where you are. This is Fairbanks, the Far North. The Last Frontier. This building," he gestured down the hall as the doors slid open, "was the farthest north concrete construction in its day. Five stories tall in a one-story town!" He must have seen the question on my face. "Built in 1933," he continued, "when I was ten. A big deal around here. We studied it in school. How to make concrete, how to build forms. That's what I wanted to do... that week."

Frank, on the phone when we arrived, waved us to chairs and watched with interest as I attempted to get myself out of my parka and seated without jostling my side.

"Fall out of bed?"

"Shot again," said Andy.

Frank did one of his double takes. "Shot again? Why am I just hearing about this? You people are supposed to be reporting bullet wounds."

We ended up telling him the whole story. I had planned to omit some of the details, but Andy plowed ahead and soon it was all out there.

"Oh, yeah," said Frank, "thanks for inviting me, again." He pointed to the badge on his shirt. "Lawman! I'm supposed to be in on this stuff. They must've known you were coming." And that's when we told him our suspicions. His response was

227

predictable.

"Nah! Hanson? He's a war hero for crissakes." He shook his head with conviction. "There has to be another explanation."

"Well," I said, coming to a reluctant conclusion. "It does help explain what happened with him and his best buddy, Chilt."

"Nothin'," said Andy.

Jacobs looked at him, wrinkling his brow. "Huh?"

"Nothin' happened. They're working together."

"Oh, come on."

"Which certainly could explain why Hanson sent us down the river canyon *shortcut*." I added.

"Yeah," he said reluctantly, "it could."

His phone rang. He held up an index finger to pause the conversation. "Gotta take this." Picking up the receiver, he listened briefly, said yes, and to my considerable surprise, handed me the phone across the desk. "The hospital, it's for you."

* * *

It happened in the Alaska way. I found out later that someone at the hospital tried unsuccessfully to call me at the rectory then tried the Coffee Cup. Rosie at the Coffee Cup dialed the school, ultimately talking to Evie, who put them on to William in his security office at Clear Station, and to Andy at the restaurant, where he wasn't. Tony, Andy's chief cook, suggested all the places they'd already called, plus this one: the marshal's office. I spoke to the nun then hung up the phone, a bit stunned.

"Bad news?" asked Frank, who heard a lot of it.

"Yeah," I murmured, still processing. "It's Kellar. I knew he was sick... and dying... but..." I stood up, stretching for my parka, tweaking my side, and winced. "The sister says he doesn't have much time

228

and is asking for me."

"Sure it's Kellar?" asked Frank, who then heard himself joking about a dying man. "Sorry."

Andy dropped me at St. Joseph's, and the nun behind the desk directed me down the old, quiet hall to room thirty-seven. I found the door ajar and, knocking softly, pushed in. Kellar, huge in the bed with tubes in both arms, looked up, recognized me, and tucked up one side of his face in what passed for a smile. Hugely jaundiced, his skin and eyes nearly glowed yellow. Somehow even with all the yellow, he managed to look gray, with dark, raccoon-like circles around his eyes. And he looked exhausted.

I couldn't help thinking of how physical he'd always been. Physically large and heavy, truly a big, tough, scary guy. Now he didn't look like he could move, let alone inflict damage.

"Just in time," he said, low but clear. "Don't think I'm here long." He turned his head to the left, to a chair alongside the bed and for the first time, I noticed he had company. "My wife, Myrtle."

I went around the bed to shake her hand, something she did reluctantly. Though she said nothing, everything about her, every nuance said anger. Without moving or speaking, she bristled.

She was small, maybe five-two, slight and hard-looking with a muscular handshake, probably in her late forties or early fifties with too-blond hair tightly permed.

"Father," was all she said, her voice lowered, roughened, and a little wheezy. In my experience, the sound of decades of persistent cigarettes and alcohol.

"Ma'am."

She leaned back in her chair, also weary, and I retreated to what seemed the safer side of the bed.

"I..." said Keller. His eyes flicked to Myrtle and then back. "I was hoping for last rites."

"Of course," I told him.

"I mean now, while I can hear them." He didn't say it, but I guessed his meaning. He wanted to be sure. He didn't want to die and somehow be cheated out of his blessing.

"I can do it now."

I carry a tiny bottle, really a repurposed Mapleine flavoring bottle, filled with oil blessed at the church altar. The oil stiffens in the cold but the bottle is small enough I can warm it back to liquid with my hands. On the trail, I carry it in my pocket or my pack wrapped in a sock for extra protection against breakage. I drew it out and twisted open the cap.

"Ready?" I looked at him, he nodded. I looked at her and she made no expression at all, a hostile blank.

Using a bit of the olive oil on my thumb, I drew the sign of the cross on his forehead and said the words. "Unto God's gracious mercy and protection we commit you. The Lord bless you and keep you. The Lord make his face to shine upon you, and be gracious unto you. The Lord lift up his countenance upon you, and give you peace, both now and forevermore." I said the "Amen" alone, as Myrtle didn't make a sound.

Kellar smiled and looked relieved. He took a deep breath, sighed, and closed his eyes. I guess I kept expecting the next breath but it never came.

"Myrtle," I said. "He's gone."

She turned just her head to look at me and say the last thing I might have expected. "*You* killed him."

CHAPTER 30

"When you live hard, you die hard," was Andy's comment. "Usually alone. The only real surprise to me is he died in bed."

We were seated at one of the red-and-white checkered tables at *Andrea's*, Whiskey Jack stretched out on the polished wood floor alongside my chair. The dining room lamps were turned off, the room dim on an overcast afternoon, with kitchen light glowing yellow through porthole windows in the swinging doors. We could hear the distant radio playing Guy Williams "Singing the Blues," and Tony whistling along as he worked, occasionally clattering big metal pots or steel utensils on the stainless counters.

It had now been most of a month since the bank robbery, hostage-taking, and getaway. In spite of all the running around, leading us in circles, it seemed the robbers hadn't gotten away — had no intention of doing so — and Roberta, their hostage, was still unaccounted for. Also unaccounted for — what had been reported as two million dollars' worth of bearer bonds.

Andy said what I was thinking. "Hard to believe Hanson could be in on this."

Although I agreed, I added, "Less hard to believe after the dredge ambush."

"Yeah." He shook his head and sipped his coffee, holding the cup in both hands. "I see you thinking. You got a plan?"

"Not a good one. I keep coming back to us going out to Chilt's for one more look. Just in case we missed something out there. And this time we'd better take Frank along."

"Yeah," said Andy. "Never saw a guy get so whiney about missing the chance to get shot at. Should be thankin' us."

"What about asking Hanson?"

Andy grimaced. "I vote we leave him home on this one." Somewhat regretfully, I nodded. I still didn't want to believe Hanson was in on it. Andy called Frank, who said he'd also been thinking about going back out, and he walked through the door in about fifteen minutes, thanking us for getting him out of the office on a slow day and for including him this time. With the temperature in the low thirties and the whole world dripping and slushy, he'd gone over to his warmer-weather uniform, including rubber boots and olive-drab lighter-weight parka.

"The breath of spring," said Andy, looking him over.

Frank snorted then sniffed the air, noticing coffee still in the pot. "I better have some of this fine Italian roast before we head out."

Andy handed him one of the glass mugs. "Bring it along." And he did.

Out at Chilt's there was actual ground showing, the first I'd seen in what had been the melt ring around the burned-out house. We heard some of the first songbirds in the nearby birch thicket. Icicles four feet long hung from the garage and cache eaves. Just as we arrived, clouds parted and sun warmed the world, chasing the gray and blue tones out of the snow and maybe out of my heart.

For all of Kellar's nastiness to me and to others, I

232

found myself mourning him a little. I knew I'd be in the minority and didn't bother mentioning it to Andy, who would — as he'd say — laugh his ass off at the notion.

Just at the end, I saw Kellar as a person, with hopes and fears, disappointments, regrets, and more than anything else, loneliness. And yes, I know — we reap what we sow.

If possible, the property looked and felt even more lonely and desolate than the last time, though in summer, here by the river, it would probably be pretty nice.

Andy studied the place. "Your buddy Chilt still ain't at home."

"What do you expect to find out here?" Frank asked, and I just shook my head. We'd already found some bonds and, in my opinion, were unlikely to find more.

"No idea," I told him. It was a question I'd asked myself. I just kept thinking we should come back out here to look around. And now here we were, on yet another wild-goose chase.

We searched through the outbuildings, even peering into the pit of the outhouse again, with no better result.

After about an hour, all searched out with not a single place left to look, I paused to enjoy the view out across the ice. Though not a big river, the Chena flowed wide here. With the thaw underway, puddles of standing melt-water dotted the ice, which would still be about two feet thick and mostly solid underneath. As before, much of the river surface lay under several feet of drifted snow, while part of it — the part previously exposed — remained clear. I still had no idea what magic in the twisting and sighing of river wind made that happen.

I watched Jack, nose down, meander out onto the ice, stopping occasionally to pee on something. I always thought of his frequent peeing as some ancient, wolfish way of claiming territory. If that were so, he'd own much of interior Alaska by now. Andy came to stand beside me, the sun warm on our faces.

"Nicer here when the sun shines," he said, and I had to agree.

When Jack reached the glare ice he stopped, looked down then jumped back, startled. I imagined he had flushed some small creature, maybe a shrew that turned on him, which they often do in spite of the size difference. Even in bitter winter, shrews, mice, and voles are active, tunneling under the snow for warmth and protection from predators as they scavenge for food. Though I couldn't imagine what food they'd be finding out on river ice. As we watched, Jack began to scratch in earnest at the ice with both front feet flying, and then to bark. Andy looked at me.

"You teach him to do that?"

"Do what?"

"Locate ice then scratch and bark at it. Neat trick, especially in Alaska where ice can be hard to find."

Jack stopped and turned to look back at us.

"Rusty on the railroad tracks?" asked Andy with a straight face. He'd been known to watch *Rin Tin Tin* on TV. Each episode featured Rusty getting himself into some pickle and saying to his dog, "Get help, Rinty!" And Rinty always ran to summon help.

So, with Jack barking at us — and because it was a balmy, sun-warmed day, perfect for loitering — we waded out through the now crunchy snow to see what kind of creature he'd rousted. But it wasn't a mouse, a shrew, or any living thing.

"Aw, shit!" said Andy.

I looked down to find a dead man staring up at me, frozen in river ice, just two or three inches below the surface in unreasonably clear water. And it made me shiver.

"Jacobs!" Andy called. "Got something for ya."

The man's sky-blue eyes looked flung open, like he hadn't been expecting the small, neat, bloodless hole in the middle of his forehead. His icy image shimmered in the sun, slightly enlarged and distorted by the ripples, bubbles, and refraction of ice. Though he still wore his white military ski uniform, I could see a bit of dark hair showing, up under the fox ruff encircling his hood. A lanyard around his neck secured an official-looking, brass traffic-cop whistle and he wore what now seemed the obligatory European-made ski boots on his feet. He had his hands up near his ears as if someone had shouted, 'Hands up!' then shot him and left him that way.

Andy bent over for a look. "Another dead guy! Who might you be?"

"You don't know?" asked Frank, joining them.

"Should I?"

Frank looked at me. "I bet *you* do."

"Andy," I said, "say hello to Chilt. The real Chilt."

* * *

The next time we saw Chilt, he was thawing on a steel table in the morgue, still fully clothed, in the basement of the Federal Building. I'd never been down there before and could certainly wait a long time to go again. Andy and I took the elevator with Frank.

"This place stinks," said Andy, as the elevator doors slid wide. He was not wrong.

"Whoever shot him chipped out a hole in the ice," Frank explained, "dropped him in, and carried enough water to freeze him there. And get this, he was frozen in clean well water, not muddy river water."

"Frozen in place, so he'd go out with the ice at breakup," I said, thinking aloud. "And when someone found him, *if* someone found him, he'd be hundreds of miles away from here, down the Chena, down the Tanana, maybe all the way to the Yukon."

Frank nodded. "We'd never have a clue what happened to him, or where it happened."

"A lot of what goes out with the breakup is never found. Gets pulverized by the ice." Andy gestured toward Chilt's brass whistle. "Here's the whistle. Who told us about that?"

I had to think. "Hanson's man, Smitty."

"Yeah," said Andy, "him." We stood silent for a moment, staring at the dead man, wondering. Andy broke the silence. "What d'ya figure? Out there about a week or ten days? I didn't see tracks and it's been about a week since we had snow and wind."

I unzipped his thawing and now soggy parka a few inches, to where the scars from the Nazi booby trap were clear to see.

"It's really him this time. Which begs the question — who is skiing around Central Alaska pretending to be him?"

"And why?" Frank turned to look at us. "You guys ready to get out of here?"

"Oh, yeah!" said Andy. And we did, none of us taking full breaths until we'd stepped out of the elevator upstairs. Even then, and for much of the afternoon, I still kept thinking I smelled morgue.

236

We said goodbye to Frank and started to walk away, but then I thought of something, calling back. "Did you get to see the autopsy on Newhouse?"

He gave me his blank look. "Remind me."

"Army guy," said Andy. "Got shot sitting in the Weasel."

"Oh, yeah." He made a face. "No, I didn't." He looked at me. "Thought he was shot in the firefight." His eyes narrowed. "You think he wasn't! What do you know that I don't?"

I shrugged, hands up, eyes wide. "I know nothing. Just curious."

"Yeah," he said, "I'll just bet."

* * *

"Ugh!" was Evie's response later, when she made the mistake of asking how my day had gone. We were in my kitchen on a kind of dinner date, companionably chopping and sautéing stuff for a mooseburger lasagna.

"I'm hungry," she said, sliding the pan into the oven and setting the timer. "We should have started this earlier."

Drifting into the living room, we settled together on the sofa and she threaded her arm through mine. It all felt so settled and married. Really nice.

"And how was *your* day, dear?" I asked her.

"Better than yours! A little. I got nowhere near a morgue. We spent the afternoon on the Palmer Handwriting Method."

"Oh gosh, are they still teaching that?"

"You bet."

"Why?"

"Well, Austin Palmer — back in the last *century!* — claimed it was faster than the method they had before, and that it would allow a handwriter to keep

237

up with an early typewriter."

"You're kidding."

"Not a bit. If it were up to me, I'd just give everybody a typewriter. I hate writing by hand, not to mention trying to read other people's handwriting.

"So..." she continued, and I could tell the conversation was moving on. She fixed me with her I'm-really-listening gaze. "Who shot Chilt, the *real* Chilt? And why?"

"Why is probably easier," I told her. "There are something like two million really good reasons. Plus the maybe ten or twelve other players who seem to have been involved in this. The partner shares — or we should say, *survivor* shares — keep getting bigger."

"You mean as they kill each other off."

"Yeah, or get us to."

"But why kill him now?" It was a good question. "I thought he was the ringleader!"

I did a face shrug. "So did I."

From my office, the phone rang. More often than not, the phone ringing was not good news and we shared an apprehensive glance.

"I could ignore it, pretend we're not here."

"Maybe it's a radio show, like Dialing for Dollars." Evie said with a grin. "Answer the question and win a fortune!"

"In Alaska?" I got up to answer. "I don't think they do long distance." It was on its fifth ring by the time I got there.

"Bet you thought about not answering." It was Frank.

"Evie said 'Don't get that, it's probably Frank.'"

He snorted. "Funny." He hesitated then moved on to business. "Hey, I got another piece for your puzzle.

238

You know how we were wondering how long he'd been there... a week, maybe ten days?"

"Yeah."

"Found a gas receipt in his shirt pocket. Not conclusive, of course. No telling how often he changed shirts or emptied his pockets."

I could tell Frank was playing this and that it would be something interesting. Evie came in, as she often did, to lean on the doorframe and listen. "It's Frank," I mouthed. She nodded.

"So how long?"

"More than a month," said Frank.

"*More* than a month? But that means..."

"Right! Somebody shot Chilt sometime before they even robbed the bank."

CHAPTER 31

Chilt's death didn't make the news. Frank put a lid on the whole thing, even going so far as to name him a John Doe with the coroner's people.

"Just a hunch," he said. "Better to let these yahoos *not* know what we know, for once."

He was right. So far, they consistently knew exactly what we knew, and maybe even before we knew it. And I had no idea how.

Andy started counting, extending fingers. "They got the bonds. They got *no* need of a hostage. It's like they're just leadin' us from ambush to ambush."

"But," I said, "we *do* keep showing up. Maybe they figure that sooner or later they'll nail us."

"But why? Why us? How do *we* even figure into this? Why not just take the money and run?"

"You know one thing," I pointed out, "each time they try to hit us, they go home with at least one fewer bank robber."

"Maybe that's the plan. Maybe the guy that's leadin' this thing just wants to keep getting 'em shot until the whole two mil is his."

"It's a lot of reasons to want to," I said. "It always seems to come back to the money."

When my telephone rang at just after one a.m., and Jack barked, I wasn't surprised, being pretty sure I knew it was the kidnappers calling. I didn't bother feeling my usual sense of dread and took my time stumbling down the very dark hall to my office. I knew they'd keep ringing.

I picked up the handset. "Hardy." Turns out I was surprised.

"It's Roberta," she said softly. "Don't talk. I don't have much time. They're all asleep. I'm not sure where I am... in a city... Fairbanks, I think. I can hear town traffic, the train, and a bell that chimes the hours. Help me," she begged. "I..."

I heard a click and the line went dead. Her voice, the sound of anxiety, real fear, left my stomach in a knot. She'd been with them too long and I could only imagine what they might be doing to her.

My office light clicked on and I hung up the phone blinking and squinting. Andy stood in the doorway in his long johns, with Jack. When Andy stayed over, sleeping on my couch, Jack abandoned my room and even his furnace grate, to sleep on the braided rug out by his friend.

Andy's brow furrowed and he tipped his head to one side looking at me. "You're not pulling on clothes and running around, so I guess nobody's burnin' or bleedin'. What's up?"

"It was Roberta," I told him, and his eyebrows arched.

"So, she just checking in, or what? No, seriously, it was really her? You recognized her voice?"

"Yes. She says she's in Fairbanks. Or she thinks she's in Fairbanks." And I took him back through the conversation. "She wants us to find her," I concluded.

"And we're just supposed to drive around Fairbanks looking for her?"

"Well, what do you want? A map? She probably risked a beating or worse to make the call." I thought about that for a minute. "Lucky she knew my number by heart."

"Oh, yeah," said Andy. "Did she?"

"I don't know why she would."

* * *

It was Andy's idea: still one more trip out to the remains of Chilt's house. I actually argued against the idea. I didn't want to go out there again, especially not alone, which was what he was suggesting. It took a lot of convincing, but I finally gave in.

"What am I looking for?"

"You already proved you don't need to be lookin' for something to find stuff. You'll just go out there and do that thing you do — nose around and discover."

I had taken to telling someone each time I headed out of town, so they'd know where to search to pick up my body. Sometimes I called Nurse Maxine, or Rosie at the Café, or left a message for Evie at the school office. Today I called Hanson's office and got Smitty.

"Yes, sir!" he said, when I'd identified myself. "The Colonel is away. How can I help?"

"I'm headed out into the Bush, not far actually, just out to Lieutenant Bradbury's rental place along the Chena. If you'd just make a note of it. I don't like to not tell people where I'm going, but I couldn't raise any of my regular contacts."

"Alone? Is that wise?"

"I think it will be okay," I told him. "We were out there the other day with no trouble. I hate to call out a whole team just to walk around and find nothing."

"Understood," he said. "And you'll be back when?"

"By four."

"Roger that. I'll enter this in the log."

I packed a lunch for Jack and me, grabbed my day

pack and the .38. Andy still had my Winchester 70, so I thought about dragging along the lever action. I decided against it.

It was the best kind of sunny bright day and the drive to and through Fairbanks was leisurely, the road mostly exposed gravel — no dust yet — and smooth sailing. With the windows rolled down, Jack stuck his head out, his ears flagging straight back in the breeze. On the radio, Fats Domino sang "I'm Walking" as the Bradbury driveway hove into view.

The last time I was here, I'd been able to drive all the way to the house. But between then and now, the season's last highway snowplow had thrown up a small mountain of snow and ice, adequately sealing the driveway. I parked the Ford in a wide spot about a hundred feet up the road, to hike back. The anxiety I'd been holding at bay actually keyed up as I shut down the engine and sat for a moment in a silence that suddenly had weight.

I debated leaving Jack in the truck, admittedly safe, but bewildered to be left behind when there was a ramble at hand. In the end I let him out.

At the driveway, the plow pile — sun-crusted enough to be weight-bearing — allowed Jack and me to climb up and over, rather than wading through, which I appreciated. Then I just strolled along the lane with relative ease, deliberately following along in one of the two melted tire tracks of exposed gravel.

It felt so good to be out of my winter parka just wearing a light jacket, gloves — no mitts — and my red felt hunting hat. The sparse birch and willow woods had come alive with song birds. I could hear a good number of ducks 'laughing' beyond the property, out on the expanse of pond water covering the top of the river ice. About two weeks to breakup was the word going around and I, for one, couldn't wait.

It would have been a sunny carefree day except for all of the questions without answers. Questions like, where was Roberta — apparently still alive but still held captive. Why? And why had Chilt, supposedly the ringleader, been killed? And more basic, could he really be the ringleader if he died more than a month ago?

Those questions led me to all the ambushes, and Andy's idea that there must be a leak. First, he thought it might be somebody in Frank's office, tipping the 'gang' as to where we'd be and when. But that hadn't panned out. Yes, we were certain it wasn't one of us, so that left only one logical place to look for a leak: Hanson, or someone in his command. We'd braced Hanson about it, and he'd been aghast... also angry, defensive, insulted, and ultimately blue, as he came to the same conclusion everyone else had: that the leaker really could be someone in his command. I'd be upset, too.

The closer I got to the burned-out house, the more I agreed with Andy's hypothesis about the leaker, and the more my skin prickled. It would be easy enough to test. If Smitty noted it in his daily report, as he indicated he would, and if I made it home alive then the problem was elsewhere.

If, on the other hand, he took my call and didn't log it then I had unwittingly told the exact person I shouldn't have exactly where and when I was going, and that I would be alone.

So, I admit I shivered as I came around the last bend leading up to the burned-out house. Grass was exposed and greening in the sunny donut of fire-melt around the block foundation, the whole place alive with flitting birds and their songs.

I wondered who they'd send, but not for long. A tall man, wearing a lightweight military parka and the obligatory balaclava, stepped out from behind the outhouse, service .45 in hand.

"End of the line," he said, still faking the rough voice.

"Who are you, really?" I asked. "You're not Chilt. Last time I saw Chilt he was stretched out, thawing on a stainless-steel table in the morgue."

He laughed a little, in a natural voice, like this actually was funny. "So, you found him!" Without shifting the .45, he used his free hand to flip back the parka hood and pull off the balaclava. Smitty. Not much of a surprise at this point.

"I don't get it," I said. "I thought you guys were a team. You were war heroes, Wild Bill Hanson's famous *team* who helped defeat Nazi tanks with skis, rifles... and pure guts. What happened?"

He shook his head firmly. "I think every one of us thought — *think* — the world of Colonel Hanson. But life goes on. You were a soldier. What are you now? Priest in a shithole village nobody ever heard of or ever will. What do you make a month? About two hundred?"

"Two hundred twenty-five," I corrected him a bit defensively. There was no sense making it sound worse than it was.

"Yeah. And that gets you what or where?"

"Do you think I got into this for the money?"

"No, I suppose not. And I certainly didn't join the Army to get rich. But imagine this. Along comes a share of *two million dollars*. Million with a capital M! It just comes marching into my life. Can you even imagine what that buys me?"

245

"You mean besides the chance to murder people, and live a life on the run?"

"Well, yeah, but also cars, boats, women, a tropical beach — *white sand!* Not just to sit on. I can *buy* the damn beach!" He pulled himself, with difficulty, back from the pristine white-sand beach of his imagination into the sordid moment a soldier hero murders an unarmed priest in cold blood, for money.

"You shot Newhouse."

"Yeah. Hated to do that, too. He was so gung ho to join the famous team. Ten or twelve years too late, though. If he'd showed up during the war, he'd have been a hero with the rest of us. For all it's worth — subsistence pay and lousy assignments — of course there's always the GI Bill. Even if he'd wanted to get into this bond deal, which I can't imagine, he'd be just one more split. One too many."

Smitty didn't seem to be in any hurry to shoot me, so I pressed on. "Seems to me, there are fewer splits all the time. Doesn't that worry you? What if someone else decides they want yours?"

"And shoots me? You kiddin'? This was mostly my idea. Soon as I heard the bonds were coming this way I started thinking about how this might go down." He was bragging now, proud of his work.

"Well, answer me this. Why all the circling around in the Bush? Why not just take the money and run?"

He shook his head. "That part wasn't my idea."

"It was a diversion," I said. "The bonds never left Fairbanks."

"You figured that out. I heard you were good at this."

"You heard that?" It puzzled me. "Who from?"

"Aaaah," he said, "can't tell you that."

246

"And you shot Chilt."

For the first time he looked genuinely regretful. "No, not me. Chilt was like my brother. He saved my life in Norway about six times. I *never* would have harmed a hair on his head. But it was all done before I knew. I came out here to help chip out the grave. He'd like that, by the way, being buried in a grave that swept out with the ice, like it was taking him off on another adventure. He was the real deal."

"Which is why he decided to not play along."

"Yeah, I guess. At first, he seemed motivated then next thing I knew we were freezing him into ice, saying goodbye."

We stood silent, him back in that moment. Me, wondering how this could all shake out. Even at a distance of fifteen feet, the muzzle of a .45 looks as big and deadly as the mouth of a train tunnel, especially with full knowledge the train is on its way.

"Well," he said, and I could see the moment had come.

"You sure you want to do this?"

"I don't *want* to do it."

"But you will anyway."

"I'll have some bad nights," he said, "but sometimes I do anyway. They'll be less bad somewhere tropical, curled up next to a sexy lady." He cocked his head quizzically. "Any more questions?"

"Still don't want to tell me who's pulling the strings on this?"

"Sorry. That's one question you'll have to take with you." He thumbed the hammer back. "Do you want to pray or anything?"

"No, thanks. All prayed up." I met his eyes. "Do you want me to visit you in jail?"

He laughed, a real laugh. "You'd probably be the only visitor I got. But that's not going to happen." He raised the .45, sighting.

They all stepped out at once. Andy, Frank, Wild Bill, and William. From the old garage, from the cache, from a 'blind' built of sticks and brush, and in the case of William, literally from under the snow — a white, snow-covered tarp that rendered him invisible at a distance of about twenty feet. They'd seen everything and probably heard most of it, too.

"Put the gun down easy," said Frank, and Smitty did, as they all moved in together.

"Oh, jeez, a trap. Fuck!" But he shook his head, actually laughing. "And they warned me about you!"

Honestly, I thought he sounded a bit relieved.

CHAPTER 32

"He wasn't the ringleader," I told Evie later. "And that was the one question he wouldn't answer, even though he planned to shoot me and I'd never have the chance to tell anyone."

She eyed me over a real salad, one that included green lettuce without the brown edges.

"That's weird." She took a bite and smiled. "*Living* green stuff! I almost forgot what it tastes like."

We were at my place eating our dinner — juicy moose steaks and green salad. Gary at the store, had called earlier to say they got in a couple of crates of fresh vegetables, the first of the season. So, we decided to go crazy, even at two dollars a head for iceberg lettuce. This was the first real salad we'd had since sometime last fall.

She waved a fork in my direction. "You know, when bears first come out of their dens in the spring they go out in the swamps and forage for plants that... *well*, clean them out." She gestured at our salad.

"Nice image," I told her. "Which reminds me, bears are out."

"I heard." She took a bite. "I've lived my whole life here and only seen a bear maybe twice. Those were black bears, not grizzlies, and I mostly see them at the dump."

"I've seen them there. Nowhere else, though...

249

yet."

"This is an especially good time to *not* see one," she said. "They come out in the spring skinny and hungry." She shivered. "People get killed by bears every year. Even people who know better. That's about the most terrible thing I can think of... to be eaten alive. Ugh!"

Fortunately, the conversation moved on, inevitably to Breakup, the thaw, and whether we'd have a flood this year. Some years, after the ice goes out here, it jams up downstream, gradually backing up and filling the valley with cold, muddy water. Town becomes a big lake, with canals for streets, and cabins — most built up — dotted here and there like islands. The kids build rafts, 'borrow' canoes, and spend their free time floating around and falling in. Everybody puts on their knee or hip boots, except for some kids who go out in tennies or barefoot to just wade, which *they* don't mind. It feels like achingly cold ice water — which it is — to someone as old as I am!

The most annoying part for most of us is having to boil our drinking water since most wells are very shallow and easily contaminated with the standing water.

But the mood changed after dinner. We were both reading, sitting on the sofa together when Evie turned a page, paused and put her hand on my arm. When I looked up, she had a tear in each eye. She blotted them on her sleeve. "I'm sorry," she said, apparently about the tears. "With all the excitement, we've never really talked about... anything."

She didn't mean 'anything.' She meant we hadn't talked about our wedding. She was right. It had been more than a month since we'd even mentioned marrying, in fact, since our premarital session with the bishop. Now, with June twelfth approaching — our scheduled wedding day — we needed to talk.

I inserted an empty flattened matchbook to keep my place, reading again: 'Free Art Talent Test, find out if you have valuable talent.' I didn't. Closing the book, I turned to her nodding, feeling my heart jag up.

Truthfully, I had been willing to *not* talk about it and just hope we were on track, hope that nothing between us had changed, and we'd soon be husband and wife, the 'danger' passed. Probably the typical male response. And yes, I probably didn't bring it up for fear of finding that it *had* all changed, and we were running completely off the track and into the weeds. Now, facing her I felt like I might not be getting enough oxygen.

"You're right. We should talk." She smiled and then just looked at me, waiting. I realized she expected me to start. Though seldom at a loss for words, they were hard to come by in this moment. I decided to blunder ahead.

"I think that you think... that something changed between us." I looked into her eyes. "It hasn't. Nothing's changed."

She smiled a little, the corners of her mouth just tucking up. I think she was trying to be encouraging. But she shook her head.

"Everything changed," she said, "though not so much for you. The bishop reminded me," she continued, "that I wasn't just marrying you. I was marrying the Church and the church life. I was dedicating my life to being a priest's wife, to smiling when you say something wise, whether I do or don't agree with it. And to chairing the altar guild, organizing bake sales to raise money for hymnals and vestments. To going around telling people 'Father wants this or that.'

"And then, listening to the Bishop talk about honesty, *how* honest? I realized I was giving up my whole independent life. I would become like one of your arms or legs. An appendage. And it scared me. I'm not knocking all the women who do it. It's a big job, and in its own way, an important one. But not for me."

From my perspective, our little 'talk' had started badly and gotten worse.

"So, I need to tell you," she continued, "I'm not sure I can do that. No, that's not right. I'm pretty sure I don't *want* to do that. And yes, I do know that puts me at square with you, and the bishop, and anybody else here who is waiting for me to pick up the slack after June twelfth." Two more tears appeared, hesitated, then rolled down her cheeks. She nodded in my direction. "Now you talk."

I took a deep breath, still feeling oxygen deprived. "I never expected any of those things." She started to speak but I waved her off. "My turn. I've only wanted — expected — a life with you and me in it. Okay, I *was* hurt when you didn't tell me about Roberta. But I worked through it. I only want you to be you, and me to be me, and us to be together. I don't care about the bishop, or the altar guild, or any of this other stuff. This is not about them. It's about us."

More tears. "You say that, but I'm not sure it's realistic." Climbing off the sofa, she picked up her parka and bent to kiss me on the lips. "I love you so much! And I do want us to be together, Hardy, I do! But sooner or later, I'm just afraid I'll resent being that person... and we'd eventually lose 'us'... we'd *both* be miserable!"

I rose quickly and held her hands. "Evie, we can work through this…"

"Oh, Hardy," she sobbed, "believe me, I've thought about it, and imagined every possible way it could be! I just don't see how it works."

She looked at me. It was clearly my turn to say the thing that mattered, that would make the difference. And with our life together hanging on it, I found myself, thoughts racing, all but speechless. I took a deep breath.

"In all the time I've known you, I've never seen you not try. Never seen you walk away from something risky or dangerous… and now…"

She kissed me gently then passionately — almost as if it were the last time — then reluctantly pushed away and went out, closing the door softly behind her.

I sat in the empty room, in her vacuum, in the silence and immense dark emptiness of a life the light has just gone out of. As if sensing, Jack came in from his furnace grate to put his head on my knee and let me scratch him behind the ears.

"I think we're in trouble," I told him, and he wagged his tail.

* * *

With only one or two days left of ice driving, best case, I drove the Ford across the river and parked it. I didn't leave it where the ferry would land, but followed a set of ruts on down to park nearer the bridge, joining a cluster of several other vehicles. Once the ice got too thin to drive or walk safely, I'd just cross on the railroad bridge — walking the somewhat narrow, very high plank path alongside the rails, ending up not more than ten minutes' distant from where I parked.

Evie hadn't come by for coffee, though when I heard a knock, I briefly thought she had. It turned out to be William, also headed across the river to park, but stopping for coffee and gossip.

Selecting a mug and filling it, he sat on a tippy stool and removed his rimless glasses, huffing on them for moisture, then polishing the lenses with an absolutely clean and ironed hanky. He was the only person I knew who ironed his handkerchiefs and looked askance at Kleenex.

"No Evie?"

Though I tried for neutral, as a trained investigator, he had no trouble reading my expression. "Ahhh," he said. He replaced his glasses by stretching the curved earpieces behind his ears. "June twelve approaches."

Shaking my head, I held up both hands in an I-don't-know shrug. He nodded. "The pressure is on." He sipped.

"She loves me. She's clear about that. And I am. But all the bishop's talk about holding teas and chairing altar guilds ran her completely off the rails. That's not how she sees her life."

"And you?" he asked, in his oh-so-mild way.

"Not how I see it, either."

"And you told her?"

I looked at him. "Of course."

"Then," he said, "it will work out."

* * *

I had to go out west of town on a sick call beyond what locals still called The Village, the more native part of town from the early railroad-building days. With my truck across the river, it meant going on foot, a mile or more of wading through good-sized

254

puddles — often over ice — and stumbling through slush, sometimes nearly to my booted knees.

The route took me past the old mission school, down a beautiful little lane of birch trees, still winter-bare. In the autumn, the leaves minted to pure gold. Evie and I loved walking there, holding hands. Of course, I missed her now and holding hands with Jack — who was fully occupied with bounding, splashing, and peeing — wouldn't be the same.

There wasn't a lot left of the mission. They'd skidded the log church into town, away from the action of the river cutting in, shearing away more and more of the riverbank. Next to be threatened was a small log cabin, known as The Bishop's Lodge, built by Bishop Peter Trimble Rowe, probably in the 1930s. There was talk of dismantling it, like Lincoln Logs, to haul into town and reassemble, maybe for a library. But it would have to be soon. Last summer the river had cut to within five feet, great chunks of bank just falling away without warning. It was a good place to not stand, so we had to keep a close watch on summer visitors.

Anyway, there wasn't much left of the mission but the main building. If the river kept carving the bank, even that would be washed away within the next couple of years, too big, old, and ramshackle to be moved. It would be stripped in place of anything useful and then in its time, allowed to teeter and fall away with the riverbank. On some spring flood, we'd see it gliding away downriver like the *Titanic*. The good news? People who had been students or orphans at the school, now living in the villages downstream, would find the hulk beached somewhere, and salvage every scrap to build homes, caches, and privies. Handy, that all those free building materials would be delivered right to them.

Beyond the mission, where I was headed today, a narrow two-rutted road threaded a small wood past what I knew to be a cattail swamp still deep under snow. From there, the ruts led to a good-sized natural clearing along the river to my destination. It was a nearly square log cabin, solidly built, circled by several small outbuildings including a tall cache, privy, a smokehouse for salmon, and maybe twenty doghouses complete with curious, bored dogs who sensed Jack and me on the road and barked us in. There'd be nobody sneaking up on this place.

An isolated and pretty spot, very quiet when the dogs let up, it was — more than anything — bear country. Yes, I did have the .38 I usually carried, but a bear might well finish me for breakfast and die of old age before I could stop him with such a small gun. In fact, what I've heard about bears is I could put a bullet into its brain and it could be dead and still kill me.

The gun of choice — bear repellant, they called it around here — is the .357 magnum, although the new .44 magnum might soon change that. No matter, I didn't have either.

I *did* now have a collection of four of the 1911-style .45-caliber semiautomatic Colts that I, or Andy had recently taken from people who wanted to kill me. Needing a larger handgun for this visit, I reasoned that I might as well get some use out of them.

Before starting out, I selected one from the bottom of the file cabinet drawer, loading in a full seven-shot magazine and pocketing a spare. Digging at the back of a closet shelf I found a shoulder holster I'd bought earlier and hardly used, slipped it on and slid in the Colt. Under my arm, in my lighter-weight spring parka, it hardly bulged at all, though if seen, no one around here would think a thing about it, especially during bear season.

And so, packing sufficient 'heat' — as they say in Humphrey Bogart tough-guy movies — I went out to anoint and pray over the sick.

Hearing the barking, Ernest Thomas came out with his shotgun to check on things, waving when he saw me on the road. His vigilance didn't surprise me. This far out from town there was always the chance that a pack of wolves or a newly awakened hungry bear might come by and see all these chained-up dogs as a tasty and available smorgasbord.

Once in the cabin, I greeted Annie, his wife, waving her back as she tried to struggle up to greet me. Complications from what her husband called 'female' surgery earlier in the season — a hysterectomy — had kept her mostly bedridden through late winter and into spring. Actually, she had come home from the hospital in Fairbanks, rested for about a week, and then tried to pack in her normal armload of firewood. She ended up bleeding all the way back to Fairbanks, having to suffer through the repair and a much more difficult recuperation.

As her husband went about his chores with the dogs, firewood, and ultimately fixing dinner, I prayed over her, anointed her with holy oil, and finally we just sat and talked about village things. She didn't get many visitors out there and Earnest didn't like to leave her to spend much time in town, so she was starved for local gossip. I didn't have a lot, but more than she did, so we enjoyed our visit.

"Is somebody fixing up the mission?" she asked. "Will it open again?" I must have looked puzzled.

"No, nothing going on over there. I'm afraid it's too close to the river to try to do much with."

She nodded, but I could see the question on her face.

"Why?" I asked.

"The dogs hear things, or maybe smell things. They all turn that way, listening with their noses up, sniffing. I just thought..." She looked at me, eyes widening. "Maybe it's ghosts!"

I thought of Solomon Esau's sightings of Deaconess Farthing. "You've lived out here a long time."

She nodded. "Almost twenty-five years."

"Have you ever seen things or heard things on your way by? Things you couldn't explain?"

She smiled a little, dropping her chin, breaking our gaze. I guess I thought she'd probably laugh at me.

Instead she whispered, "All the time."

CHAPTER 33

I had hoped to see Evie in the morning but didn't. And I hoped to see her after school, maybe for dinner. We could fix something together or walk over to the Coffee Cup to get something. But she didn't show up then either.

For my dinner, I fixed a small pot of rice, mixed in canned peas, and had it alongside moose meat sliced from Sunday's roast. It was probably all good, but I found I didn't have much of an appetite. I couldn't get past the notion of being at an impasse with Evie, with no idea how to work it through.

I had an evening meeting, so no time to sit and stew about it. The altar guild, made up of five dedicated women, gathered monthly in the parish hall across the street. Yes, they gathered to visit and gossip, but also to handle details of church service upkeep, such as re-stitching pulled seams in choir robes and polishing the altar brass. They didn't need me — knew exactly what they were doing — but I added an official something to the mix that they seemed to appreciate. So, I went and sat, drank perked coffee from the red can, and gossiped with 'the girls.'

But tonight, we hadn't been meeting more than ten minutes when I heard the door open behind me and all eyes rose from me to whoever had just come in. They smiled, so I knew it was someone friendly, and turned to welcome the late-comer. Evie! She came in, shedding her parka, greeting me with a warm kiss on the cheek and a wave to the women, most of whom she knew well.

"Sorry I'm late," she said to the group. And then to me, "I've got this."

"But…" I said, surprised and a bit alarmed at this sudden about-face.

"Whatever I don't know, the ladies'll fill me in, right?" They nodded enthusiastically. "So, you go do what you do, and we'll take care of business here."

"Uh… o-kay… thanks, honey," I said, getting back a smile that would launch at least a thousand ships. I snagged my jacket off the back of my chair and left the ladies to 'do what they do.'

It was still light out — would be for hours — the sky clear and the temperature balmy, just above freezing, the street and yard still a vast, partially-melted wasteland of snow, slush, and melt water. But splashing back across to the rectory, I felt the load lifting and the world seemed like a pretty good place. As Browning observed, 'God's in His heaven — all's right with the world.'

But we need to talk! I thought, still puzzled, yet cautiously optimistic.

* * *

We were all off the river now, with temperatures in the thirties, ice too thin to drive, and scattered melt making even walking out too dangerous. Earlier in the week a sled dog got loose and ran out on the ice in front of town, to great consternation. Wisely, no one tried to go out for him, instead tossing out a trail of smoked salmon bits that finally lured him back safely to the river bank.

Evie and I walked down after dinner to view the black-and-white striped, four-legged 'tripod'. In late winter, they froze its base into Tanana river ice, tethering its top by a long cable to the green-painted tower on shore. There behind glass sat the clock that would officially stop when the ice moved.

"Almost spring," she said, viewing the clock face through reflections of our faces and the blue sky behind. Even with warmer temperatures and snow melt all around, patches of bare earth revealed that it wouldn't be spring until the ice broke up.

Why such a big deal about ice melting? That's what I thought when I first got here. Like all the old jokes about watching paint dry — watching ice melt. And it's true, some rivers just melt, no big deal. But since the Tanana flows mostly north, and its more southern feeder rivers melt first, breakup could be dynamic, with lots of water pressure and other ice behind it. So, our breakups happen with a roar, huge sheets of ice sliding, slamming, grinding, pulverizing. An ice jam downstream would flood us in a day, leaving us with nothing to do but slosh around and wait until the jam melted, broke loose, or rarely, when the army dropped bombs on it.

"I think she's dead," said Evie without preamble as we walked back across the tracks for home — my home, at least. Soon to be ours. We'd had this conversation before. It didn't go anywhere. It couldn't. Maybe that's why, when we got to my front vestibule, just at the door, she paused.

"I'm not ready to go in. You want to keep walking? Maybe out by the Nenana?"

I did want to. It was the perfect time, with mosquitos not yet out and plenty of evening. Not only would the sun not set until after ten, we wouldn't see full dark again until late summer. We'd caught Jack napping on his furnace grate and when we spoke to him, he only blinked drowsily, so we left him to it.

Chandalar's other river, the Nenana, joins the Tanana just below town. Smaller and less wild than its unruly big brother, ice on the Nenana just melts the old-fashioned way, or after the Tanana breakup, slides out quietly without the big fuss. And certainly without anybody betting on the outcome. In fact, the river is so well mannered, they tie up steamboats for the winter a half mile upriver to be frozen in ice — even the older wooden ones.

Both wearing knee-high rubber boots, we strolled, talking about us. Okay, mostly about the wedding. I suggested eloping, not really seriously. We had the bishop scheduled to perform our service, and our guest list had expanded into a general invitation, not just to Chandalar folks but to friends in Nenana, Minto, and even some from Fairbanks.

We waved at the watchman and poked around the boats. The steel diesels, the *Yukon* and the *Tanana*, were here. Also the wooden, steam-driven river tug, the *Taku Chief.* The covered remains of the old steamboat, *Hazel B*, torched just last winter — with Evie, me, and William aboard, plus a Federal witness he was protecting — was also frozen in place. I could still hear the crackling and popping of that old wood burning bright and hot in my dreams.

"Remember that?" I pointed to the remains.

"Until I die!"

Evie wanted to walk farther but I hesitated. "Bear season," I reminded her. "I didn't bring a gun."

She laughed. "You've been carrying that .38 all winter. Fine time to not have it." I threw my head back, hands up in an expansive shrug.

"People keep trying to kill me!"

"I *know*," she said, "and you're such a nice guy!"

She looked out at the river, ahead at the trail then back at me. "Just a little farther. If I go home I have to grade papers. It's more fun being with you."

"Oh," I said, "when you put it like that…"

We walked another half hour, slowly, probably about a mile. It was an easy trail. It ran just a little wider than a dogsled, right along the river bank through a young forest of willow, birch, and the occasional small evergreen. Each tree stood displayed in its own little dimple of melted snow.

Snow was slushy and in some sunny spots even melted to good old solid brown dirt, now feeling wonderfully firm if not a little odd underfoot. It had been a long time since last fall.

We smelled it first, bear scat, then saw the pile mid trail, about twenty-five feet ahead. It looked and smelled very fresh.

"Uh-oh," said Evie. As one, we turned. Things weren't better behind us.

We'd been followed. Not difficult with us talking and dreaming. There were two of them, one was the big cop, Burton, whom we'd last seen out behind the Bide-A-While. The other, wearing the requisite balaclava mask, was a slight figure, shorter than either of us, wearing a day pack and training another of the 1911 service Colts in our direction. I knew who it was — had suspected anyway — and the voice clinched it.

"Hands high," she said, in her whisky-and-cigarettes voice. She waggled the Colt for emphasis, not that she needed to. We'd raised them quickly enough when we saw the gun.

"You're a hard man to kill," she said, pausing to grab a breath and to wheeze. "But I don't know why. I coulda shot you plenty of times on the walk out."

"Your husband said he had nothing to do with this," I told her.

"Damn!" Surprised to be recognized, Myrtle yanked back her parka hood and snatched off the balaclava, stuffing it in her parka pocket. "He didn't.

She saw Evie looking back over her shoulder at the fresh bear pile.

"Bear got you worried?" she taunted. Keeping the gun trained, she slipped out of her backpack, pulling out a length of cotton clothesline cord which she extended to me. "Tie her."

"You don't want..." I said.

"Shut up," she snarled. "I *do* want. Tie her hands behind her and tie her to one of these willows. Tight!" And she demanded to see me yank on the cord. Then she handed Burton a similar length of cord. "Tie him. And don't get between him and the gun." In another minute or so, it was done.

"Get out of here," she said to Burton. "Wait for me at the car."

"But..."

"Go!" She actually waggled the gun at him. He left quickly.

"What's this about, Myrtle?" I asked her.

"My husband wanted you dead and now I'm doing it."

"He didn't want me dead. He came to see me when he was dying, and to tell me he had no hard feelings."

"Bullshit!" she shouted. "You humiliated him, stole his gun, got him disciplined at work and ... and ... drove our sons away! Broke Kell's heart... just lost his will to live. The boys wouldn't even come back for the funeral!" Her fury had ramped up to a scream. "*They're gone... and he's dead because of you!*"

Off in the woods, as if in response, we heard brush crackling and a distant low growl.

She looked back over her shoulder to make sure Burton had gone. He had. We'd watched him walk down the trail, only turning back to look once just before going out of sight around a bend in the trail.

"Okay," she said, as if satisfied, and again reached into her pack. She pulled out a large Thermos, like she intended to stand and drink coffee in front of us. She twisted off the cup and pulled the stopper, slogging toward us through the wet snow. *Death by coffee?* If only.

She splashed Evie and me with blood, not hot but warm and thick, contrasting vividly red on my tan parka and khakis, and against the snow. Out here in the fresh air it smelled at once oddly sweet and metallic, the smell of blood iron. This was all a little confusing and she must have seen it on my face.

"You don't know how much time I spent doping this out. I thought I was gonna have to drag you out here. It's the perfect Alaska crime. I'm gonna be gone — out of here — with an alibi. You two are gonna be back here screaming and crying! Your buddy Frank Jacobs, that son-of-a-bitch, will come out here, sniff around and just shake his head. I only wish I had him tied up there on the next tree!"

She shook the last few bloody drops against my pant legs and stepped back, looking pleased.

"Goodbye," she said, "and good riddance!" She turned abruptly, snatching up her pack as she went past, sliding it back over her shoulders while striding down the trail, clearly in a hurry.

It was then I noticed the breeze in my face, blowing our way, just as it blew the blood scent out behind us. We heard fresh growls and crashing in the underbrush, now not as far off, closing rapidly.

There was a name for what we'd become. Bait.

CHAPTER 34

Evie had cut herself loose, probably about the time Burton got me tied. While knotting her ropes, I'd slipped the Buck Knife out of her back pocket into her hands. With Burton occupied tying me, and Myrtle watching him, she'd quickly gotten her very sharp knife open and begun slicing at her bonds.

With Myrtle walking away, about halfway to the distant trail bend, Evie slashed me loose from the tree. It took another thirty seconds to free my hands, Burton's ropework proving a lot tougher than mine. All the while, I had my eyes on Myrtle, just in case she turned, saw we were loose and started shooting — not that she'd be likely to hit us from that distance with a handgun. Even making her getaway, she had no speed. She wobbled and staggered like she didn't walk much, a likely result of her bar stool workout program and trying to get air through her ruined lungs.

They say a bear, with its over-large scent receptors, has the most sensitive nose of all animals. So it seemed. Crashing blindly through the woods, it headed right for us. Closer and closer came the frantic hungry-animal racket. The bear crashed through underbrush, roaring and huffing, propelled by what must have been the maddening aroma of fresh blood. I turned just as my ropes fell free to see the creature explode from a small copse onto the trail, about a hundred yards from us, a younger grizzly. He saw us immediately, stopped and rose on his hind legs, paws held wide and studded with three-inch claws. All the while we could see his nose working as he snuffled and snorted — slavering — perhaps his smallish brain trying to work out which dinner wine goes best with human.

"Okay," I said, "here's what we do."

Evie looked at me. "About the bear?"

"We run." I said.

"We can't outrun a bear!"

"We can try."

"You're forgetting I'm faster than you."

I knew that. I'd tried racing her before.

"Oh, I see, your big idea is the bear eats you while I run away?"

I shrugged. "Who knows? I might turn out to be faster than you."

"You're not."

She glanced at Myrtle, just disappearing around the bend. We glanced at each other. Then we ran!

We must have surprised the bear. Sometimes they chase instinctively. This one hesitated, standing like a big kid playing tag, giving the obviously slow kids a sporting chance. I imagined him snorting out, 'Ready or not, you shall be caught!' But there were limits. As I chanced another glance over my shoulder, he dropped to all fours and shifted into drive.

I never ran so fast. Evie, ahead of me, continued to increase her lead. We made it to the trail bend in record time. So did the bear. Huffing and snuffling, it was right behind me. I swear I could feel the heat of his breath! Somehow, even while sprinting, he managed to pull up a paw and whack me on the back of my thigh, but I managed to stay upright and, if anything, increase my speed. I knew I couldn't last. I used to do a lot of long-distance running and sprinting when I was boxing every week, to build wind and speed. But I hadn't intentionally run anywhere since last summer. My lungs burned, and muscles in my arms and legs felt impossibly hot and tight. My feet felt like they'd turned to lead. But to stop was to die — slowly, terribly.

On the trail ahead of us, probably feeling flushed with success, Myrtle turned to face an Alaskan's worst nightmare. Evie flashed past on Myrtle's left, as I passed on her right, not so much a flash as a prolonged smear, my breathing like thunder in my ears.

"Oh shit!" she screamed. I counted eight shots fired, as fast as she could pull the trigger. And then just screams until abruptly there was silence.

A little farther on, we found her car, a blue Oldsmobile, the engine running. Burton, oblivious, had the radio turned up listening to Little Richard singing "Tutti Frutti." He hadn't heard the screams, but the shots popped him out of the driver's side like he'd been ejected, the door standing wide.

Evie raced around to the passenger side and wrenched open the door, sliding in. It was a good idea. I sure couldn't run any farther. So, I collided with Burton, knocking the wind out of him with a great *oof* of stale cigarette breath as I threw myself into the driver's seat, jammed the column shift into first and floored it, music blaring, tires spinning, the door slamming itself shut with the acceleration.

"Slow down!" Evie called out, as I narrowly skidded around a tight corner. "Nothing's chasing us now."

Most likely, the bear was having lunch. And Burton, if he went back to check, was losing his. We drove back to town with Little Richard singing, "A whop bop-a-loo-la, whop bam boo!"

* * *

Nurse Maxine swung open her door and saw my face. "You again?" Then she saw the rest of me — and Evie — splattered with blood. Her face went white. "What happened?"

I held up a shaking hand. "Relax, most of it isn't ours."

"Most of it?" The two women helped me out of my soggy pants. Maxine held them up with two fingers. "You saving these?"

"It's just blood. It'll wash," I said. She turned them around. It wasn't just blood. The side and back of the right upper thigh — lower butt — had been shredded, four parallel jagged slashes extending from the side seam across much of the back.

"Toss 'em," said Evie, sensing my hesitation and making the executive decision. To me she said, "I'll go home and get you a fresh pair." I liked the way 'I'll go home' sounded coming from her lips.

"Up here," said Maxine, indicating that I should slide up on her examination table on my belly. I heard Evie's sharp breath intake.

"That bad?"

"I've seen worse," said Maxine. "But yeah, bad enough." She exhaled slowly through her teeth. "When did this happen?" We told her. It had now been more than an hour since we stopped to phone Frank Jacobs.

"Bleeding's pretty much stopped, just oozing. You need stitches." She shook her head. "I'm gonna wash these, put a pad on, and start you on antibiotics. You don't know, and don't want to know, where these claws have been. And I can give you a local."

270

She looked at Evie. "He needs to go to Saint Joseph's. I think this is going to be more stitches than he would want me to do here. Certainly more than I want to do."

Evie nodded. "I'll go get pants," she said. With the pickup across the river, we were still driving the Oldsmobile. I gave her the keys.

So, Maxine cleansed my wounds and I gritted my teeth. It hurt to begin with, and for some reason only got more painful until finally she filled a massive hypodermic syringe with a javelin-like needle and gave me a shot, which also hurt.

"You practice veterinary medicine?" I asked. It looked like a horse syringe. Bad timing. I *swear* she pushed the needle in an extra millimeter! I sucked a noisy breath through my teeth when she pushed the plunger.

"Man up," she said.

"Bedside manner needs work," I muttered. She snickered. "I get that a lot... from the ones who live."

"Will I be among them?"

She leaned back to squint at me through bifocals. "If you play your cards right." Just my luck. A nurse with attitude.

It was a long painful walk and then ride to Fairbanks. With river ice punky, we had to walk the railroad bridge then slowly make our way down the rough trail to where I'd parked the truck. Even with the local anesthetic, every misstep hurt... a lot. And then I had to sit on my sore side, or try to not sit on my sore side for sixty miles. I wished we could have brought the Oldsmobile so I could have stretched out in the back. It was still too cold to stretch out in the truck bed.

They knew me there, too. "Father!" said the night

nurse when she saw me limping, her face a question mark.

"Grizzly," said Evie.

"Oooh. Third bear mauling today." She hesitated a beat. "You're the first one alive. Where did he get you?"

"Out by the Nenana."

She pressed her lips together, bunching her cheeks.

"Where on your *body*?"

I pointed at my rear. "Thigh."

"That's your butt," she announced for all to hear. "Need a wheelchair?"

"Hurts to sit."

"Bet it hurts to walk, too." But I did.

Once again, life got better with morphine. One hundred forty-eight stitches. They were still working on my backside when a sister intruded on my drugged reverie to hand me the phone.

"For you, Father."

I think I said, "Who would call me here?"

"Jacobs," said the voice. "That's who. In Chandalar. Just came in from the site. What a mess," he went on. "Hard to believe that used to be Myrtle. No sign of Burton, though." He paused. "Did you see her gun?"

"Oh, yeah. She definitely showed it to us."

"Looks pretty much like those other guns you took from people trying to kill you."

"That's what I thought."

"So how bad are you?" I craned my neck to look at the doctor and two nurses who were finishing up on my backside.

"Marshal Jacobs wants to know how bad I am."

The doctor looked at me over his glasses.

272

"A hundred forty-eight stitches and about two weeks of pain, assuming we prevent an infection. If this gets infected, we may have to amputate your buttock." He laughed, and the nurses laughed. I wasn't laughing. It must have been medical humor, or the late hour, now after midnight.

"Apparently I'll live," I told Jacobs.

"Good to know," he said. And then, "Looks like we're gonna be here all night."

"Really?"

"Had to send out for a come-a-long. Got several hundred pounds of stiffening bear to haul off what's left of the victim. She killed the bear, but not until he'd pretty much torn her up and then fell on her. A bad last minute or so."

"Yeah, I'm sorry we had to hear it," I told him.

"Swell," he said, "that'll stay with you." He was right. I could still hear screaming.

With the morphine in my system, I walked out pretty well, to find Andy waiting with Evie.

"You two are stayin' here with me," he said. "Not driving — and walking — all the way back to Chandalar. But no hanky-panky. I'll chaperone."

Evie, looking at him, pressed her lips together and suppressed a smile.

"If there's no hanky-panky, why would we even *want* to stay with you?" He laughed, but cautiously, glancing at each of our faces to make sure she was kidding. Our good behavior had always been a particularly big deal with him.

We followed him in the Ford back across the Chena River to the small place he rented near his restaurant. Even at midnight, there was enough light to see a small, old log cabin in good condition, with just a bit of yard and, of all things, a picket fence. In

273

summer he even had a postage stamp of lawn he mowed. Andy loved this little bit of lawn and I'd seen him out there of an evening with his push mower, walking along in the scent of cut grass, a contented look on his face.

"Hardy, you take my bed," he commanded. "Evie in my 'guest' room. I'll be on the sofa." I tried to argue that I'd sleep on the couch but was too tired and by now, too dopey. Evie tucked me into bed under Andy's watchful eye, kissed me goodnight and went out. I think I probably went to sleep the instant she clicked off the light, because I remembered nothing more.

I slept until eight, late for me, and woke up smelling coffee even through the closed bedroom door. Like a fool, I tried to sit up and swing my legs out of bed, forgetting that only yesterday I'd been serious bear fodder. The pain was incredible, and I may have yelped. Okay, I did yelp. In seconds I heard a quick knock and Andy came creeping in to check on me, shadowed by Evie. They both looked concerned.

"You okay?"

"No."

"Hurts?"

"Oh, boy. You don't know…"

He grinned. "I do know. Coffee'll help. Need a hand up?"

I did. "Slowly," I directed. It still felt like someone poured gasoline on my right buttock and lit it. Evie helped me into my pants, with Andy hovering. Then the two followed me as I made my tentative way toward the kitchen. They had pills for me, which I took, and within the half hour felt the pain start to ease. With one 'cheek' perched on a wooden chair, the sore one hovering, I accepted my properly doctored coffee — real cream, sugar, and just a bit of cocoa powder. I had just taken the first sip when we heard a knock.

Andy cocked his head, his face a question mark. "I never get company."

"You're never home," said Evie and went to answer. She came back with Frank Jacobs and William. The two had flown back from Chandalar and the grim, all-night job with the bear and its victim.

"Grisly," Frank said, when asked how it had gone, and gratefully accepted coffee. "I picked up this guy," he aimed a thumb in William's direction. Frank sipped, sighed then said, "Hey!" and reached for the parka he'd hung on a chair. "Check this!" He pulled out a white paper evidence bag, smashed to the shape of Myrtle's Colt. "We've already pulled prints," he said, and handed it to me, grip first. I took it and checked it. Safety on, clip out, and chamber empty.

"It's an empty gun," I observed. He made a face.

"Notice anything else?" I looked it over. It appeared to be a match for the guns at home in my file cabinet. A 1911-style Colt, an older model but little used. Actually, it didn't appear used at all. He got tired of waiting for me. "No serial number," he said. "In fact, no engraving... no print of any kind. No country of origin. Not even a patent."

"Ground off?"

"It was never there. And I'll bet they're all like that."

I held up the gun to examine it. He was right. Not a word engraved on it and no abrasion marks.

"So," I asked, "how does that help? We don't know anything about these guns and have no idea where they came from."

"Well," he said, "that's the weird part. According to William here, that tells us *exactly* where they came from."

CHAPTER 35

William told him the story, though Andy and I knew it. About secret shelters the federal government built in Alaska early in the Cold War. They did it with the fair certainty the Soviets would overrun the Territory and try to hold it.

Called *Operation Washtub*, originally an idea of J. Edgar Hoover and the FBI, the program recruited and trained eighty-nine "stay-behind-agents" to resist the occupying Soviet forces, and to secretly radio reports of Soviet troop movements. The government also built and fully outfitted secret caches throughout the state. They were fully stocked with food, radio equipment, medical supplies, guns, and money — lots of it — in greenbacks and unprocessed gold. According to William, nine of these shelters contained a total of more than a million untraceable dollars.

Only last winter, implicated in a murder and on the run from the late Chief Kellar, Andy and I had been guided by William to one of the secret sites, snowshoeing out through darkness and a bitter blizzard to seek shelter.

William took a sip of his coffee and made eye contact with each of us. "The rifles are standard military issue, .30-06. Common in Alaska, anyway. The handguns are pre-CIA .45s — OSS-issued during the European war. They are unmarked. I am wagering..." he set down his mug, pulling off his wire-frame spectacles to massage the bridge of his nose. "This gang of bank robbers has also plundered money and guns from these top-secret sites."

"While distracting authorities and the rest of us," I added, "with their slow-speed, meandering getaway. And it worked."

"But how did they know?" asked Frank, sounding a bit exasperated. "How did they know about the sites... about the money? It's the first time *I've* heard any of this, and you civilians already know!" He swept a hand at Andy and me. "And have already been there! If these are top secret sites, how did they find them?" We didn't know, though I had the beginning of an idea.

"More coffee?" Andy got up to pour another round.

Evie turned to smile at me. "More drugs?" she asked. I said yes to both.

Shaking his head, Frank pointed out the obvious. "It's a big territory. We don't have a prayer of finding these guys!" He turned to me. "Do we?" It was an old joke of Andy's. Predictably, Andy laughed.

I set down my mug, shifting the weight on my chair, trying in vain to make sitting not hurt. "There's one more problem," I told them. "One we need to solve before we can do anything else."

* * *

It took a full week to walk and sit without wincing.

"Still sore?" asked Evie in the parish hall after the eleven o'clock service on Sunday.

"A little."

"Anything I can do?"

I lowered my voice. "Kiss it?"

She looked around to see if we could be

278

overheard. We couldn't. "Hardeee!" she protested, actually blushing. Then she added, "In your dreams!" and walked away smiling.

Solomon Esau approached me cautiously, an old china coffee cup with the handle broken off, cradled like a chick in both hands. As with the previous times, he reached out a finger to touch me.

"I have seen her again," he confided.

"The Deaconess?"

"Yes." He nodded solemnly. "In her shawl." He started away then turned, his eyes flicking to either side. "And your blond lady," he whispered. "I saw her. She told me to warn you about a bear."

"Blond lady?" But I knew. "When did she give you this message?"

"It was..." and his eyes looked up and off to one side. "In the past," he said. He didn't know. Time, days and weeks, had ceased to work for him. Assuming it ever had. A twinge from my backside made me wish he'd been quicker to pass along the warning.

Later that day, with trepidation, I called Wild Bill Hanson. "I got a tip about men on skis," I told him, and filled him in. Including the part about the possible leak at the marshal's office, and Andy being out of town.

Why did I volunteer to be the bait? I don't know. Evie asked that question, too. "Why is it always you?"

"It's the most plausible," I told her. "Frank or William wouldn't have to go out alone. They have helpers. It's only me who would have to call someone, so I will."

"Just you and me," Hanson said without hesitation. "Sure, I'll go with you."

279

We arranged to meet the next day. I didn't sleep well that night, tossing and turning, palpably anxious. Setting out in the morning, I deliberately left Jack at home and out of harm's way. Evie knew to check on him after school.

"Oh, Hardy, be careful," she'd said with some anguish, and then, "I hope it's not him! I like him."

I hoped it wasn't him, too, for the same reason, plus not wanting him to shoot me.

The meeting place would be halfway to Fairbanks, a trail Andy knew about, leading to a small cabin about a half mile in. Which meant once again I had to get there by walking across the Tanana River on the railroad bridge and down the steep trail to my truck. It was a balmy day, temperature in the high thirties, great for walking, and this time I reveled in how easy the trail had become while not lacerated and bleeding from my backside.

"It's easy to find," Andy assured me. "For one thing, there's a plowed pullout, and it's right across the road from a twisted evergreen. A spruce, I think." It seemed pretty straightforward compared to some of his directions, like 'turn when you see the moose.'

Across the river from town, the steep hill stood up earth-colored, its snow almost completely melted under a vivid blue sky. It looked heavenly. Snow had melted from the railroad tracks and ballast, and even the foot path from the bridge to my truck lay smooth, firm, and clear of snow.

The river, on the other hand, remained a vast wasteland of unstable rotting ice interspersed with blue pools of standing water. "Any day now," old hands advised over steaming mugs at the Coffee Cup Café. Any day would be fine. Even though my 'winning' ticket date had passed, I was ready for breakup. We all were.

I carried a small day pack over my shoulder, the .38 in my jacket pocket, the .45 under my arm, and my father's old .30-30 deer rifle in my hand. For the first time on one of these walks, I carried no snowshoes. I wouldn't miss them.

About a half hour up the Fairbanks road, I saw his military jeep parked at a roadside pullout with Hanson leaned against a front fender, jaw working the ever-present stick of Juicy Fruit. I checked for an evergreen directly across and then wedged the Ford in alongside, the pullout still steeply snow-shouldered thanks to winter snowplows. The road itself was bare and damp, but not yet summer dusty. Come July, what seemed like a permanently suspended haze of road dust would be the first sign of Fairbanks for an approaching highway traveler.

He greeted me, shaking hands, extending the Juicy Fruit pack. I took one and thanked him, unwrapping it and stuffing the gum into my mouth and the wrapper into my pocket.

"So, what's the story? Men on skis out here?" He made a questioning face. There was clearly too little snow left here to be skiing.

I shrugged. "I didn't get it firsthand. Frank called me. Maybe they were carrying skis." Hanson shook his head, making an I-don't-know face and stood up, grabbing his day pack and M1 from the Jeep hood.

"Another false alarm?" he asked as we turned toward the trail.

"That's how I'd bet," I told him.

"Got to check it," he said. "Besides, it gets me out of my office."

We started up the trail, me in the lead, a trickle of electricity coursing up and down my spine. I was already sweating. For one thing, if Hanson was dirty, if he'd sold out, we didn't have to get all the way up to the cabin. He could shoot me right here on the trail and go home happy, never mind that I had reinforcements hiding at the cabin.

At the same time, I felt like seven kinds of slime for leading Hanson on. That is, unless he was here to kill me. He'd always been straight with me. Well, as far as I knew. And now I was deliberately deceiving him. *Has to be done*, I told myself.

"So, there's a leaker in Jacob's office? Damn." He spoke quietly. "Why can't people just do their jobs and be trustworthy?"

We went slowly, cautiously, like we would if we thought we were sneaking up on bad guys. About fifteen minutes up the trail, rounding a bend, the cabin came into view. I began to relax a little, knowing that if anything did happen, I had backup here. I found myself trying to spot Frank, Andy, or William in their hiding places. I knew they'd be fairly close in. But they'd done their jobs well. I saw no sign of them. Nothing.

"They're supposed to be holed up here?" Hanson nudged open the cabin door and we both peered in. Nobody had been here for a long time. Most of the window panes had been punched out or shot out. An old wooden table near the iron woodstove lay furry with dust and rodent droppings.

Hanson looked at me, thinking something. "Not here. Never were. Was this a credible witness?" I feigned a disgusted face.

"I don't know. Sorry I wasted your time."

"No," he said, "it's no problem. Never hesitate to call me. Like I said, any excuse to get out of the office — and off the base — is a good one. Besides, this is a thing you don't want to do alone." He hesitated and looked around. "We out of here?"

I looked around, too. I could find no clue that humans had been here since the melt. I credited Andy for getting them up here and concealed so well.

"I'll lead," said Hanson, as we started back down. "They could still hit us." Rifle ready, he eased off down the trail toward the highway.

I felt an enormous sense of relief, walking back down the trail. This had been Hanson's chance. If he were really in on this, he could easily have shot me and walked back down, driven home with no one the wiser. Instead, we walked back to our vehicles together, shook hands, and drove away.

"Remember," he said at the last, "call me anytime." And I said I would and waved him away.

I started breathing again as I shifted into gear and drove most of a mile back toward Chandalar before rounding a curve to find Andy, Frank, and William standing by the side of the road looking puzzled. I pulled over.

Andy stuck his head in the window. "Where you been? Hanson cancelled?"

I looked around, only now seeing the highway pull-out and twisted evergreen that had been my road signs. Somehow, I'd driven right past, stopping, parking at a different trail simply because Hanson had and not noticing that the signal evergreen wasn't twisted, like this one obviously was.

"Well, I..." was as far as I got.

"You went to the wrong trail." Andy made his disgusted face. "Didn't I tell you, *twisted* evergreen? But, no…"

Thankfully, Frank cut through his little tirade. "So, you went up, saw the cabin, he didn't shoot you, and you walked back down." I nodded.

"That's the proof we need," he said. "It's not Hanson." He made eye contact. "Luckily for you." And I nodded. He didn't say the obvious thing. *Or I'd be dead.*

CHAPTER 36

On Friday night over dinner — moose steaks with home-grown potatoes and canned peas on the side — Evie and I talked about seeing dead people.

"Solomon saw Mary," I told her, "and he mentioned the bear — passed along her warning about it — without me telling him anything. Come to think of it, I didn't tell him about Mary, either. Did you?"

"No," she said, "of course not."

"Why does he do that? Reach out with his finger and touch me?"

She laughed. "He does that to make sure you're alive, not talking to a ghost. He's always had trouble telling the difference between the live ones and the dead ones."

"That's pretty weird. Seeing dead people. Especially seeing so many that he has to check."

She did a face shrug. "So, he sees dead people. Why not? You do." She had a point. She took a small bite of steak and chewed it thoughtfully. "I was about three when I arrived at the mission, for all practical purposes an orphan, though my father was still alive.

"Most of the older kids out there were orphans from the flu pandemic... whole families died. Sometimes whole villages. Trappers or mail carriers would come mushing in and find everybody dead. Nobody buried, of course.

"We heard stories... really terrible stories... a man

285

found frozen with his arms wrapped around his stove. Starving huskies eating the remains and spreading the bones. Ugh!" She shuddered and pushed away her plate. "It used to give me nightmares... and may again.

"When I go out to the mission," she continued, "I don't *see* people, but I feel them all around me, just like I used to. And I hear them again, crying in the night. That's what draws Solomon. The spirits. I'm not surprised he sees the Deaconess." She took a sip of coffee and looked thoughtful. "I guess I'd be surprised if he didn't."

After doing the dishes together — she washed, I dried — I walked her home. She was days from the end of another school year, with lots of assignments to read and evaluate and grades to calculate and enter. At her door, the last thing she said, "You have an idea, I can tell."

"Half an idea," I told her.

She grabbed me by both shoulders. "Listen to me, Hardy! Before you act on your idea, let's talk it over. I know how you are. You end up thinking you have some perfectly good reason to go off on your own and try to get killed. You don't. Okay?"

"I hear you," I told her, and I really did. I resolved to 'sin no more.'

Back at the rectory, trying to read, but not reading. Trying to think, but not thinking so well, either. What did I know? I knew the bank had been robbed and the bonds stolen. I knew that the original five robbers had somehow turned into a whole gang of them, though many — maybe even most — were now dead. I knew that Chilt, the so-called ringleader, first identified by Roberta at the bank, was probably dead even before the robbery. How did that add up?

286

I knew that instead of making a clean getaway, which they easily could have, the gang hung around apparently shuttling among the government-stocked shelters that were supposed to be secret, plundering them. The more I thought about it, the more it went from random and shapeless to a well-planned, well-executed crime scheme that netted, by my estimate, nearly three million dollars. Not bad for six weeks of work.

And then finally, because of something Evie had said, it all settled like random Lincoln Logs that had been flying loose around in my head, suddenly dropping into place to form a perfect cabin. Though it was late, I called Evie, pretty sure she was still up. When she answered, weary, stifling a yawn, I told her, "I know who, I know where."

"I was sure you would," she said.

* * *

Early on Saturday morning I gently closed the door on Jack — who really wanted to come along — and hiked the mile or so out from town in the direction of the old mission. According to my Winchester ammo calendar, illustrated with a nearly irresistible clutch of chocolate lab puppies, this was the fifth of May and still no ice breakup.

The day was solidly overcast with the temperature in the low forties, a good day for walking. A two-to-three-foot berm of chunky, dirty snow still lined most of the way, though the roadbed had melted back to native river sand, pot-holed and puddled. More than once I was glad for tall boots. I strode along, comfortable in my Woolrich jacket, red felt hunting hat, a pair of cotton work gloves, carrying the .38 in my pocket and the .45 under my arm. No rifle. With any luck I could avoid shooting.

I was frankly soul-weary from carrying a gun, shooting and being shot at, and from blessing and performing last rites over bodies with bullet holes. These were people who had made the bad decision to take a job and score some easy cash, and then died. Period, end of story. Not what they had signed on for. Certainly not how they thought their lives would end. It all seemed so pointless.

I passed over the railroad tracks and along the still-frozen river, past the slipways where they hauled out and launched the river boats and barges. Farther along, I walked under the latticed railroad bridge trestle then through the native village with its low, scattered log cabins and tar paper shacks, seeing almost no one. At the end of the road where the snowplow turned around, I climbed up and over the crusty snow pile. Continuing out the birch-lined lane I soon arrived at what was left of mission property — that hadn't been cut away by the river — a several-acre knob of land set in a smooth curve of the Tanana.

Solomon said he'd seen the Deaconess through a window in the main building, so that's where I headed. I still had keys for everything. In fact, when I took over the mission I'd inherited a beer box full of old keys and padlocks, few of which matched, but it made an interesting Sunday afternoon project in midwinter.

Seen from the air, the building would look like a U. The two-story main section included a dining room, tiny library, main office, and a nurse's office. From that, sprouted separate wings for boys and girls.

Solomon had been very clear about which window he'd been looking through to see the Deaconess, so that's where I started. I risked a quick peek, trying to not make too big or stationary a target

288

of my face. But it's hard to get a look, otherwise.

What I saw froze me — Roberta, gagged, sitting in a straight-backed wooden chair, hands tied behind her, in an otherwise empty room. She saw me, her eyes flying wide. She jerked her head convulsively in the direction of the door and the corridor beyond. Apparently that's where her captors were. I reached into my pants pocket, reluctantly pulling out the .38. As I walked, I found myself wondering, why gagged? She'd been captive for weeks. Someone must have seen me approaching.

I followed along the wall to the main front door and used the biggest of the old-fashioned keys, about four inches long, to ease myself in. To my considerable surprise and relief, the door operated silently, unlocking, swinging in without squeaking or groaning. It seemed a good sign. Stepping into a small foyer, closing the door gently behind me, I stood in the dim silence with a few dust-moted sunbeams and the pervasive smell of old clothes, old wood, and probably old souls.

I'd been here quite a few times before, so had no trouble picking up the fresh overlays of cigarette smoke, food, and a hint of perfume. But unlike previous visits, even in the near-deafening silence, I sensed at least one living being and knew that this time I wasn't alone here. But still I saw no one.

Walking as softly as I could, I made my way down the hall to the room where I knew Roberta sat. I reached for the knob where it should have been, but it wasn't. I'd forgotten. In an orphanage with many small children, all the knobs had been installed about six inches lower. I felt again, found and turned it. Unlocked, the door swung in. But now, no Roberta.

In the time it had taken for me to go from the

window to the door, they'd moved her. Or... there was one other explanation.

"Roberta?" I called, and my voice echoed down the bare halls and up the wooden stairs.

She didn't answer at first, then stage whispered from somewhere. "Be quiet! They'll hear you."

"No," I said, speaking normally, "you're here alone. It's just you with your money. Nobody else. Like you planned."

"It worked," she said, after another long pause, no longer whispering. She sounded pleased with herself.

I put the pistol away. Stupid maybe, but it just seemed wrong. The memories of her as a belligerent teenager sitting in my office chair were still fresh. The .38 in my pocket had belonged to her father. I couldn't very well pull a father's gun on his daughter. Besides, I was mightily tired of pulling guns on people.

A door creaked from about halfway down the hall and I moved to look. She had been hiding in a broom closet and stepped out, causing me to rethink my gun policy. She leveled a scoped rifle in my direction and expertly shot the bolt. I found myself looking down the barrel of Andy's missing Mauser. Abruptly I found it very difficult getting air in or out.

"You don't need that," I croaked. "I'm just here to talk."

"No, you're not. You must think I've been asleep these past few years. You're known for finding the one who did it. Solving the crime. Which is why I always knew it would come to this. Me and you. Sorry to be the one to break this to you, but you're here to die."

She had changed since I'd last seen her. Older, of course. More attractive. Under some circumstances, one might even say 'fatally attractive,' though she looked a bit weather-beaten now, after weeks on the run. Her luxurious black hair, down to her waist the last time I'd seen her, had been hacked short. Even so, she'd had time to apply lipstick this morning, no doubt Persian Melon.

"You've got... what? Three million dollars? All your partners are dead. Why are you still here? Why kill me?"

She smiled and cocked her head in what, in a different situation, might have looked sweet and pretty.

"I don't like you. I never liked you. I don't like the way Evie kowtows to you... 'Hardy this and Hardy that.' She admitted you wouldn't have liked her helping me. I kept hoping that nutcase Myrtle would find someone to finish you. But she was a loser magnet."

"You gave her guns."

"I had one of the guys do it — I try to help out. Besides, I had some spares."

"From the government bunkers you cracked."

"Yep. Nice of them to leave me all that cash. Not to mention plenty of food and places to hide."

"They were supposed to be secret. How did you find out about them?"

"Poor dumb Chilt told me. You know — pillow talk," she said winking seductively at me. "At first I couldn't believe the federal government would leave all that cash laying around in the wilderness. But I got him to take me out to one. Cash *and* gold dust! It was like Christmas. And he had a map to all of them, something to do with his Army job."

"I'm guessing he didn't like the idea of you taking what you wanted."

291

"Yeah, it was crazy. He went all Boy Scout on me."

"And you shot him."

"He went happy. I screwed him first. Gave him everything he wanted. *Then* I shot him."

"I'm sure that made it okay."

She laughed. "Funny." We were quiet for a minute. "You know, Evie told me you'd come alone. A long time ago, we were talking about something else, and she said you always thought you could handle things by yourself. Said it drove her crazy. So, I always knew we'd have this moment, just you and me before I shot you."

"Then I'm sorry to disappoint you." I gestured toward Evie, behind her, just stepping out the kitchen door into the hallway, revolver in hand. She'd managed to unlock the back door and slip in soundlessly, just as she'd been able to sneak out that way as a rebellious teen.

Roberta laughed. "That old trick," she said, but then a floorboard creaked. She turned her head cautiously, the Mauser still pointed at my middle.

"Evie?" Evie holding a gun on her seemed to surprise her.

"Yes, Roberta," said Evie.

"You'd take his side against me?"

"Oh, yeah."

"So that was all just an act, trying to help me?"

Evie shook her head. "Not a bit. I really thought I could help you not turn out like I had. Or like I had before I met Hardy. Or like this!"

Roberta seemed confused. "I've got three million bucks here... plus gold. I was hoping we could share it."

"We can't," Evie said flatly. "It's not your

292

money... not mine. Not to even mention all the guys you suckered to be able to get it, the guys that you killed or someone else killed for you. What's the body count on this three million? Do you even know?"

Roberta shrugged. She didn't. "Now I'll have to kill both of you."

Evie thumbed back the pistol hammer. "Not today."

"You won't shoot."

Evie fired the .45, like a clap of thunder in the old wooden hallway, plowing a furrow in the fir floor boards between Roberta's feet. I saw her blink and startle, but not much more.

"Okay, you will shoot," she said. "But you missed me."

"I won't the next time. Put the gun down."

Moving deliberately, Roberta changed her grip on the rifle, sliding her finger away from the trigger. I began to breathe again. Holding it in front of her, she bent as if to place the rifle on the floor then tossed it at Evie. The high, pop-up toss gave Evie time to see it coming, but made her wait for it to arrive. It seemed to take forever.

In the meantime, Roberta ran.

CHAPTER 37

Evie caught the Mauser in one hand while thumbing down the hammer on her .45. Down the hall we heard a window squeak up, slamming at the top, old window counterweights clattering.

Evie looked at me. "Where's she gonna go?"

I said the obvious thing. "She has a plan." She'd had a plan for everything else, even making sure the window would open quickly. I'd tried opening windows out here before, to let in warmth on a summer day when the temperature inside still felt like freezing. I never could find one that would open. Most were painted shut.

Jogging, we followed the sound down the hallway, pausing at a window at the end to look out.

"There!" Evie pointed. We saw Roberta sprinting flat out for the river.

"Oh no!" Evie threw me a round-eyed look.

No one in his — or her — right mind would go out onto the ice now. Though one good thing for her... if she survived to the other side, she was out of here. No one in *their* right mind would follow. She probably had a car stashed across the river near my truck. We'd never see her again.

I vaulted out the window with Evie right behind me, both of us running, hoping to catch her while she was still on solid ground. I'd been out on the river this late in the season and knew how scary it could be. In fact, just the year before, I was crossing on the ice as it began breaking up, barely making it to the far shore. From one minute to the next, the whole expanse of river ice shifted into motion, ice grinding and gnashing and threatening to sweep away with me aboard. I *so* didn't want to do that again!

As with the bear chase, Evie flashed past me.

"No, let her go!" I shouted, realizing the perversity. I'm running to catch Roberta but expect Evie to not do the same. No matter, Evie's pace never faltered and she steadily expanded the distance between us.

Making her getaway, Roberta wore a small canvas backpack. I had no trouble guessing what she carried... probably a big wad of cash and two million dollars' worth of bearer bonds. She'd never need to work another day in her life, if she had one.

It was less than a quarter mile to the riverbank. On a smooth and flat terrain under a scattering of birch, the ground was a mix of bare, slushy, and puddled, with scattered patches of crusty snow. Evie ran, dodging the patches and puddles like a quarterback dodging blockers, always seeking bare earth and solid footing.

Though just eighteen, Roberta couldn't have been in such great shape. She smoked and had been hiding out for six weeks, probably eating poorly, not exercising much and not running at all. Evie closed on her like a locomotive. Just at the riverbank, stretching out both hands, she grabbed Roberta by the backpack, and yanked back hard.

Somehow Roberta managed to tear free, leaving the backpack in Evie's hands. Hardly breaking her stride, she took a flying leap off the five-foot bank, landing on ice or shallow melt out of my view. Evie paused, considered the icepack, and made as if to jump and follow. Still about thirty feet back, I shouted.

"Don't!"

Evie hesitated then shot a glance back at me. She turned back to the river, as if to jump anyway. I shouted again and she froze. But it wasn't my voice that stopped her. It was the shrill wail of the Ice Pool siren, all the way out from town, thin and distant — but unmistakable. Breakup!

The ice shuddered like a freight-train starting to move. I saw Roberta stumble and sidestep with the unexpected motion of it. The far shore, with the tall hill and the railroad tracks, never too close, suddenly seemed an eternity away.

From one blink to the next, the river shattered into large slabs that, ever so slowly began to move. From what had been glacially still, sheets of ice as long as boxcars now began to lift and fall, exerting pressure on those downstream, gnashing and grinding, sometimes riding up over and submerging other pieces of the floe, building into a blood-chilling roar.

Still, Roberta ran, leaping cracks and narrow channels, somehow believing she could make it to the far shore and safety. It wasn't how I'd bet.

I found myself holding my breath, hoping, trying to will her to make it across the next open lead, and the next, like this was a running race or a contest I wanted her to win. I allowed myself to believe she could win, like a favorite runner in a race.

How deep was the river? Not too deep. I'd heard it could be as shallow as six feet out in the middle, especially at the end of a long winter. But to fall in, to sink beneath the ice, even if it somehow happened without grinding her to pulp, would mean never rising again.

Feeling — in spite of everything — heartsick, we watched her grow smaller with distance as the river bore her away downstream. Near the middle of the ice, inevitably, she slowed to a walk, then finally eased to a standstill, her back to us, staring ahead at the far shore. I saw her shoulders settle, saw her turn to face us. No more running.

My mind raced to come up with something we might do to save her. A boat out there would be just as doomed. A helicopter? Fat chance.

Unexpectedly, she waved, a full arm semaphore, like from the deck of an ocean liner, the *Normandie*, the *Queen Mary* — the *Titanic,* pulling away.

She waved again and we waved back. She was departing and we were seeing her off. But there were no horns, no streamers, no celebratory fire boats with water cannons. It was just the river wind, the distant siren, the roar of the ice, and absolute certainty we were watching her die. Making the sign of the cross in the air, large and visible in case she could see me, or cared, I said the words.

"Unto God's gracious mercy and protection we commit you. The Lord bless you and keep you. The Lord make his face to shine upon you, and be gracious unto you. The Lord lift up his countenance upon you, and give you peace, both now and forevermore. Amen."

Another minute or two, as she turned away from us to face downstream, she dropped straight through and disappeared. One second there, the next second gone, the ice quickly jamming closed where she had fallen.

Evie stood for a time, staring out at the now swiftly moving ice, tears streaming down her cheeks. Not wanting to intrude, but not wanting her to be there alone, I went to stand alongside and, after a time, she put her arm through mine, still weeping.

"I thought I could make a difference."

"I think you did."

Evie sniffed and dabbed at her eyes. "You must be kidding."

I shook my head. "She had plenty of people who would have liked to run away with her. The only one she thought to take was you. In the Roberta world, that's a big deal."

"I suppose."

We stood a few more minutes, not talking, just watching ice sweep by. Off in the distance the siren finally quit. We stood a few more minutes then turned together, as if by signal. We locked up the mission building and walked the mile home, saying little, thinking much. And yes, vastly relieved that this whole thing was now finally over.

CHAPTER 38

That was the night Andy threw what he called a pre-wedding dinner for us, actually closing Andrea's on a profitable Saturday night so our friends could come. I knew Frank would be there, so I carefully wrapped a parcel to bring him. Just a little something I thought he'd appreciate.

Since the breakup cleared the river earlier in the week, the little sternwheel ferry, *Princess of Minto,* had been slid down the ways, and was back into summer service. There were two cars aboard, in addition to my truck, filled with Chandalar friends heading to the party. Caravanning up the Fairbanks highway, we arrived at Andrea's at about suppertime, nose-in parking in front of the restaurant. Car doors opened and then slammed as we climbed out of our highway-dusty vehicles and filed into the restaurant. We left Jack to snooze in the truck bed.

Andy was there with Rosie, of course, also Molly and Henry, Oliver, William and Alice, Adele and Big Butch, and Nurse Maxine. From Fairbanks, Frank Jacobs appeared, also Wild Bill Hanson with a date, a tall, thin, athletic-looking blond he introduced as Annika.

"She's a skier," he told me. He looked happier than I'd seen him yet, though with an overtone of something that Frank soon explained.

"Hanson and I are on the hook for two million in lost bonds. There'll be an investigation. We managed to recover 90% of the bunker cash and gold. That may save our jobs." He looked understandably glum.

Henry saw me, came running, and I rocketed him up toward the high, pressed-tin ceiling. He saw the nude portrait and when I set him back down, stood mesmerized. I knew how he felt but tried to distract him by helping him find his seat and get him settled. Molly saw him staring and looked at me.

"He is a boy," she said.

Coffee arrived in glass mugs — the good stuff — and we found seats, the red-and-white checkered table tops all pushed together to form one long table. Very Italian. It was centered with wax-encrusted, wicker-bottomed wine bottles, their candles lit. With the restaurant lights dimmed, the candles cast golden light on happy faces we loved.

I couldn't help sighing, reaching for Evie's hand as she reached for mine. If this wasn't perfect, I didn't know what would be. After a hard winter, we were all here together, safe, happy, intact, drinking good coffee and getting ready to eat a meal I already knew would be delicious.

Andy tapped a butter knife on a wine glass, the gentle tinkle gradually quieting conversations that ran the gamut from ice melting and upcoming weddings, to people who'd had their butts gored by bears.

"We're here to celebrate friendship," said Andy, "and a wedding." He raised his glass in our direction.

And celebrate we did, but I couldn't help thinking of my visit to Roberta's parents, Teddy and Effie. I'd gotten there as quickly as possible. News, especially bad news, travels like lightning in the village. Teddy had opened the door and looked at my face.

"You found her." He paused. "She's dead." He invited me in and called Effie. We sat in the kitchen at a chrome and Formica dinette set and Effie poured strong black tea into a matched set of mugs emblazoned with *North American Grand Champion Dogsled Races, 1956.* Teddy asked if she suffered. I said I didn't think so, it was quick. In the end they thanked me for coming, for hurrying to them. They told me they weren't surprised, had seen this coming and, I suppose, had been preparing. Now it had happened, their worst fear, and they would go on.

I didn't tell them, though it would come out, how involved she was in the whole thing. They'd hear plenty before it finally faded and everyone began talking about something else.

Andy concluded his speech, as we'd arranged, by wishing Frank a happy birthday. We all sang happy birthday, heartily, and presented the gift we'd wrapped and brought along, which confused him.

"This is great, folks, but it's not my birthday."

"Sure it is," said Evie. "Open your present."

"Open it," urged Henry's small voice.

Frank picked up an unused butter knife and began cleanly slicing the wrap, which turned out to cover a smallish shoe box. "Not my size... or style," he remarked, seeing 'pumps' on the label. I don't know what he expected, certainly not two million bucks in bearer bonds. He sucked in a breath when he saw the tidy stacks, and I think, for a time, he forgot to let it out. He looked at me.

"All here?"

"Yes," I told him, "but you'd better count them... later." And then, finally, I saw him begin to breathe again, and smile.

"You didn't say you had them."

"No one asked."

It was true. With Frank and Wild Bill off to Fort

Yukon on a case, a deputy and tech assistant had flown in to Chandalar on the morning after breakup and Roberta's death. They asked us everything possible about the death, took a ton of pictures, checked the window she jumped out of, even measured the distance from the Mission building to the riverbank. In the end, they asked us about everything but bonds.

For our part, Evie picked up the small pack as we left the mission, casually slinging two million dollars over her shoulder as we walked home, without either of us thinking much about it. We knew what it was — assumed — but it wasn't heavy or bulky. When we got back to the rectory, Evie tossed the pack onto the small sofa in the front room, and there it sat.

Biting off a bit of bread stick, Wild Bill caught my eye. "And this was all Chilt's idea?"

I shook my head. "I don't think any of it was. I think he met a new girl, liked her, trusted her, and never considered she might be working him for information. He never meant to sell you out. His fate was probably sealed when he told her about the bonds and the bunkers. She came up with a plan and offered to cut him in. He must have been horrified. Chilt was a decent guy, loyal to you and to the Army. She said, 'He went all Boy Scout on me.' So, she shot him, and probably shot some of the others, too. Her plan was always to end up with everything and she almost did." Hanson's relief was palpable.

At about this point, Evie went out to the truck and brought in Andy's Mauser. She'd cleaned and polished it, and tied a wide, red ribbon around the barrel — saved from Christmas and the rifle she'd given me. Andy's eyes went wide and even a little misty. He'd pretty much lost hope of ever seeing it again. The two had history and it was good to see them reunited.

Lingering over coffee, the group thoroughly subdued by a really delicious meal, Rosie looked up, her coffee mug held contemplatively in both hands.

"I know they robbed the bank to get the bonds. That makes sense. What I don't get is why the 'getaway' never really got away. They just circled. What's that about?"

I looked at Frank but he just looked back. "Take it," he said.

"Roberta never intended them to get away. They used all the reported sightings to find and plunder the *Operation Washtub* sites. I'd be willing to bet they called in their own sightings to keep us looking the other way. It worked. William says they hit all of them — for close to a million bucks and a bunch of unmarked CIA handguns."

"There was something else," added Evie. "Attrition. With Smitty's help — in fact it was probably Smitty's idea — she busted out military convicts from jail in Anchorage because she needed the manpower. She got them to participate by promising a cut of the bonds, apparently without any intention of ever paying out."

"She just paraded them around so that we could shoot them," I said.

"But there was something else," Evie added. "Roberta knew that Myrtle had put out a bounty on Hardy, originally five thousand dollars. That's why, when they ambushed us, most of the shooters were trying to hit him."

"I wondered about that," said Andy. "Even with all the incoming, I didn't have much trouble. Usually they're trying to knock me out — the shooter. They were pretty much ignoring me."

"Tell me this, Sherlock," said Frank to me. "Why hit the sporting goods store for pistols? According to you, they already had a bunch from the bunkers."

I shrugged. "My guess... I think they just ran short. They were hiring Kellar's crooked deputies, and I'll bet one of them cleaned out the pistol supply. And we kept taking them away from people who showed up to shoot me. I have a drawerful back at the rectory. Well... five."

"I need those back, too," said Frank. "Evidence."

"And government property," added William.

Frank sipped his coffee thoughtfully. "We looked all over the Territory for this gang — for her — and then out of the blue, you went right to her." His gaze shifted to Evie. "With backup, for a change. How'd you know she was there?"

"Solomon Esau."

Frank made a doubtful, questioning grimace, squinting one eye. He knew Solomon. "He just walked up to you and said Roberta's hiding at the Old Mission?" The others shifted to look at me.

"Yeah," said Alice, "I was wondering about that, too."

"It turned out Solomon had been telling me she was there the whole time. I just didn't hear him." And then I corrected myself. "I *did* hear him, but I didn't *understand* him."

Andy made a face. "Huh?"

"You remember I told you he was seeing ghosts... the Deaconess?"

"Yeah."

"He was seeing Roberta, with a scarf or a shawl over her head."

Andy sniffed, doubtful. "She deliberately showed

304

herself while hiding out?"

"Well, she knew what he was like. Had known him all her life. I think she was bored and decided to have a little fun with him."

"She knew," said Evie, "he'd think she was a ghost."

I nodded. "Each time she saw him coming, she set herself up in the window so he could see a ghost. She knew, most people here — not me, until recently — knew that Solomon can't tell who's dead and who's alive without touching them. Seeing her there, in a frankly spooky place, he just assumed she was dead."

"And he couldn't just reach through the glass to find out!" Rosie said with a well-that-explains-it roll of her eyes.

"I was pretty sure who he was seeing as soon as Evie explained that to me. And as for backup..."

"I told him he wasn't going without me," added Evie, netting a laugh.

Frank had the last word. "Good job, everybody. Somehow, we all survived this."

As chairs began to scrape back, people taking last sips of coffee, pulling themselves together to go out into the perpetual twilight, Andy asked Evie, "After all this, you still want to marry this guy?"

Never at a loss for words, Evie picked a good one. "Indubitably."

CHAPTER 39

We caravanned home the way we had come, through the long subarctic twilight. Even though it was late, we found the *Princess of Minto* snubbed up to the shore, waiting. Yes, we'd called ahead.

Riding back across, we stood at the bow rail watching the river surface slip past, the muddy water shifting and sliding into endless swirls, rips and whirlpools. Maybe it was the hour, but even the splashy battering of the orange paddlewheel blended into the murmur of a gentle good night.

Mosquitoes were out, the first few, but not on the river. I closed my eyes, picking up the cool scent and sensation of water overlaid with the perfume of cottonwood trees amid a myriad of other unknown — to me, anyway — green plant life now rising to replace the snow.

"Almost home," I murmured, thinking again with a bit of wonder how this somewhat ramshackle river town had eased its way into my heart and soul, into my life. I would live here, be married here, have children here, maybe even live to see my children have children here. On this night, I could see my whole future laid out here in this dusty little town, far, far away from everything and everyone I'd known before. And it was all good. As if sensing my thoughts, Evie threaded her arm through mine to pull me close, and I looked at her, loving her.

It *had* been a long, deadly winter, but somehow

we and the people we loved had survived. I felt Evie shift at my elbow.

"I love you," she said.

"Why in this moment?"

"Because everything feels right in this moment. We're heading home together — with our dog." I liked the way she said *our* dog.

"And because, day in and day out, you're simply the best person I know. The one I want to spend my days with. All of them."

"And your nights? What about the nights?"

"I would say *especially* the nights."

"Oh, boy!" I said. "Me, too."

ABOUT THE AUTHOR

Photo by V. Judy

Raised in the interior of Alaska, Jonathan Thomas Stratman infuses his novels with all the excitement, color, and adventure of life in the rugged 49th state.

Whether in his much acclaimed **Cheechako** adventure series or in his **Father Hardy Mystery** series, Stratman's characters call on reserves of courage, stamina, and resourcefulness — not just to prevail, but to survive.

No wonder so many readers say, *"I couldn't go to bed without finishing the book!"*

A NOTE FROM THE AUTHOR

Dear Reader,

If you enjoyed this book, would you please go to Amazon.com or Goodreads, type in 'Jonathan Thomas Stratman,' and write a short review? I'd appreciate it very much. The more reviews Amazon sees, the more they promote my work.

Check out my Facebook page, also, by typing in 'Jonathan Thomas Stratman, Author.' A "LIKE" would be very helpful, too.

Thanks!

*P.S. **Godspeed Honeymoon**, Book 6 in the **Father Hardy Mystery series** will be available in 2020.*

Made in the USA
Middletown, DE
31 May 2021

40728890R00187